Carmel Bendon's superb novel ta[l] intriguing premise into a world of [m] mysticism, the limits of spirituality and the different ways in which we all approach the truth. In a world of carefully spun stories that are whispered in dreams and to doctors and nuns, can we ever really reach a rational conclusion in a world where nothing can ever be certain? And can we ever firmly conclude the facts that lie at the heart of fantasies? This is a tremendous, playful and richly poetic book that speaks to the storyteller inside all of us.

Walter Mason, author of *Destination Saigon*
and *Destination Cambodia*

Grasping at Water beguiles with its strong sense of mystery, history, character and place. When an inscrutable young woman is plucked, alive, from the glistening waters of Sydney Harbour, her psychiatrist, Kathryn Brookley, becomes immersed in a tale that defies logic and time. As Kathryn's quest for truth morphs into a voyage of self discovery, this spiritual page-turner draws you under its spell.

Michele Seminara, *Verity La*

Finely written historical mysticism entwined with a modern mystery, Carmel Bendon's stunning debut sizzles with originality and intrigue. *Grasping at Water* is the thinking-person's thriller that's sure to whet the literary appetites of readers the world over.

Amanda Hickey, journalist and filmmaker

GRASPING
AT WATER

carmel bendon

To Jan

Happy reading,

Carmel Bendon

ODYSSEY
BOOKS

Published by Odyssey Books in 2018
www.odysseybooks.com.au

A catalogue record for this book is available from the National Library of Australia

Author: Carmel Bendon
Title: Grasping at Water / Carmel Bendon
ISBN: 978-1-925652-41-3 (paperback)
ISBN: 978-1-925652-42-0 (ebook)

Cover design by Michelle Lovi

To Adrian, Laura, Erin and Bridget—

my loves, my lessons, my life.

❧ I ❧

Once there was a garden, lush and languid by the sea. And into that garden came a handsome soldier and an innocent young woman. And in their delight at each other, the young woman delightedly and innocently conceived a child. And the handsome soldier returned to the war, leaving the young woman with only a memory and the precious souvenir of a baby girl. But it was in the days of misunderstanding, when love was limited to respectable people; and so the baby was taken from the young woman's arms and given into respectable arms. And, after that, all the young childless mother had left was the gaping wound in her heart.

7 May 2013

Unnatural. That's how he'll later describe the atmosphere that hangs like the dark clouds over the harbour this morning.

It's early, the sun just up, and the light winds of the previous day have intensified to whip the harbour into a washing machine. The ferry from Manly to Circular Quay slips and dips and rises and rolls in the churning ocean and he is not surprised to be the only passenger who has chosen to stand near a deck entry door and look out onto the threatening sea. He stares toward the steep sandstone cliffs of North and South Heads; they offer no protection to the harbour today and loom, instead, like failed sentinels letting in an enemy that will swamp all in its path. Very unnatural.

Most days the ferry ride to work is a pleasure. When Sydney Harbour glistens under a generous sun, there is nowhere else in the world he would rather be. But today the sun has been swallowed by the deep, angry water, and the air is cold, very cold. Too cold for so early in May.

What's wrong with the harbour today? What's wrong with me? he thinks as the ferry falls off an impossible crest. He knows the answers to both questions. The first one is a straightforward matter of an east coast low pressure system that imposes itself on Sydney a couple of times a year in late autumn and winter. An early arrival, yes, but understandable. The answer to his second question is far more complex: a knot of sadness and love that last night's argument with his wife has tied more tightly; and anger, too, that she is not interested in participating in the untangling. Such a beautiful, brilliant, headstrong, puzzling woman. A mystery to him. A mystery to herself. He shakes thoughts of his wife away, filing them in the 'too hard basket' for the moment as he steals himself to stay upright against the boat's rocking motion.

Once the ferry is past the heads, the sea settles into a less chaotic, more predictable rhythm and he decides to step outside the crowded, stuffy interior of the main passenger cabin to get some fresh air on the port-side deck. He ignores the waving hand and shaking head of a crewman who gestures to dissuade him and, instead, continues opening the heavy door. He steps onto the slippery exterior boards, closing the door firmly behind him as he goes. He pulls his coat collar up around his ears then, spreading his newspaper on part of the sea-damp wooden bench that encircles the vessel's lower level, he takes a seat and a very deep breath. Seaspray smacks his face, but he sits doggedly, willing the water to wash away his disappointment.

He starts to relax, taking in a vista that never fails to enthral him. The parade of harbourside beaches, still lovely under grey skies; Watson's Bay with its pub and restaurants; Lady Jane beach (minus its nudists today); the expanse of Rose Bay with one of its seaplanes even now taking off into the blustery sky; exclusive Point Piper with its multi-multi-million dollar houses; the picnic areas of Shark Island. In the distance, even in the overcast weather, the Harbour Bridge presides over the scene. Above it, a Qantas A380 glides southward on its final descent to the airport.

Suddenly, as they pass Garden Island and Woolloomooloo, and with only about five minutes of the journey to go, the wind stops. Completely. Not a breath. Calm. Eerily calm.

Unsettled, he leaves the bench and steps forward to lean on the railing, his eyes darting between the approaching cityscape and the navy blue water beneath the boat. The ferry takes a wide, smooth sweep around the Martello-towered Fort Denison, the small, steep island where, over two centuries earlier, some of the young colony's most difficult convicts had found themselves imprisoned, marooned in clear sight of the growing Sydney town but with no way of getting back there. And, always in view of course, but now coming closer, floating like a giant ship with unflappable white sails, is the Opera House. It captures his gaze, holds it utterly, till a shaft of sunlight breaks through the clouds and reflects so brilliantly off the building that he is forced to look away.

And then he sees it. A shape in the water. Pale but distinct. Small, but growing larger as the ferry bears down on it. A shape ... with a head ... and legs ... and outstretched arms. A body. Floating. Face down. A body. A human body.

'A body. There's a body. In the water. Stop. Stop the boat,' he screams, to the air, to the water, to anyone.

He runs, waving his arms wildly at those inside the main cabin.

'Help. Someone. Anyone. Stop this ferry now!'

Somehow, people appear from everywhere. Shoving. Shouting. A crewman is calling the captain. The ferry is slowing ... but oh, so, slowly. The blade of its prow prepares to slice through the body. Time suspends. All those crowded on the decks inhale as one and are silent.

The ferry stops. It stops within inches of the body. Group exhalation. Time recommences, accelerates. Ropes, hands, life buoys are lowered, thrown over the side, a young crewman jumps in and, somehow, the soaked body of a young woman is brought to lie on the deck at his feet. A thermal blanket is placed over her; people offer coats to the shivering crewman who has retrieved her.

'I'm a doctor,' he confesses, looking toward the ferry captain who has materialised by his side. 'I'll help her ... if it's appropriate ... you know ... usual protocol.'

'There's nothing usual about any of this,' responds the captain, rubbing his hands together. 'I just didn't see her. I don't understand. This is a busy part of the harbour. Why didn't anyone report this earlier?'

'Are you all right?' he asks, stepping in the captain's direction.

'Fine, good. The important thing is, how is she?'

He kneels beside the body, feels the neck for a carotid artery pulse, registers the surprising warmth of the body, observes the even rise and fall of the chest, scans the face for signs of trauma but notices none, notes the remarkably healthy colour of the woman's face and finds, on picking up one of her hands from under the blanket, that the fingernails are pink.

'She's alive,' he announces.

'Thank God,' the captain sighs, the relief obvious. 'Okay, well, Doctor, if you can stay with her, I'll get us to the quay. Marine Area Command has already been notified. There'll be an ambulance waiting.' Turning to the passenger throng, he shouts, 'Move back folks. Give them some room. We'll be on our way now. There in five minutes.'

As the captain hurries off, the doctor kneels beside the woman. He is close enough to hear her breathing. He gazes at her face. The skin is clear, unlined, and he guesses her age at around thirty. He wonders at the delicacy of the brown-fringed eyelids. As he wonders, the lids flick open. Steely blue eyes stare back at him, sear him. His heart jumps, his nerves twinge, a sick panic seizes him. How can she be alive? So alive, after this ordeal, he wonders.

Several seconds pass before the veneer of medical competence can assert itself. He is aware of other passengers and crew staring at him from various vantage points, expecting information, intervention.

'You're safe,' he hears himself announce. 'I'll stay with you until you're moved from here to a hospital where you'll get appropriate treatment. No need to try and talk but, perhaps, you can nod your head if you've understood what I've told you.'

The woman's eyes remain fixed, unblinking, on him. She does not nod.

'Are you in any pain?' he tries. 'I'm not going to examine you here; best not to move you about. From my brief visual assessment, I can tell you that your vital signs seem good. But, perhaps, you've got pain somewhere. Can you let me know if that's the case?'

Again the unblinking eyes, the unmoving head.

'Well, perhaps you could tell me your name,' he coaxes.

At this, she turns her head away from him and the fringed lids clamp shut. And remain shut during the short trip into Circular Quay where assistance is waiting. Dutifully, the passenger-doctor offers the paramedics his thoughts on her condition.

'All noted, Doctor,' says one, as the patient is transferred onto a trolley and into the ambulance. 'We're taking her to the emergency department at Royal Harbourside. Do you want to accompany us?'

'No, I'm afraid I can't. Very busy.'

'Well, thanks for what you've already done. It was doubly lucky that you were on that ferry. I mean, what are the chances? You have the medical skills, of course, but to be the one who spotted her … the only one outside on deck at the time. Great coincidence, huh?'

'Yes, quite a coincidence,' he agrees over his shoulder as he hurries away.

{ 2 }

This is what she said:

All things begin, and all things end, or so it seemed to me. But what if there is no beginning and no end? Only flow. What if everything I had believed all my life was revealed to be completely wrong? What if the world that I have seen for the years of my life was shown to be an illusion? Would I discard the solid illusions of a lifetime in favour of the truth?

She sat behind her desk, staring at the clock on the wall, her eyes fixed on the monotonous movement of its second hand. Tick, click, tick, click. Time moving on, and I am not, she thought as she bowed her head to observe the ringless fingers interlaced in her lap. As the experienced psychiatrist that she was, she made a mental note of the wry smile that accompanied the observation.

The sound of the mobile phone, as sudden and loud as a gunshot in the early morning office, threw her back in the chair. An intake of breath, a moment's hesitation, and then she slipped into her professional persona to reach for the phone and answer, 'Dr Kathryn Brookley here.'

She heard the caller make a false start, then a clearing of the throat before a young, male voice rushed, 'Hello, Dr Brookley. Sorry to call before office hours ... but, um, pleased you've answered personally. It's Tim Mason here. An on-duty doctor in the emergency department.'

'Yes, Dr Mason. How can I help you?'

'Tim. Please. Just Tim. Ah, there was a woman admitted around seven-thirty am. I think she needs a psychiatric ... I think a psychiatrist's opinion is needed.'

'I see. Can you tell me something about the woman?' Kathryn placed the phone on the desk and hit the speaker button, providing a space between the caller and her lack of enthusiasm.

'Yeah, I can tell you something. And it's pretty interesting.'

'Proceed, then. Give me the details, Dr Mason.'

'Tim, just Tim. Okay. She was fished out of the harbour early this morning. A passenger on the six-thirty ferry from Manly spotted her, floating between the Opera House and Fort Denison. Not long after sunrise. Lucky to see her at that hour, the Marine Area Command officer told me. They were there within minutes of the call. Still, they couldn't believe she was alive. Eyewitnesses reported that she was floating like a dead person one minute; the next minute, breathing and eyes wide open. Amazing, huh?'

Kathryn covered a yawn but, registering the young doctor's earnestness, she made an effort to inject some warmth into her tone as she said, 'Yes, fascinating. So, she's alive. But who is she? Young, old?'

'Good questions, Dr Brookley. And that's what makes it even more amazing. There was absolutely no ID on her and no one fitting her description's been reported missing in the last forty-eight hours. From the look of her, though, she couldn't be older than thirty.'

'Did she say how she came to be in the water?'

'She hasn't answered a single question, hasn't spoken a single word, since being found.'

'Maybe she fell off one of those big cruise ships. Maybe she's from overseas and doesn't speak English,' Kathryn suggested, flicking off the speaker and taking the phone to her ear again.

'No, no cruise ships in or out of Sydney since late yesterday afternoon, so if she fell overboard she's been treading water for a very long time.' Kathryn heard an awkward laugh before the young doctor continued. 'And the dress she was wearing when found—looked like it was made from a sack.'

'Yes, hardly your holiday cruise wear. So ... are you thinking she just jumped in, from some point round the harbour foreshores?'

'I wondered about that,' offered Tim. 'It's possible but, as the officer pointed out to me, there are always people about the quay area and no one reported seeing her jump in. And, in addition, she was right in the middle of the main ferry lanes so … um …'

'Yes, I see. A bit of a mystery,' Kathryn said, hoping she sounded sincere. 'So, where are we? I presume the process of notifying the appropriate authorities to assist in the identification is underway? And what about the physical examination?'

'Yep. The police are across it; they've already started the process of posting bulletins with a general description of her going to all relevant agencies and authorities, and to social media so, hopefully, that'll turn up some relatives or friends or, at least, some information. The Social Work department is onto it, too. As for the physical examination, there was a doctor on the ferry when she was brought in from the water and he reported that she looked fine the instant she was retrieved. The paramedics, too, found the vital signs to be good, strong. And, my examination … same thing. Remarkably healthy; no discernible physical damage.'

'Well, perhaps you're right. It sounds like she might need a psychiatric assessment. I'll be down to Emergency in about an hour. See you then, Dr Mason.' Kathryn cut off the call and returned her focus to the wall clock. Tick, click, tick, click. She decided to stare straight ahead for another forty minutes. Tick, click. Then she stood up from her desk, brushed her hair, applied her lipstick, picked up her phone, handbag, and notebook and walked, one foot in front of the other, to her meeting with Tim just Tim, and the mystery woman.

Kathryn knew Tim instantly—the awkward-looking young man bent over tying the laces on his running shoes. As she approached, he jumped up to his full height of two lanky metres, tucked an escaped corner of his shirt back into his pants, took a very deep breath, and thrust his right hand at her for shaking. She ignored the gesture but tried out a smile as she introduced herself, saying, 'I'm Dr Brookley. But you may call me Kathryn, just Kathryn.'

'Aw. Great to meet you, Kathryn. Great that you got here so quickly. So, she's in there.' Tim indicated a room to the left of the ward desk where they were standing. 'Should I come with you?'

'Why is the door closed? If this patient is as unstable as you seem to have been suggesting, she should be under careful observation.' Kathryn did not try to hide her irritation. 'I'll do this initial evaluation on my own, thank you. And I'll contact you later, Dr Mason, with my opinion. Your mobile number, please,' she demanded, holding a flat palm out.

'Here it is, Kathryn. Dr Brookley. Here's my card. Yeah, sorry about the door. It was open … I don't know why it's now closed. And I checked the patient myself only about ten minutes ago. All good. She was quiet and comfortable in the bed. I'm sure I left the door open.'

Kathryn wasn't listening. She snatched the card from Tim's fingers and stormed toward the door, twisting its handle and flinging it open before disappearing into the room and closing it firmly behind her.

Kathryn was glad to find the woman's room was darkened and still when she entered. Perhaps my temper outburst and door-slamming didn't disturb her after all, she thought as she paused, leaning against the closed door, taking a moment to allow her eyes to become accustomed to the dim surroundings. And, if the woman was asleep, she didn't want to startle her by flicking the switch and flooding the room with the harsh glare of a hospital ceiling light.

'Please, please, come in. Come and sit with me.' Kathryn heard a strong female voice of precise vowels and clear consonants speaking to her. She looked in the direction of the voice and there, to the right of the bed, sitting up perfectly straight in a green vinyl armchair, was a petite but very striking young woman with closely cropped brown hair and wide blue eyes staring intently at her.

'Did you say something?' asked Kathryn, mentally trying to square Dr Mason's description of an uncommunicative patient with the confidently spoken woman in front of her.

The woman didn't answer. Instead, she raised her left arm in a beckoning motion, and smiled as Kathryn approached and took a seat in the plastic chair opposite her. At first the two women sat in silence. Kathryn averted her glance sideways so as not to appear to be staring, but she could feel the other woman's gaze searching the top of her forehead.

Finally, Kathryn looked up and, summoning a smile, ventured, 'I'm Dr Kathryn Brookley, but please just call me Kathryn.'

'Yes, I know who you are, Kathryn,' the woman whispered.

At this, Kathryn felt her breath catch in her throat, felt her mind shuffling through names and images of past patients, but coming up with no matches. 'Well, I'm at a disadvantage, then,' she replied as her breath settled. 'I'm very sorry but I don't recall having met you before.'

'You are correct, Kathryn. We have not met.'

'Oh, then how ...' Kathryn stopped herself, realising that she should be careful to avoid being swept up into any game this woman might be playing. She settled her thoughts back into their professional box, straightened her spine, and continued. 'Well, as I said, I'm at a disadvantage as you know who I am but I don't know you. So, please, what's your name?'

'I am me. I have many names. Choose one for me if it's necessary for you; if it makes you more comfortable.'

'I, that is we, all of us here, want to help you. You're in a hospital, but do you know why?' Kathryn could not pinpoint why she was struggling to keep her own tone calm. She was aware of the rising tension in her voice. 'If you tell us who you are, we can make sure that you find your way safely home. And, if there's some reason you don't want to return home, we can help you with that too.'

'Thank you for your kindness, but there is no need to trouble yourself. I am always safely home.' The woman smiled, revealing small, even teeth.

Kathryn arranged her face into an understanding look and said, 'Well, that's great. That's really great that, ah, that you feel safe here with us. But, um, we could make you even more comfortable if we knew a bit more about you. So, do you mind if I ask you a few questions?'

The woman shrugged and replied, 'Ask me anything, but I cannot promise to know the answers. Or, perhaps if I do know, I cannot promise that you will like my answers. But I shall do my best.'

While Kathryn listened, her mind raced. She made mental notes based on the woman's somewhat formal way of speaking. Accent: English? Definitely well educated. Direct and confident? Or clever and manipulative?

'Yes, do your best.' Kathryn smiled in encouragement. 'Why don't we start with your name?'

'Dear Kathryn, I've already answered that one. I am me. I am. But, again, feel free to put a name to me if it helps you.'

'Well, I don't want to put just any name to you. Maybe if you tell me a little about yourself I'll be better placed to choose a name that I think suits you,' suggested Kathryn.

'Ah yes, that makes sense,' said the woman, nodding and leaning forward in the chair. 'I'll tell you a short tale and perhaps you'll see something of me in that tale, and then you'll feel more at ease with me.'

Kathryn fought to keep the annoyance from showing on her face. This patient is trying to wrestle control of this meeting from me; I'll have to tread carefully, she thought. 'Yes, please proceed,' she managed.

'Thank you, Kathryn. I shall.' And, closing her eyes, the woman said:

Once, there was a young woman who, for reasons that are not relevant to this tale, became very ill. Her illness took the form of a high fever, accompanied by a paralysis first in the legs and then progressing to the chest so that the woman found it increasingly difficult to breathe. Her mother, whom she greatly loved, called a doctor. When the doctor came, he prodded and probed and prognosticated, but it was all to no avail. The illness increased in severity but the woman herself began to decrease … in size. She became smaller and smaller so that by the afternoon of the second day of her affliction, she had shrunk to a size no bigger than a hazelnut. Her mother, distraught at the progression of the illness, picked up her tiny daughter and placed her on the palm of her hand. 'What am I to do for you?' wailed the mother. The young woman said, 'I am the same person that I was yesterday, just in another form. So all you need to do is love me as you have always done.' The mother mouthed agreement to this proposition, but her heart and mind could not grasp it, and so she put her tiny daughter in her pocket and carried her about with her wherever she went, seeking a cure that would restore the girl to her former form. Until, one day, the pocket developed a hole in it, and her daughter fell out and rolled into the sea. And there she stayed until the water renewed her, changed her form again. And so she was found.

The woman leant back in the chair, indicating that her tale had concluded. Kathryn shifted uneasily.

'An interesting tale,' she managed. 'So, you're telling me that you've been ill? And that your mother has been caring for you. Is that correct?'

'We are all ill in some way, at some time. And it is in the nature of mothers to care for their children. So, yes, in some ways, you are correct.'

'Where is your mother?' asked Kathryn.

'Right here.' The woman placed her hand on her heart, not taking her gaze from Kathryn's face.

'Oh,' breathed Kathryn, as she felt the room beginning to spin around her.

'You know about locking things in your heart, don't you, Kathryn?' whispered the woman. 'And locking other things, other people, out.'

Kathryn was conscious of her legs beginning to tremble. 'I'm not sure what you mean,' she replied, 'but, in any case, this is not about me.'

'In this case, Dr Brookley, you are wrong. Talk to your husband. You will see it has everything to do with you.'

The silence that followed seemed to be choking Kathryn. She could not utter the expected doctor-to-patient words and, instead, only coughed out, 'I think I'll let you get some rest … We'll talk again later.'

She managed to steady her legs just long enough to get out of the chair and stumble from the room.

Tim came across Kathryn later in the day in the staff cafeteria. He recognised her from the back as she sat at a corner table, her head rigid and her face turned to a blank wall. She didn't seem to notice him walk up to stand behind her and she reacted with a start when he tapped her gently on the shoulder, saying her name.

'Dr Brookley? Kathryn? Hi. I didn't mean to startle you, just noticed you sitting here, alone. I, um, I thought you were going to let me know when you'd finished your assessment of our mystery patient. Are you okay? Should I … um, do you mind if I sit down?' he asked.

'Please. Yes, take a seat. Sorry I didn't get back to you earlier. And I feel I owe you an apology for my bad temper earlier.'

'No problem,' he said, dropping onto the seat. 'I'm thick skinned. Nerdy, and nervous, but thick skinned. And I probably deserved it.' Tim thought he saw a flicker of a smile cross Kathryn's mouth and, encouraged, he continued. 'So … what did you make of our patient?' He heard the excitement in his own voice, was aware of leaning a little too far across the table.

'I'm not sure yet,' Kathryn began. 'She spoke, you know? But she didn't, or wouldn't, tell me anything. Well, that's not quite true. She told me some story about an illness. Shades of Thumbelina about it. But, then again, not like it at all. Far more disturbing. And something about her mother, but not really. She's mentally unwell, that's for sure, but I wouldn't, I couldn't, at this stage, make a diagnosis.'

Tim shook his head. 'I'm not sure what you're telling me here. I don't know what thumbelina is.' He felt his face redden as the awareness of his inexperience with both psychiatric illness and women struck him. He tried to read the psychiatrist's reaction to his confession, and knew she was sneering at him when she said, 'Thumbelina is not a disease, you know. It's that fairy story of the teeny little girl. Didn't your mother ever tell you any fairy tales?'

'I didn't have a mother. Or father,' Tim muttered, trying not to sound pathetic.

He noticed Kathryn give a minute shake of her head before she said, 'Oh, Tim. I'm so sorry. That was insensitive of me. Very unprofessional too.'

Tim relaxed back in the chair. 'No, really, no need to apologise. I never knew my father. And I can't really remember my mother. I've been told she died of an overdose when I was about two. After that, I was taken into institutional care before being fostered by several very nice families until I reached eighteen.'

'That's tough. You must have been tenacious, resilient, and smart, to get yourself to university, into medicine.'

'Yeah, I worked hard at school. I didn't really have much else to do. I was hopeless at sport; home life was pretty ordinary. Don't get me wrong, though—my foster parents were good people.'

Tim thought Kathryn's features were softening. He hoped she wasn't going to cry. 'So, any other thoughts on the patient?'

'Well, there is something that's really unsettling me about this one. I can't put my finger on it. It almost felt as if she were attempting to diagnose me, as if she knew me, somehow. But, of course, she doesn't. She's clever, insightful. And I'm sure she's manipulative. I just don't understand her motivation yet.'

Taken into her confidence, Tim felt more confident himself and dared, 'You know, the mention of an illness in that story of hers, and those changes in perception of body size, might mean that there's some other pathology involved here. Maybe we should order a neurological consult.'

Tim saw Kathryn's eyes come to life. She thumped her hands on the table. 'Oh my God, That's it. Well, that's part of it. Part of what's been niggling me all afternoon. I don't know why I didn't think of it sooner.'

Tim knew a silly smile had crept across his face, knew that the way he rested his elbows on the table stamped him as too eager, but he decided he didn't care. 'So … you know what's going on with her?'

Kathryn took her time before saying, 'Not really, but you've triggered my memory of a possible link. Quite some years ago, I was a young doctor at the Royal East Sydney Hospital. One morning in the staff room, Dr Anderson, a consultant neurologist, was telling the story of how the renowned psychiatrist, Dr J J T Smith, had enlisted his help on a case at Harbourside. It involved him conducting a series of neurological tests on a young woman who was found, alive and well, in Sydney Harbour, but who seemed to have no memory, no clue, of who she was or how she got there.'

'Great,' said Tim. 'This is probably the same woman, at it again. Let's speak to Doctors Anderson and Smith.'

'That's the problem. Both Dr Anderson and Dr Smith are dead. I'm now forty-five years old so it's about twenty years since this incident. And the case Dr Anderson was speaking of was another twenty years before that. So … sometime in the 1970s. What I'm trying to say is, there'll be no help for us from the "originals". But, in reality, what help could they be anyway? You see, it doesn't fit. If that woman was still alive she'd be at least forty years older than the woman we're dealing with today. Our patient looks about thirty at the most, not seventy or more.'

Tim's eyes widened. 'Hmm, what are we talking here? Extreme facelift? Or, it could be some weird syndrome. Maybe we should do a search for that earlier case. It might give us some clues in dealing with our current mystery woman. Do you want me to go to Medical Records in my break?'

Kathryn shook her head. 'No. They don't hold records that go back that far. But …' She didn't finish the sentence. Instead, she sprang up. 'Dorothy, Dr Smith's secretary. She's still there, working for the group of psychiatrists who took over his practice. She's been there forever.'

When Dr Brookley had called to inquire about records or information on a mysterious woman who had been pulled from the harbour decades before, Dorothy knew exactly what was being asked of her. She knew where the file was kept, and she knew what it contained. Every day for the past forty years she had thought about the woman who was the subject of that file. Oh, how willing she had been then to be judge and jury. Now, very often, she wondered what her life would have been like if she had been courageous enough, all those years ago, to agree with her employer, Dr Smith. She suspected that she would have ended up like Margery. But would that have been so bad? Was her own lonely, tedious life any better than that of the deranged but happy and outrageously wealthy old nun?

This office had been the centre of Dorothy's life for forty-five years. Now, at seventy-seven years of age, she was well past retirement but, as she had nothing and no one else to fill her days, and as she was still competent and had been willing to keep up with the technology that modern offices required, she'd kept working. On many winter mornings her bones ached as she set out from her little one-bedroom apartment, but the aches of loneliness, guilt, and regret were more acute and propelled her onto the crowded train and into the office that had once been her joy but was now her penance.

And now this. All these years later. Would it be the end, or was it another chance, a very late, last minute chance? Yes, it's said that there are some things that happen in life that offer us the possibility of change, present us with an opportunity to completely renew our way of being in the world. There are some individuals who come into our lives and make an impact so startling that we can, if we choose, go into the future seeing ourselves and others in an astoundingly different way. Dorothy knew this, but she also knew that many people miss or reject the opportunity when it's presented. People like her. They respond with fear; they put up their walls and retreat to live behind them, denying that they have ever glimpsed what's on the other side. They move in comfortable and familiar patterns. They choose the delusion of security and surround themselves with friends who share the same delusion. Dorothy had often wondered if such delusion-sharing was the definition of sanity or of madness. She had concluded, at different times and depending on her mood, that it was neither—and both.

Dorothy made her first decision. She would give Dr Brookley the whole file. She would take more time with the second decision. Perhaps, when the moment came, she would answer all the questions; and, perhaps, if given the opportunity, she would see this young woman from the water. But not today. For today it was enough to hand over the file.

From the back of the top drawer of her desk, Dorothy took out a single key attached to a souvenir keyring of the Sydney Harbour Bridge. She used the key to try to open the middle drawer of the old filing cabinet in the corner. She was not surprised when the lock resisted the key's entry—it was at least twenty years since this drawer had been opened. Dorothy trudged back to her desk and picked up a tube of lotion that she used throughout the day on her dry, wrinkly hands. She squeezed a few drops of the lotion onto the key and, on returning it to the lock, was pleased to find that it did the trick.

The drawer contained only one item. She took out the slim, yellowing manila folder and then placed it into a larger plastic document satchel, tied a string tightly around the satchel and wrote in black permanent marker across the front and back surfaces the word 'Confidential'. Picking up the satchel she walked out of her office, not bothering to close the door behind her. She gave the satchel to the receptionist, Mrs James, with instructions to respect the 'Confidential' nature of the material and to hand it directly to Dr Kathryn Brookley, and no one else.

'Thank you, Mrs James. And please inform my employers that I am retiring as of today,' she said. Dorothy left without looking back.

{ 3 }

This is what she said:

Those who look carefully see that the mundane and the everyday are alive with the pulse and possibility of the miraculous. Think about your kitchen table. It is very familiar in its ordinariness and practicality. A flat timber surface, scratches here and there, four straight wooden legs. It is not a big table but it is well made, the tabletop perfectly rectangular in shape, with its longer sides exactly ninety centimetres apart along the entire one hundred and fifty centimetre length. In Euclidean geometry those longer sides of your rectangular table are defined as being parallel—and parallel lines, by definition, do not meet or intersect. But imagine that both long sides of your kitchen table happen to rest perfectly on two meridians of longitude. You remember from your school days that meridians of longitude meet at the poles, and here we move from the kitchen to the great circles of hyperbolic space. Planes versus spheres. Parallel versus non-parallel lines. Limits versus infinity. What you see versus what is. Things viewed from a greater perspective often look very different to things that exist within the limits of our day-to-day vision. What do you really know of your kitchen table?

Kathryn sat at her kitchen table, a glass of red wine in her hand, the forty-year-old folder from Dr Smith's archives in front of her. On its cover, in the 'Patient's Name' box, she read 'Known as Julie X'. She took a gulp of wine, put the glass down on the table, and brought her hands together, raising them to let the tips of her index fingers rest on her lips, prayer-like. She stared at the folder, hesitating to look at its contents. She lowered her hands, spread her fingers out on the table's surface, and thought of the rings that once circled the fourth finger of her left hand. She lifted the glass for another gulp and was aware of the earthy flavour in her mouth. She placed the glass down again, noticing the dark knot of honey-coloured wood next to where the glass sat. She listened to the silence of the late-night kitchen.

She opened the folder and fanned its contents across the table. At a glance, she could tell that it was a collection of medical reports, newspaper clippings, records and transcripts of interviews, miscellaneous jottings, and a small faded photo. On closer inspection she saw that someone had taken the time to give each item a number and a heading of sorts—a description of the item's origin, type, and a date. She began to read.

Item 1: Xeroxed copy of Emergency Department admission notes; attending doctor not named.

7 May 1973, 7.30 am

Female, age uncertain but estimated to be around 30 years, brought to Emergency Dept by ambulance at around 7.20 am after being pulled from Sydney Harbour by a ferry crew. Crew members reported woman was breathing when rescued. Ambulance officers attending reported breathing and blood pressure normal, and no apparent signs of trauma to head or body. No signs of hypothermia.

Examination on admission:
- Temperature: 36.5C
- Respiration: 13
- Blood pressure: 120/70
- Pulse: 65
- Non-communicative; uncertain if this is due to lack of

comprehension or of speech, or both. At this stage, patient is unable to be identified, and cannot/will not identify herself. Social Work assessment ordered. Patient to be transferred to a general medical ward for overnight stay by which time, hopefully, family will be located.

Item 2: Newspaper clipping, *Herald Sun*, late edition, 7 May 1973.

A young woman was pulled from Sydney Harbour early this morning by Manly ferry crew members after a passenger spotted her floating near Fort Denison. The ferry immediately called for assistance and Water Patrol Officers responded. Ambulance officers were contacted and were at Circular Quay when the ferry docked to transport the woman to the emergency department of Royal Harbourside Hospital where she remains in a stable condition and under observation. The woman showed no signs of physical injury, but is apparently confused and disorientated as she is unable to give any account of herself. Police are appealing for help in identifying her. She is described as being about 30 years old, 5' 2" tall, and of slim build. She has light brown, closely cropped hair, pale complexion, blue eyes, and was wearing a long, grey woollen dress but no shoes or jewellery. Contact North Sydney Police Station if you have witnessed anything in relation to this incident or if you have any information about this woman.

Item 3: Typed copy of Resident Medical Officer's report on incident of 8 May 1973; attending doctor not named.

Re: unidentified female patient, admitted one day prior (7 May) following her discovery in the harbour.

11.20 am: paged to urgently attend a patient on Level 4 Medical Ward experiencing sudden onset of breathing difficulties and paralysis of the lower limbs. Arrived within 5 minutes of being called but, on examination, found patient to be breathing normally, lower limbs mobile and responsive to stimuli. All other vital signs normal. Patient was still unable/unwilling to identify herself, still not speaking, but did shake her head when asked if headache was present. Appeared somewhat drowsy but otherwise well.

Recommendations: allow patient to rest but continue half-hourly obs.

(Note that patient was seen by psychiatric Dr J J T Smith yesterday pm; Dr Smith to be informed of this latest development. Note, expedite Dr Smith's recommendation for neurological consultation for this patient.)

Item 4: Transcript from tape recording of Sister Margery Plimsoll's account of her first meeting with mystery woman, which took place on evening of 8 May 1973. Recorded during interview with psychiatrist Dr J J T Smith on 25 May 1973.

I remember every detail, every thought, word, and action of our first meeting. It is etched in my mind like a woodcut design, which I have used as the stamped background to my life since that time. Many nights I dream of it; many nights I dream of the other meetings. All of the meetings, all of our conversations, inspire my days and soothe my nights.

When I came on duty at ten pm for the overnight shift, I was told by the head nurse of the departing shift that the woman had slept for some hours following a short episode of breathing difficulty and partial paralysis earlier in the day, but had awoken at around six pm and appeared bright-eyed and alert. She had eaten all of the evening meal before falling into a normal and very peaceful sleep as soon as the main ward lights were turned off. But, so far, the woman had not spoken a word.

I admit to being intrigued by the woman's flawless skin—very pale, but very beautiful, as if it had never seen the sun. Strange, though, that her hands were quite calloused, indicating manual labour. There was something about the woman that disturbed me. Something familiar; a chord of recognition, but I could not find the melody.

'Are you all right, dear?' I whispered, placing my cool hand on the woman's forehead. Here, I thought I detected a slight rise in temperature and so I reached for a thermometer.

'Just pop this in your mouth, dear. You seem a little warm. That's right, just hold it there gently. It won't take too long,' I assured her. I took the woman's right hand in mine and held it as I waited for the temperature to register. When I removed the thermometer, I saw that her temperature was indeed elevated and she seemed a little agitated. She began to make a series of small, sighing sounds, forming her mouth into shapes that suggested speech.

'What is it, my dear?' I asked, leaning my head closer to her quiet utterances. 'What can I do for you? If you tell me your name, I'll be able to help you.'

'Ju, jul … ju,' the woman breathed, the quality of her voice as gentle as bubbles in dishwater.

'Is your name Julie?' I prompted. (I have a particular liking for that name. If I'd had a daughter, that is the name I would have given her.)

'You must tell me, my dear,' I tried again. 'I see now that you can speak after all and, if you tell me your name, I'll be able to contact your family to take you home. I'm sure you'd like that.'

The woman shook her head, rapidly and vehemently, and then she fell back against the pillow and, reaching her right hand toward me, patted my arm. Such a kind touch. And, as no other patients called for my attention, I remained with the woman, gently stroking her forehead and close-cropped brown hair, until the first pale rays of dawn tapped at the east-facing window at the end of the ward. The woman seemed to respond to those rays. I noticed her eyes moving under their fragile lids; I saw her fingers twitch; I heard her take a solid inhalation, and then she awoke.

'How are you feeling?' I asked.

'I am well. And you are well. And all is well, and all shall be well,' she answered, even though I had asked only about her health. Later, of course, I would understand what she meant but, at that time, I just thanked God that the woman was beginning to communicate. It gave me confidence to try, again, to find out something about her.

'Yes, you *do* seem well,' I began. 'I'll check your temperature again in a minute but, perhaps, you've now remembered your name.'

'I have not forgotten it,' she said.

'Oh, that's good. If you tell me, I can let the right people know and we can help you get home to your family.'

'What is *your* name?' she asked, not seeming to be ignoring me but, rather, enlarging the communication. It seemed a reasonable question so I answered, 'I am Sister Margery.'

'Sister Margery.' She said it as a repetition, not an address. 'It is a good name. But do you understand that even though you have told me your name, I cannot help you get home?'

'Yes, I see. But I'm not a patient, I'm a nun, so my home is here, in my work in this hospital, in my prayers, in my dedication to others, and to God,' I tried to explain.

'Then we are the same, Sister Margery. Like you, I am home already.'

I was confused, and I told her so.

'Then I will tell you a tale, and you will see something of me in the tale, and you will understand better ...'

Once, long ago, there was a woman who delighted in the ordinary things of her everyday life. She loved the high heat of a summer's day, and the deep chill of winter evenings. She loved the fragrance and colours of her garden in spring, and the way that the bees gathered sweetness from the garden's flowers. She loved the way in which the rain tumbled in plump drops over the eaves of her cottage on darkening autumn afternoons. Best of all, she loved the open arms of her husband and the laughter of her children. But one day, there were no more children—they had grown and gone on with their own lives and her husband had died and her work in the cottage was no longer joyous; it was hollow. But her heart was still full, for, in her ordinariness, she had learnt to love and to suffer; she had embraced the lessons of everyday life. The sun still shone, and the rain still fell, and the bees still gathered. And so she knew that she too must be useful. But her home was no longer the place of her usefulness. And so she left it, to find her work in the home of the world.

Something in that tale moved me. I cannot describe what it was. I stopped asking her for details of her life after that. I just called her 'Julie' because that name had come to me when she had made those first sounds. I know it didn't really suit her. Julies are outgoing, pretty, and popular. She was nothing like that, but I hoped that giving her an ordinary, happy name would stop others pestering her about irrelevant details.

Item 5: Handwritten note in Medical Ward nursing file of morning of 9 May 1973. Authoring nurse not named.

Sister Margery reported at shift changeover this morning that during the night, the mystery patient gave her name as 'Julie'. Files relating to this patient will now be marked as 'Julie X' until more conclusive identification comes to light.

Item 6: Carbon-copy of original letter of referral from Dr J J T Smith to consultant neurologist, Dr M Anderson.

Dr J J T Smith (Psychiatrist)
Suite 45
Sterling Medical Building
Pacific Highway
St Leonards NSW 2060

17 May 1973

Dear Dr Anderson,

Attached please find the 'official' referral for the patient known as 'Julie X', whom we discussed in our recent phone conversation. From that conversation, you will understand that, unfortunately, I can give you very little in the way of substantive personal information about this woman, but I shall attempt to summarise my thoughts on her to date.

Julie X is about thirty years old and appears to be in generally very good health, despite her ordeal in the harbour and retrieval some ten days ago on 7 May. She is reluctant (more than unable, I feel) to identify herself, but has expressed a willingness to be known as 'Julie', at least for the time being. To this point, no friend or relative has come forward, and no missing person report has matched her description. She is articulate and intelligent and, intriguingly, gives accounts of herself in what she terms 'tales'. From the psychiatric point of view I at first thought these tales might be representative of some sort of dissociation, perhaps a dissociative amnesia, but Julie's apparent control of what she reveals, and to whom she reveals it, leads me to suspect that there is something more complex going on. What this 'something more complex' might be I have yet to discover, but one of Julie's tales in particular has prompted me to request your assistance. The tale concerns a young woman who, after becoming ill with breathing difficulties and lower limb paralysis, experiences a significant decrease in body size (Julie actually described it as becoming the size of a hazelnut) and, thus, it has occurred to me that there might be some sort of frontal or temporal lobe abnormality, or other more diffuse neurological problem, giving rise to such physical symptoms and changes in perception. Your assessment of this patient, therefore, is sought and will be greatly appreciated.

Personally (and I realise that what I am about to admit puts me at odds with the bulk of my medical colleagues), I find Julie's explanation of an alternate reality—which I also touched on in our recent conversation—quite compelling and, possibly, more consistent with good mental health than what often passes for sanity in the general population. Perhaps this says more about me than about Julie X and, as such views are probably best left outside the professional consideration of this patient, I offer them only as 'off the record' comments, which might, or might not, add to the overall picture of this unusual young woman.

I await your opinion with interest.

Yours sincerely,

J J T Smith

Item 7: Xeroxed copy of typed report by occupational thera-pist, Robyn Hideman, following incident involving Julie X at psych unit, 31 May 1973.

I, Robyn Hideman, declare the following to be a true report of an incident that happened during an 'Activities of Daily Living' session on Ward 10 at Northern Psychiatric Centre on Thursday, 31 May 1973. I write this report on the afternoon of the same day.

I had been one of the occupational therapists for Ward 10 for only three weeks when I was directed by my supervisor to provide a session in basic kitchen activities for a group of the ward's patients. Being new to the position and, in fact, having only recently graduated, my experience was not vast but I can truly say that I was conscientious and saw my work in the psychiatric sector as a vital part of the rehabilitation process. In my view, encouraging and assisting these patients to begin to look after themselves in preparation for their possible release from hospital, was of equal, or even greater, importance than ensuring their medication was in order. Yes, making morning tea for yourself might seem the simplest of chores for most people, but when you are seriously out of touch with reality such ordinary tasks are a challenge, and a challenge I was hoping the patients under my care that morning would embrace and benefit from. This is my way of explaining that I was confident when I led patients Julie X, Bruce W, Cheryl D, Arleen P, and Rodney R into the ward kitchen.

I had prepared carefully for this session. Earlier that morning I had gone through every drawer and over every surface of the kitchen removing knives and other sharp objects to a locked cupboard. I returned to the kitchen, this time with my charges, at a few minutes after ten am. No one, with the exception of Sooty, the kitchen's cat, was present when we entered and he was dozing in his regular morning position on a sunlit patch of linoleum under the end of the stainless steel bench opposite the garden window.

I said something along the lines of: 'Okay, let's get started. Good, I see you've all put your cigarettes out and just a reminder that we have to keep it that way in the kitchen. So, it's morning tea for six of us and we're going to work together to make it a really enjoyable occasion.'

I further encouraged and directed the patients by saying: 'I've divided up the jobs so listen carefully for your part. Julie and Arleen, you're in charge of setting the table. You'll need to choose and spread a tablecloth, set out the cups and saucers, the plates, and spoons and forks. Rodney, the cake is in the fridge, already cut, but you'll need to arrange it on a serving plate and also put together a selection of biscuits on another plate. Bruce, you'll be making a large pot of tea, and Cheryl, you'll be getting the milk into a nice jug and refilling the sugar bowl. Are we all clear?'

Nobody answered but I knew they had heard and understood because they all began to move around the kitchen with a purposeful air. Arleen was already taking a gingham cloth from a drawer and Julie was following her to the table with some cups and plates in both hands. Bruce, I noticed, had filled the large kettle from the sink's tap and placed it correctly on the largest hotplate.

'That's right, Bruce,' I said, and I recall that I put a hand gently and tentatively on his back as I instructed him. 'Now turn it onto the highest setting. That will make the water heat more quickly.'

Apart from me, nobody said a word but there was enough activity to assure me that this session was going well. I felt even more confident about this when, within ten minutes of commencement, four of the five patients were sitting at the table, eyeing the cake and fiddling impatiently with spoons and forks. I took up a position with them, on the longer side of the table, where I could keep a good view of Bruce and the final component of his tea-making. On cue, the kettle began to whistle the water's readiness, and I called across the table to him, 'Okay, Bruce, time to take the water off the heat. Right. Now just pour it onto the tea leaves that you've already got in the pot.'

I saw Bruce duly lift up the kettle and begin to turn toward the teapot but, quicker than a blink, he swung the other way and emptied the entire boiling contents onto the sleeping Sooty. The cat's horrific howls were short-lived. It seemed he was dead of shock within moments. It was a shocking thing for all of us. The group around the table were frozen to their seats. I stepped out from behind the table but could not move any further—my legs were jelly. And, I'm mortified to say, from somewhere deep in my stomach I heard a scream force its way up my throat and out of my mouth. Quite soon after this I heard people running along the corridor. Help arriving, but too late. A wardsman moved to restrain Bruce, but no force was necessary; he had begun to hum and was more than willing to return to his room in exchange for a cigarette. Other staff appeared from everywhere to escort the other patients from the kitchen. Some went willingly, distressed by what they had just witnessed and wanting no more of it. But not Cheryl; she began wailing into a handkerchief and, proclaiming her deep love for Sooty, she moved toward me and linked her arms around my waist, anchoring herself to the spot. And not Julie. Julie gripped the corner of the table when Dr Prescott rushed in and tried to coax her on her way. She shook her head violently in protest and pushed past the doctor to reach the dead cat in what seemed like one leap. She bent down and laid her hands on the animal's wet, scorched fur. For a moment she was perfectly still, perfectly quiet, and those of us watching took her cue and shuffled to form a still, quiet circle around her. Slowly, Julie began rocking back and forth in her crouched position and from her mouth came a mumble, a tumble of incoherent sounds. Her rocking increased and the sounds arranged themselves into words, but not words that made sense to her audience. And then the words ceased and the room seemed to become a vacuum—no sound, no movement, no breath. Suddenly, Julie scooped up the limp cat, holding it close to her chest, cradling it as if it were a newborn baby. With her next movement, Julie stood, lifting the cat's body closer to her mouth as she did so. Strongly, deliberately, she inhaled and, with a powerful puff, exhaled completely over the cat's head.

We all saw it. Later that day, all but Dr Prescott would describe seeing exactly the same thing. All but Dr Prescott would describe catching our own breath as Sooty's chest expanded in receipt of Julie's breath. All but Dr Prescott would describe the cat's chest continuing to contract and expand in an unmistakable show of life. All but Dr Prescott would tell of seeing Julie place Sooty back down on the kitchen floor and of seeing him roll immediately from his side to his four paws and walk vigorously back toward his sunny spot underneath the bench, pausing briefly to lap up a bowl of milk on the way. We would all tell of our amazement at realising that Sooty's scorched fur and skin had reconstituted into its former glossy pelt.

'It's a miracle,' all but Dr Prescott said.

'The cat was obviously just stunned,' said Dr Prescott. 'Julie picking the animal up so suddenly started it breathing again.'

'But what about the scalding injury?' we all said.

'Obviously the water wasn't as hot as you all assumed,' said Dr Prescott.

'But we saw it with our own eyes,' we all said.

'I suspect magic, or group delusion,' said Dr Prescott. 'As for Julie, I suspect temporal lobe epilepsy. I will schedule another brain scan.'

'Why don't you have the fucking brain scan?' screamed Cheryl. 'You're the only one who can't see the bleeding obvious.'

'Get them back to their rooms now,' barked the doctor to a young orderly whose mouth had formed into a poorly disguised grin at Cheryl's words. I think Dr Prescott saw that I grinned at this too because he then turned on me and shouted, 'Obviously you did not take the expected precautions for this activity. These are all very disturbed people and you have acted unprofessionally in allowing this incident to develop. You'll be expected to provide a complete report on what went on here this morning. Make sure that what you have to say is factual, not fanciful. Your job's on the line so I'm sure you understand what I mean.'

Here ends my truthful report.

Item 8: Handwritten note stapled to front of the occupational therapist's account, dated 8 July 1975.

Tried to follow up on this report and on the young woman who wrote it. Discovered that the report was never tabled. Miss Hideman resigned the same day she submitted the report and apparently moved away from Sydney shortly after. She did not renew her registration as an occupational therapist and there are no records showing her as working in any health-related facility since the reported date of the incident. Her current whereabouts are unknown.

Item 9: A handwritten note on the subject of witches.

Witches cannot be drowned.

'This old woman, suspected of being a witch, was taken to a great river nearby, to see if she would sink or float. Her legs were tied and she was thrown in and it was observed that, though she tried to stay under the water by the pumping of her hands and arms, she instead did swim like a piece of cork. Above twenty persons were there to attest the truth of this.' (*English Chronicle*, late 1600s)

See also the *Maleus Malificarum*, Part 3, q.15, (Sprenger and Kramer, 15th century).

Item 10: Two short notes, handwritten. No date.

'There's only one lesson, you know.' (Julie X)
And then he showed me a little thing, the size of a hazelnut. And I wondered at it and he told me it was all that was made. And I wondered how it did not fall away to nothingness because it was so small. And he replied that it was preserved because he made it and cared for it and loved it. (JN, 14th century).

Item 11: Photograph labelled: Julie and Margery, Xmas '73.

Item 12: Newspaper clipping, *Sydney Morning Herald*, 7 May 1974.

A young woman, who was found in Sydney Harbour under mysterious circumstances one year ago to the day, is believed to have drowned after falling from a residential wharf on Sydney's Pittwater. A man on a yacht, at anchor some distance from the Cottage Point waterfront property, saw the woman tumble into the water early yesterday morning and alerted authorities. A thorough search of the area has so far failed to find any trace of the woman whose identity, since her discovery last year and despite extensive investigation, has remained a mystery.

Kathryn woke with a start, her head lurching up suddenly from where it had been resting on her forearms on the table. She had been dreaming of watching the moon rise over a still bay. The evening was warm, and the air was full of the scent of night-jasmine. She could taste the salt that the breeze had picked up from the bay's water, and she could hear the laughter of the two women with her. One of them was her young mystery patient; or was it Julie? And who was the older woman?

She sat back from her kitchen table with the questions still in her head, but the images of the dream were already vanishing as the chill of a pre-dawn May morning settled on her body. She realised that she must have fallen asleep immediately after completing her study of the contents of the folder. The kitchen light was still on but the heating had switched off in obedience to the automatic timer, leaving the room icy. Her body felt stiff with the cold and the long sitting, reading, re-reading, and thinking. She inclined her head to one shoulder then the other in an effort to undo some of the kinks jamming her neck. She wriggled her toes in her slippers to get the blood circulating there again before she stretched her arms overhead and yawned loudly. Then she stood up, flicked on the heater, and headed for the kettle and a strong cup of tea.

As she waited for the water to boil, she looked out her kitchen window at the night retreating from the garden. The first stripes of yellow and pink were appearing over the back fence. It was going to be a beautiful day.

The hot tea, followed by a hot shower, refreshed her and she decided that she would go straight into work. This nonsense with the current mystery woman needed to be sorted out promptly. Kathryn was sure that the woman must have heard or read about Julie X and was mimicking her now; but for what purpose? I'm a psychiatrist, not a detective, thought Kathryn as she rummaged through her bag for Tim Mason's card. For the moment, Kathryn regarded Tim as the most appropriate sounding board for this situation. In their brief meetings of the previous day she had summed him up as open and non-judgmental. True, he was a little awkward but he was also young, unjaded. At some level, Kathryn acknowledged that she needed Tim's energy and enthusiasm to deal with the sweep of challenges and possibilities that the mystery woman seemed to be presenting. And, in the light of their reactions to her own recent host of personal problems, she was reluctant to share any more than was absolutely necessary with her senior medical colleagues.

Kathryn texted Tim as she left home, asking him to meet her in the staff cafeteria before his shift. She explained that she wanted to update him on what she'd discovered in the folder. He responded immediately that he would be there waiting for her.

The cafeteria was busy when she arrived and she wondered about the wisdom of meeting there when she'd hoped to have an uninterrupted discussion with Tim. She caught sight of him in the queue at the service counter. He noticed her at the same time and waved her over.

'It's going to be too noisy here for us to talk,' she said when she reached him.

'No, it's okay. Look, see that table over in the corner? I've left my jacket and a pile of books on it. I rushed in here as soon as I got your message. What can I get you?'

'Just a black coffee, strong, please,' she answered, not bothering to argue with him when he refused the money she held out to him. Instead, she crossed to the corner table and got Julie X's folder out in preparation for their conversation.

'Well. Anything interesting?' Tim began as he started unloading the tray—the coffee for Kathryn; a large plate of eggs, bacon, sausage, and toast, and a mug of hot chocolate for himself.

Kathryn cleared a space to the side of Tim's array of food. 'See for yourself,' she instructed, spreading out the folder's various content pages. 'Or would you prefer me to summarise?'

Tim formed a distorted smile around his mouthful of sausage and egg and managed, 'A bit of both.'

'Okay, you eat. I'll begin,' she said. 'The folder's contents consist of both original and transcribed, typed and handwritten information. Oh, and on the subject of identity, the mystery woman from the 1970s came to be referred to as "Julie X", so I'll also refer to her in that way to avoid confusion with our present mystery woman.'

Kathryn paused for a sip of coffee and then pointed to the first page in the folder's pile.

'Item 1. Emergency admission notes. The woman in these notes is Julie X, admitted forty years ago. But her description, as given by the admitting doctor in Emergency, is very similar to our current woman. I'm reminding you of this because I have to keep reminding myself of the same thing. Look here,' she said, tapping her index finger on the page. '"*Female, age uncertain but estimated around 30 year … brought to Emergency Dept … pulled from Sydney Harbour by a ferry crew*" … and so on. Sound familiar? The notes also say she couldn't identify herself. And check the date: 7 May. The same day that our current woman was discovered—just forty years earlier.'

Kathryn could see she had Tim's attention, could see by the way he tilted his head to one side and slowed his chewing that he understood the seriousness of what she was telling him. She went on: 'Item 2 is the newspaper account of a woman being pulled from the harbour, unscathed; again so similar to our own mystery woman. And it gets really interesting after this with these next items giving details, from a variety of perspectives, of what happened to the 1970's patient. Look at Item 3. It's a copy of the resident doctor's notes on what happened to Julie X on the day after she was admitted to the ward. Lower limb paralysis and breathing difficulties. These were the symptoms that our patient attributed to the woman in her tale; you know, the Thumbelina story I told you about. Anyway, it's all weird and, I tell you, if our water woman starts having paralysis or breathing difficulties today, I'm going to need specialist treatment myself.' Kathryn allowed herself a little laugh and Tim smiled back.

'Yeah, that would be too creepy,' he agreed. 'Sorry, I don't mean to interrupt you but do you mind if I take a minute to check if they need me in Emergency yet? Officially I was on-duty ten minutes ago. Steve's covering for me, but I'll have to go if it gets busy,' Tim explained, looking at his phone. 'No, so far so good. Keep going, Dr Brookley. Kathryn.'

'Well, this next item *is* a bit creepy, I think. It's a transcript from a recording of someone called "Sister Margery Plimsoll" and it seems that she's the one who gave the woman the name "Julie". It also seems that Julie had quite an impact on Sister Margery. A life-changing impact. But what struck me especially about this account was the way that Julie X told a story when asked about her name and home. Tim, that's when I got the strange tale yesterday—when I was trying to get some personal details from her. That's more than a coincidence, don't you think?'

Tim took up the transcript and studied it.

'It is strange. Still, it might be part of an unusual syndrome. You know, like a storytelling neurosis, or something,' suggested Tim, smiling but without much conviction.

Kathryn laughed again. 'No such thing. Or, are you going to say that we've discovered this new syndrome? Are you planning to write it up for the journals?'

'Maybe. I hadn't thought of that, but why not?'

'Well, you might want to hear the rest of my summary before you get to that. I think there's a bit more investigation required. For example, Tim, why would a nun be nursing Julie X? I mean, this is a public hospital.'

'Believe it or not, I might be able to answer this,' said Tim. 'I read—yes, actually read—a brief history of this hospital when my residency here was first confirmed. For many years, right up into the early 1970s, there was a reciprocal arrangement with a Catholic private hospital that saw some of their nursing nuns working here, and it also allowed for some of the public, post-emergency patients who needed only observation and some gentle care to be transferred there. I would imagine that Julie X (presuming her breathing problem and the paralysis turned out to be transitory) would have been a good candidate for a stay in that private hospital, you know, until her identity was sorted.'

'Tim, that really does explain it,' said Kathryn. 'So, maybe Sister Margery or one of the other nuns might still be alive to tell us more about the mysterious Julie X.'

Tim shook his head. 'One or two of them might still be alive but I don't know where we'd find them. According to my reading, that little hospital closed in about 1975. And, I didn't read this, but I heard it somewhere, the sisters who ran the hospital were a small order that, for some reason—some sort of scandal—was discontinued … if that's the right word for a religious order … when the hospital was shut down.'

Kathryn shrugged. 'Well, perhaps we won't need to find anyone. Hopefully someone will turn up soon to claim our mystery woman, and all this will start to make sense. There's got to be a rational explanation. Which brings me back to my summary. Item 6, for example, is Dr Smith's referral of Julie to the neurologist, Dr Anderson. I was quite pleased to find that because it confirms my memory of Dr Anderson having assessed the original woman. It would be helpful to know if he turned up any brain dysfunction, but I don't know where we'd look for that. And, anyway, the next item has Julie in the Northern Psych Centre so I guess we can assume that her problems turned out to be mental and not physical. And this is where it gets really strange. Have a read of Item 7, the report of a strange incident that happened during an occupational therapy session. And the little attached note, Item 8, says that the OT quit her job, disappeared, straight after the occurrence.' Kathryn rifled through the papers and handed the relevant pages to Tim.

She sat very still while he read them. This drama is the last thing I need, she thought. And yet, it's the first thing that's interested me in months. Last and first. First and last. Last and first. First and last. The words clicked over in her head.

'Kathryn. Kathryn. Dr Brookley?' The voice seemed to be coming from far away, muffled, underwater.

'Sorry, Tim. I was just thinking of something. What were you saying?'

'I was saying that this OT's account is pretty amazing. Disturbing. Do you think it was a miraculous healing? Of the cat?'

'No, of course I don't. There's got to be a logical explanation.'

'Like what?'

'Any number of things … perhaps some kind of group hypnosis went on in that psych hospital. Don't tell me you believe in miracles?'

'Who knows? If something like that cat thing happened before *my* eyes, well, that would be … well, that would be very hard to discount. Maybe I would believe, if that's what my experience was.'

Kathryn made no effort to disguise her irritation. 'Tim, get a grip. You're a doctor. Objectivity should be your guide. Science doesn't countenance miracles.'

'Science itself is a bit of miracle, I think.'

'Rubbish, Tim.' Kathryn noticed Tim's smile fade, his eyes now downcast. She conjured a softer tone. 'Why don't you get us another coffee?'

Tim nodded, sprang to his feet. She watched him walking over to the counter to order. So tall, so thin, so awkward. And yet, so bright, uncomplicated, non-threatening, and eager to help. She regretted her stridency. There were details in the remaining items that had unnerved her and she spent the short time waiting for Tim's return to the table weighing up whether she should share them with him. She and Tim weren't friends; they were not even colleagues, really. But, for present purposes, young Dr Mason was an ally in the sorting out of this annoying case. With his surprising collection of background knowledge,

Tim might be able to offer insights that had not occurred to her.

'Here,' he said, placing the coffees down before he sat again. 'And I got some pastries as well. So … we're set. Continue.'

Kathryn ignored the pastries but picked up the coffee and lowered her voice to say, 'Tim, this next item is a note about witches. It's handwritten, in the same hand as the note about the OT quitting, but there's no indication of the writer.'

Tim put a half-eaten pastry back on the plate and gave his attention to the note. 'This mention of witches not being able to be drowned is interesting in light of both Julie X and our own mystery woman, isn't it? I mean, they were both pulled out of the harbour, and were apparently unscathed by the immersion.'

'Surely you're not saying you believe in witches too?' asked Kathryn, her eyebrows moving into a frown.

Tim had returned to munching his apple danish and finished it before replying. 'Well, yes and no. I guess if you'd somehow come to know that witches can't be drowned, then it's something you might jot down when you've got a patient who's survived a watery ordeal. Like, even if you're the world's top psychiatrist or neurologist, you still might read about other stuff. Now, take me, for example. I'm a very committed young medico who really likes vampire books and movies.'

Kathryn's little smile at his confession seemed to encourage him and he went on: 'And, I also happen to know, from my wider reading and movie viewing, that when all those women who were accused of being witches were tested as to their floating or sinking potential, it was at a time when most women, most people, couldn't swim anyway, so of course it was only the few, very cluey, women who kept afloat. And, naturally men were, and still are, wary of clever women. Not to mention the fact that, in these witch tests, the women usually had their hands bound to their ankles so there was no other possibility but drowning unless you were smart enough to escape the binding. Again, that would make you cleverer than the men who bound you, wouldn't it? See, it's all about male anxiety about women,' he concluded with a folding of his arms and a broad grin.

Kathryn didn't smile back this time. Instead, she put her elbows on the table and, resting her chin in her hands, stared across the cafeteria to the window overlooking the hospital garden. She held the pose for a minute or two before shifting her eyes back to the young man. 'Tim, I know you're trying to lighten the atmosphere here and I appreciate it. But, actually, what you say makes a lot of sense. What if someone did feel threatened by Julie X, not just because she survived, apparently unharmed, from a potential drowning, but because she didn't conform to the norm in other ways? It seems she disturbed a lot of people.'

When Tim made no attempt to disagree with her, Kathryn straightened up, took a breath and expanded on the point: 'It's this quality of disturbing people that interests me a lot about both of these women. And, actually, I'm speaking personally here. Take a look at these last three items,' she said, carefully picking up a scrap of paper, a newspaper clipping, and the small photo and handing them to Tim.

'Okay,' agreed Tim. He took his time reading the two short items and then studied the photo. 'This Julie here looks a lot like our patient, doesn't she?'

Kathryn nodded and began tapping her index finger at one of the items on the table. 'That handwritten scrap with the quote from someone named only as "JN, 14ᵗʰ century"—does it remind you of anything?'

Tim narrowed his eyes, cocked his head to the side and then slowly shook it. 'Ah, I don't think so.'

'Look again, Tim. Here, let me read it to you,' she said, moving the page so they could both look at it at the same time. '"*And then he showed me a little thing, the size of a hazelnut. And I wondered at it and he told me it was all that was made. And I wondered how it did not fall away to nothingness because it was so small, And he replied that it was preserved because he made it and cared for it and loved it.*" In a way, I'm relieved that you don't recognise anything in particular. It helps me explain away my initial uneasiness about it. I'm probably reading too much into it. But, anyway, for what it's worth, we're back to yesterday's tale again where our patient referred to a sick young woman shrinking to *a size no bigger than a hazelnut*. Here is someone, all those years ago, putting a note in Julie X's file that also refers to something about a hazelnut. A hazelnut. I guess it's a coincidence and I'm just being oversensitive, don't you think, Tim?

Tim was about to speak. Kathryn watched him as he tried to form his mouth into a meaningful reply, but she stopped him before any words came.

'Just while you're deciding whether it's odd or not, Tim, there's one more thing in those items that I've found unsettling personally. You'll have noticed in that final item—the newspaper clipping from 1974— that Julie X is reported to have disappeared after falling from a wharf. The wharf was at Cottage Point, on the Pittwater. Do you know it?'

Tim shook his head, so Kathryn continued: 'It's a small community, a very small community; within a national park, but out of the way. And I know that because it's also where my husband and ... er ... where I have a holiday house. Why doesn't *that* feel like a mere coincidence to me?'

Again, Tim's mouth worked on a reply. He shifted awkwardly in the chair.

'Let's just think about this,' he replied. 'Sure, in these early stages there are a lot of inexplicable things we're discovering but, as you've reminded me, that doesn't mean we won't find a logical explanation in the future. And I really don't think that your holiday house and Julie X's disappearance from the same area is any more than a coincidence. And hazelnuts ... well ... I eat them sometimes, so that's not super-strange either, necessarily.'

'Tim, it can't all be coincidence. Both women were pulled, unharmed, from Sydney Harbour on the same date, though forty years apart—Julie X on 7 May 1973, our own patient on 7 May 2013. Both are described as being not much taller than five foot, with light brown cropped hair. Neither woman could identify herself and, in the case of Julie X, no one ever came forward to identify her and, in the last twenty-four hours, no one has identified our mystery woman either. Yes, granted, in Julie X's case, some other pathology ... you know, that instance of neurological symptoms ... was present and that doesn't seem to be so with our patient. But then there's the storytelling: Julie X told Sister Margery a story; our mystery woman told me a story. And then we come back to the "hazelnut" and the "Cottage Point" coincidences. I know it's got to be some kind of a trick, a scam, but why? I don't know what to make of it.' Kathryn stopped speaking and stared at her coffee cup.

Tim puffed out his cheeks, sighed, then rubbed his eyes. 'Kathryn, I don't know either. But, we're going to know. I'm going to help you on this, I promise,' he began, just as his mobile phone made them both jump with its sudden ring. 'Excuse me, again,' Tim said. 'Call from Steve. Let me just see what's up ... Yeah, Steve, what've you got?'

'Everything okay?' asked Kathryn as Tim returned the phone to his pocket.

'Well, yes and no. Steve's going to keep covering Emergency for me while I go up to the medical ward and assess our mystery woman—who's experiencing breathing difficulties and lower limb paralysis.'

'Oh my God.' Kathryn realised she was shaking. Still, she managed to call after him, 'Let me know what happens.'

❦ 4 ❦

This is what she said:

The sun rises and the sun sets; we call this a 'day'. The moon waxes and the moon wanes; we call this a 'month'. The Earth makes its great circuit around the sun; we call this a 'year'. All the rising and setting, the waxing and waning, the making of great circles; we call this a 'life'. 'Days' and 'months' and 'years' and 'lives' are words for the accumulation of our experience; 'death' is the word we use to describe our perception that the accumulation ceases. We have made life and death about words, about description. We have described life in terms of 'time passing', but, in reality, time does not pass, and therefore life does not pass. We simply choose to perceive life in that way because we prefer to think in words. But what if words are only a part of the whole; what if accumulation is only part of experience; what if there is no time? Can you imagine life beyond time, before and beyond words?

It was late in the afternoon when Tim called Kathryn to let her know that the woman's brain scan had returned a normal result.

'That's good news, I suppose,' Kathryn responded, 'but the normal scan and your earlier news of the lightning-quick resolution of her paralysis and breathing difficulties this morning makes me even more certain that she's up to something.'

Kathryn could hear the confusion in Tim's voice as he asked, 'Do you think she was faking those symptoms?'

She felt her thoughts whirling around an angry centre. How could she tell him that she suspected the woman was trying to undermine her, to embarrass her in front of her peers? And that she had no idea why. She took a deep calming breath before saying, 'Tim, I don't know how to explain it, but there's more going on with this patient than meets the eye. She really *did* speak to me, you know …'

'I believe you, Kathryn.'

'I know you do. But the question is, why has she only spoken to me?'

'Perhaps she trusts you,' he offered.

'Maybe … but I doubt it's as simple as that. To be honest, she's really starting to get to me. Anyway, any news from the police on her identity? Any inquiries from relatives or friends?'

'No, nothing, no progress at all there. And, in view of your suspicion of our patient, I sort of hate to tell you this but, in the absence of neurological problems, the move is to hand her over to the psychiatrists; you, specifically. And, as far as the team is concerned, they're hoping that you'll recommend some kind of in-patient care in a psych facility because she can't take up a public medical bed for much longer.'

Kathryn moved the phone away from her ear and closed her eyes for a moment.

'Kathryn, are you still there? Are you okay?'

'Yes, I'm fine, Tim. Actually, this little conversation has helped me come to a decision. When you rang I was just finalising some leave for myself. I'd thought about going to the holiday house for a break, but now I'm thinking of doing my own bit of investigation into this woman, and her mysterious predecessor, Julie X. Frankly, the whole thing has thrown me and I need to get to the bottom of what's going on. It's like a pebble in my shoe—annoying, slowing my progress on other work I should be doing. Once I give my full attention to it, I don't think it will take long to figure out this woman's motives. I've been making provision for other patients in my absence and, as the team has now requested, I'll also make sure our water baby is secure, somewhere, before I play detective. I'll be over to see her in an hour or two. Perhaps we can meet after that so I can handover the paperwork?'

'I finish my shift around six. Do you think you'll still be with her then?'

'Yes, very likely, Tim. Come up to her room when you're free. I'll see you then.'

Kathryn walked quietly into the room, aware that, just as in their first meeting, the lights had been dimmed, casting the woman's bed into semi-darkness. After the glare of the hospital corridor lights, Kathryn's sight took a few seconds to adjust, but when it did, she saw that the woman was lying on her back, breathing softly and steadily. Her eyes were closed and Kathryn stopped some metres from the bedside, debating whether to disturb the woman's rest. As she hesitated, she noticed the woman's lips had begun to move, as if in speech. Keeping her feet on the same spot, Kathryn leant her body forward slightly in an effort to hear what she was saying. The volume was low, barely a murmur. At first Kathryn thought that the woman was speaking a foreign language, but it was more than the words that were strange. Her intonation, still as quiet as a breath, rose and dipped gently as if she were singing some strange song. The beauty of it caught Kathryn by surprise and, to her further surprise, she felt tears beginning to sting her eyes. She squeezed her lids shut, tried to push the inexplicable welling of emotion away. When she opened her eyes she saw that the woman had also opened her eyes and that they were fixed unblinkingly on the empty space at the end of her bed.

The woman's murmuring increased. Kathryn thought she heard the words 'mother' and 'love', but otherwise it seemed an incoherent babble, the sounds running together, vowels without consonants now. Sometimes there were pauses of several seconds between the murmurs when the woman appeared to be listening, and then the rush of sounds would continue. After several minutes of this murmuring and listening, a silence filled the room and the woman shot her arms forward, spread her fingers wide apart, and then closed them firmly as if grasping at something. The silence shattered in the instant that she moved her hands back to rest on her chest, over her heart, and she began to sob uncontrollably.

Kathryn's own heart suddenly ached with an indescribable sympathy for the woman and she was torn between rushing forward to comfort her or maintaining her position and observing the process that was unfolding in front of her. It was with reluctance that Kathryn chose the latter course, rationalising that she would be able to help far more effectively if she had a clearer picture of how this scene resolved itself. She was just seconds into her decision when the woman laughed, loudly. Kathryn jumped, startled, and instantly the woman turned her head and stared straight at her. Then she beckoned, and Kathryn responded by walking a few steps to take a seat at the bedside, just as she had done the previous day. This time, she didn't ask for the woman's name. Instead, Kathryn looked deeply into her eyes and, for no reason that she could put words to, asked the woman what she had seen that had made her laugh.

'You can call me Sophia,' the woman said, 'though it is not my name. My real name, your real name, all real names, are written in eternity. But we're in time, for the moment, aren't we, and so we have a name that can be written in time. We have a true name and a timely pseudonym. And that's funny when you think of it; and that's why I was laughing. And I'm laughing because dear Dr Mason thinks he and all of you are here to help me when, actually, it's the other way around. I am here to help all of you.'

Later, Kathryn would wonder at this conversation. She would wonder at the woman choosing the name 'Sophia'. She would wonder about time and eternity and what her own eternal name might be. But mostly she would wonder why Sophia had affected her so profoundly. For the present, however, Kathryn fought a mounting agitation to maintain her professional composure, determined to find out more about this strange patient.

'Well, Sophia. That's a good name,' Kathryn began. 'I have a young niece with that name, though mostly we call her "Sophie".'

'A niece,' repeated Sophia.

'Do you have nieces or nephews, Sophia?' Kathryn ventured, but the woman was not to be drawn.

Instead, she laughed again and said, 'I will tell you something of my life, of your life, of all lives. But you must promise that you will listen without judgment. You must promise to open your heart, fill it with light and lightness; see the grand scope of my life as one glorious play of hope and love and suffering, all mixed. If you can promise, I can help you.'

Kathryn was annoyed, uneasy. This was not how the doctor–patient relationship was meant to go. Ethically, even more than personally and intellectually, she felt herself resisting.

'Perhaps I should hear what you have to say before I commit to such a deal,' said Kathryn, trying to smile, trying to appear unconcerned.

'Ah, dear Kathryn. But you should know, far better than I, that promises don't often work that way. We might all commit to a great many things if we were assured that the outcome would always be favourable. Every patient who submits to the surgeon's knife is acting in faith and hope. Those who marry take a great leap of faith. Every traveller who sets out on a journey expects to arrive safely at his destination but it is not always so. Still, does that deter him from setting out? Every time a woman gives birth, she places her hope above fear, trusting that all will be well with that child. But we know that it does not always turn out as we expect. Sometimes a baby breathes only for a moment, or not at all; but even in that circumstance, would the woman give up the joy of knowing her child, of holding the child even for a moment? Love overcomes all fear.'

Kathryn felt the ground falling away from under her. She had no choice but to whisper, 'I promise.'

Sophia smiled and reached for the control that adjusted the bed, pressing the button that raised the top half so that she was sitting upright, legs stretched in front of her. She plumped the pillows behind her back and head and settled in comfortably. In response, Kathryn leant back in the chair and placed her hands gently in her lap. The room held its breath and Sophia began:

'My life is the same as your life, the same as everyone's life, except that I am someone who has chosen to see things differently. I do not see time passing. I do not live by the clock. A clock's hands go round and round but they never move forward. I choose to move forward. I see my life as an unending chain of points—points of light, points of experience. If you think about your own life, you are really living a continuous series of points, a cavalcade of tiny and big moments, an unending flow of thoughts and actions that sometimes amount to very little, and at other times beget huge consequences. It is like flicking through thousands of photos. Some catch your eye, some remind you of happy or sad occurrences; some you have forgotten, or wish that you could forget; some you store in your heart, others you let go.'

'Yes, I think I can relate to what you're saying, Sophia. Some things are significant, some are not,' said Kathryn.

'All things are significant, Kathryn. It's just that we choose which ones we embrace, and which ones we discard. Sometimes we make the wrong decision.' Sophia paused, looking at Kathryn as if expecting disagreement. When none came, she smiled and continued. 'I shall try to explain more fully. Once, I understood life as you, as most people, understand it but I was granted a vision of a different possibility. I was proceeding, blinkered, along what might be described as the horizontal axis of earthly life when, suddenly, eternity broke through—a shock, a shaft of energy split my horizontal path with a vertical one that reached all the way to heaven. At that moment of intersection of the horizontal mode and the vertical mode of being, time was cut open and filled with eternity for me, and the ordinary became the extraordinary. Think of the shape of that intersection, Kathryn. The intersection of the horizontal with the vertical, of two straight lines bisecting each other; it forms a cross, a very powerful symbol. And it is the cross that we all bear, the cross of our blindness to the Truth, to Reality.' Again Sophia paused, inclining her head toward Kathryn in a gesture that seemed to be seeking some sign of understanding.

Kathryn was struggling. 'When you speak of eternity, of the extraordinary ... Are you saying you have lived before? That you have had other lives? That you have been reincarnated?'

'No. I am saying that I live; that I have lived and that I continue to live. Simply live. Not a series of lives, just a different life, a life of continuity.'

Kathryn sighed heavily as the thoughtful lull into which she had fallen was replaced by the more familiar irritation that this woman induced in her. 'Okay. So are you suggesting that you're immortal? Or is it that you time travel?'

'Of course not,' replied Sophia. 'I am as mortal as all humans. As for time travel—all I can say is that I understand there is a commonality to people's joy and suffering that transcends time and place and that I have seen much of human experience.'

'Hmmm.' Kathryn's mind raced. 'So, would it be correct if I described your life as one that has spanned more years than most people's lifetimes? Many more years?'

'Kathryn, I do not see, or speak, or think of years. But, as you do, and if it will help you understand: yes, I have been alive for many years beyond what you would consider the usual lifespan. I have lived since I understood. Though it is not always what you might regard as an earthly life at all times.'

Kathryn pressed a hand to her forehead. 'Sophia, it would really help me if you would put a number … a rough number … to how many years we're talking about for this "different" life of yours.'

'I came to understanding in what you would call the fourteenth century,' Sophia replied, matter-of-factly. 'Before that, I do not know where or what, or even *if*, I was. Because, before we understand, we are not truly alive.'

'The fourteenth century. That is a long time ago,' said Kathryn, straining to remain composed. 'And … and when you say you came to understanding, you are referring to that moment when you were shown a different reality? Am I correct?'

'It is difficult to put into words because understanding happens beyond words. But, I can say that, yes, it is the sudden arrival of an absolute clarity in which one's immediate existence is seen from the perspective of eternity.'

'I am trying to grasp what you're telling me, Sophia, I really am, but I'm sure you know that it is very strange, especially for a person of the twenty-first century, and a doctor at that.' Kathryn tried to control her impatience. 'Perhaps if you tell me something of the life in which you gained your understanding, I will have some context to help me.'

Sophia's eyes moved rapidly from side to side several times before she spoke. 'Very well. Perhaps it *is* appropriate to speak of that life, as the impact of the insights I was given at that time are etched on my mind. Even those events that were pre-cursors to my understanding—such as my own birth, marriage, death of loved ones—are carved in my heart. With the advent of my understanding, all and everything crystallised into part of a greater reality. But be aware that when I say "I", and when I speak of events that happened around me in the fourteenth century, I am referring to an accumulation of impressions of a particular existence in a particular era and they are only a tiny part of the whole.'

'Yes, I acknowledge what you're saying,' agreed Kathryn, though she really wasn't comfortable in giving acknowledgment to anything Sophia might say.

Sophia, however, seemed to take Kathryn at her word. She nodded and, turning her face away from Kathryn, fixed her gaze straight ahead, as if peering through the opposite wall, and began to speak:

These are the points of light, some of the flashes of the existence associated with the advent of my understanding:

I am born and christened "Ailith". Counting backward from the winter after I gained my understanding I would say that, in your current way of designating years, the year of my birth was 1342 or 1343. Again, according to this counting, the Black Death came to my town in 1350 and took my father and sisters away. My father had been a merchant and had done well in the years preceding his death but, as our town was thoroughly devastated by the plague, there were few left to tend the harvest and so there was little produce for purchase, and my mother and brother and I were beset by the gnawing emptiness of hunger for many months. However, the town was a trading centre and it eventually revived, attracting people back with the return of its thriving market.

I can describe for you points of light, happy childhood memories, as they flash by: a busy, prosperous town; the market in its bustle, and shouting, and colour, and chaos. And there am I, a little brown-haired girl sitting with my mother by the hearth, learning to spin, listening to tales of saints, accompanying her and my brother to the marketplace. And now, I am passing the cook-shop and inhaling the delicious, steamy scent of savoury pies baking. I imagine tasting one of those pies, even though my mother is telling me that Merle, the cook, is not to be trusted, that she sometimes fills her pies with tainted meat and rotten rabbit. Still, the warm aroma tempts me and I am thinking of the twenty-five herring pies that our town is required to render to the Crown each year. How I wish to sample one of those herring pies. How I wish that old Merle—toothless of face and bulging of body—was charged with the baking of the important pies. In my wish, Merle would fill twenty-five bready, crispy pie cases with salty herrings and when they were all baked and warm and resting on the great oak shelf near the shop's entry, she would take a sharp knife and cut the biggest pie into a hundred even pieces; and then she would call all the town's children to line up for a slice. And I would be at the front of the line. And my brother would be second.

Another flash, this one of searing sadness: my brother, being older, in due course has taken over our father's business, reinvigorating it and taking it to a level of prosperity far beyond that which my father had achieved. But continued comfort is not to be our lot. It happens that, in the year 1358, my brother is set upon by robbers who are envious of his success and, in his efforts to evade them, he falls from the Fye Bridge over the River Wensum and drowns. My mother and I mourn him sorely and it becomes imperative that I marry to ensure security for us. In truth I had little wish to marry, having vowed my devotion to Our Blessed Lord when I was eight years of age and wishing to suffer for His sake as he had suffered in his own death on the Cross. At that time I had heard the priest tell the story of St Cecilia and the wounds she suffered for the love of God and I wished to do likewise. I wished to suffer. This childish wish and promise cannot be honoured in the face of my mother's despair and so I consent to be married to a young woolmonger named Hugh. To my surprise and delight, Hugh is a kind, attentive and loving husband. Here, a shining moment, as he first takes me to his bed, kisses my lips, my mouth, my breasts, my arms. His own strong arms are around me, his sweet face smiles on me and his body moves tenderly above me. We are one. And I count myself blessed, the most fortunate woman in Norwich, save for the fact that, despite the passing of two years and more, I seem to be unable to conceive a child, and I wonder if it is God's punishment for my abandonment of my early promise. Hugh and I make many prayerful petitions at St Leonard's in the cathedral priory and travel together to Holy House in Walsingham and finally, in the spring of 1364 I feel the presence of a child in my womb. Our joy is overflowing, but life is harsh and such happiness necessarily fleeting. And in the winter of that same year, my darling Hugh falls from his horse and dies while his child within me continues to grow.

And then it is winter in the great town of Norwich in East Anglia. A bleak wind is blowing from the sea across the flat fenland, picking up cold moisture as it roars in, and dropping it as icy rain onto the town. In the town, the street that I see is not cobbled but is of packed dirt and the freezing torrent has turned it to sticking mud. The surface gutters are clogged with putrefying waste, causing animal and human excrement to overflow and mix with the mud, all congealing into a sickly stew that coats traversers' legs up to their knees in solid filth and fills their noses with a stench so vile that it liquefies in their lungs. Inside my house, a peat fire burns in the open hearth and warms the inhabitants but its smoke is thick, odorous and irritating. I am lying on a low settle bed in the corner of the dim, low-ceilinged room and I am coughing, the choking spasms adding to the severity of the pains of my labour that is now in its second day. The blinding rain that has beset the town for three days has prevented the gathering and strewing of fresh rushes and fragrant herbs on the dirt floor of the lying-in room. No men are permitted near a birth but, nevertheless, I think of Hugh and long to see his face and have him touch my hand and kiss my mouth once more. He cannot. He is gone. Matilda, the midwife, and my mother attend me, tiredly but lovingly rubbing my belly and flanks with rose oil, and giving me a mixture of vinegar and sugar to drink. I am shivering with cold, with fear, with effort. Matilda unpins and loosens my hair, my mother opens a cupboard door and unties the knots in her apron cord so that the room is animated with opening and loosening in the hope that my labouring body will similarly slacken and open. St Margaret, the patron saint of childbirth, is invoked in fervent prayers. My pain increases, more slow hours pass, and still I labour without reward. Matilda and my mother speak to each other earnestly in whispers. A decoction of flaxseed and chickpeas is prepared and Matilda rubs this on her hands and then pushes her hands into me to rotate the baby who cannot find its way into the world because it is trying to enter feet-first. I am helped to the birthing chair and Matilda crouches between my shaking legs, easing, encouraging. My mother stands behind the chair, supporting me under my arms. I can barely stay upright let alone push so Matilda must pull. Amid screams and wails, a tiny, whimpering but beautiful boy is born. I am cleaned and assisted back to the bed. He is bathed, rubbed with salt, warmly swaddled, and placed on my breast. At first, his tiny, mewing mouth seeks nourishment but, like me, he is weak. I stroke his head, willing him to suck, but he does not. Such has been the stress of his arrival that he dies, pale and cold before he has had the chance to be pink and warm in my arms.

My mother and I use the last of our money as dowry to secure our entry to the female Benedictine community in Carrow. And here I reflect on the fact that, though this enclaustration in a nunnery was the fulfilment of the ardent wish of my eight-year-old self, it was now no more than the refuge for two widows who were without funds and the support of husbands, brothers or sons. Bitterly I reflect, too, that my childish wish to suffer has been granted, not by taking the veil (as my infantile imaginings directed me) but in the heartbreaking loss of those I loved most dearly, save for my mother who has also suffered without respite. No wonder, then, with such a dispirited attitude, that in the beginning of my convent life, I am disturbed, beset, tormented by strange fits and debilitating headaches and pains of all variety. Many remedies are applied but to no avail and soon I am thirty winters old and praying for death as a release from my miseries.

And then, at this lowest point of my experience, when all seems lost, I am engulfed by understanding, swept up in insight, and to me is revealed the workings of life, of its joys and sufferings. In a tiny point of light, I am changed. And I can no longer think and feel and live as I have to this point. Now I see clearly.

Now, it is the day of my death to life, and of my death to death. The bishop, resplendent in rich, shining black vestments, is reciting the "Rite for the Enclosing of an Anchoress". I am the focus of the rite. I have spent the previous night in prayer and vigil and I have fasted for some days. Earlier on this day, I made my confession. Now is the Mass for the Dead during which all present pray for me as I lie prostrated before the altar. The mass ends and I arise and follow the bishop in procession with the others of the congregation. I carry a lighted taper. We all process from the church to the door of the anchorhold, but only I and the bishop cross its threshold. In some anchorholds there is a pre-dug grave but my cell is not one of these. Nevertheless, the bishop administers the Last Rites and then I blow out the taper and the bishop leaves me alone in the dark cell, locking the door as he goes. He will hold the key but, for me, the door is now permanently closed. I will spend the rest of my days immured here. I am dead to the world, but my spirit is alive and soaring.

Sophia stopped speaking. 'It is enough,' she said emphatically, her face no longer fixed, trance-like, on the opposite wall but looking directly at Kathryn.

It took Kathryn several seconds to switch her attention back to the present time and place. Despite her determination to maintain a professional and rational objectivity, Kathryn knew that tears were rolling down her cheeks. It was not only that she found an authenticity in Sophia's story; it was also that it reflected something of her own life, something that she preferred to keep in check. She wiped her eyes and face with her sleeve, and, composing herself, said, 'Sophia, thank you. It is an extraordinary tale. Well, I mean, you've described an extraordinary life. And it's filled me with so many questions I don't know which one to ask first.'

'Dear Kathryn, you may have many questions and that is a good thing. Questions are usually more important, more enlightening, than answers. How sad to know it all and have nothing left to ponder and wonder at. Certainty is the most crippling of illusions.'

Kathryn nodded. 'Yes, that can be true, and I agree that not every question has an answer. In the medical world, of course, we strive for answers in order to help our patients. But, in this instance, I'm hoping you can explain what an anchoress is? Or was? What did an anchorhold look like? I've never heard of these things; I just can't picture them.'

'These are straightforward questions, easily addressed,' replied Sophia and Kathryn thought she detected a note of relief in the young woman's voice as she began her reply. 'Prompted by the religious understanding and fervour of the age, an anchoress was a woman who, feeling called to serve God and her community by assuming a dedicated and largely solitary life of prayer and contemplation, chose without coercion to be permanently enclosed in a small cell built onto the side of a church. There were also, at that time, men seeking the same sort of life and they were called *anchorites*. The little cell in which the anchorite or anchoress lived out his or her days was called an anchorhold. It has been sometimes also referred to as an "anchorage".'

'How big were these anchorholds? Tell me more about them.'

'They were small. Usually dark and cold, being built of stone and situated on the north side of the church, next to the graveyard. You will know that, in the northern hemisphere, the north side receives the least of the sun's warm rays when the summer has passed and thus the anchoress was hidden from the light not only because she was locked away but also because of the location of her enclosure. Inside the cell, the floor was usually of packed earth and its walls featured two small windows covered with skins or cloth but never glass. One window gave access to the outside world and through this the anchoress received the physical nourishment needed to sustain the body while the second window, called a "squint", gave direct access into the church and through this window the spiritual nourishment of the Church's sacraments were received.'

'How did the anchoress manage the basic things of life? You know, food preparation, toileting, removing rubbish?'

'Well, usually the anchoress would have a servant who would take care of those daily needs. Sometimes there was even a little anteroom for the servant who could, of course, come and go as required.'

'But the anchoress, or anchorite, stayed locked in there alone, for life?' Kathryn was incredulous.

'For life, yes, but she was not totally alone. As I've said, one of the windows gave access to the outside world. In that way, though the anchoress was separated from the community by the walls of her anchorhold, she was also living in one of the most public parts of town, right next to the church. And, remember, in the fourteenth century, almost everyone attended church. People would come to the window and consult with her, ask her advice and seek her prayers for their need. So, in a way, she was like today's psychiatrist, but with spiritual insights added in. The anchoress was the responsibility of the ordinary people as well as the clergy. It was they who contributed to her upkeep, bringing her food, leaving a bequest for her in their wills. It seems an unusual life from today's perspective, but it was not lonely. It was a life of special contribution.'

'You described moving from being a nun to entering the anchorhold, didn't you? Was that how it was for all anchorites and anchoresses?'

'I cannot speak for all, but the progression you describe as pertaining to me was the one common to the majority. For me, too, the spur to this life was the receipt of the revelations that enabled me to understand,' she clarified.

'What were those revelations, Sophia?' asked Kathryn.

'You have strayed from questions with easy answers to a question of great import and I do not wish to elaborate at this point. The answer to this will unfold for you when the time is right. In response, then, I shall say only this: there were several revelations, but all were one in that I was given to understand many things about the nature of life, and sin and suffering; about the human condition. That is, the message was singular.'

'What do you mean by singular, Sophia?'

'I mean, as we all already know in our hearts and souls, there is only one message, only one lesson. And that lesson is Love.' At this, Sophia closed her eyes.

'Perhaps we could discuss more about that lesson at another session,' Kathryn said encouragingly.

'You do not discuss Love. You live it.' Sophia was adamant. 'Is there something else you wish to speak with me about?'

Kathryn felt panic knotting her stomach. She needed more information from Sophia, but was uncertain in which direction she should push. It seemed that the topic of a life in the fourteenth century was exhausted for the moment, but she wanted more details, more insights into this strange world that Sophia was detailing. Rationally, of course, Kathryn knew Sophia had not been alive over six hundred years ago, but she had spoken with such clarity and conviction about it that Kathryn was unwilling, and unable, at this stage, to append a 'delusional' label to the young woman and the experiences she was describing. Kathryn decided to pick up on Sophia's offer of speaking about 'something else' and, swallowing firmly, she inquired, 'Would you be able to tell me something else about your life in … well, what should I call it … another time period? Say, the seventeenth century, for example.'

'No.' The volume of Sophia's voice rose. 'It is of no benefit to you. Between the beginning of my understanding and now is less than the snap of your fingers. Do not concern yourself with things that are of no benefit to you, no value to your life; things that are meaningless to your soul, your happiness, and to the souls and happiness of others.'

More cautious, more measured, Kathryn tried again. 'There's wisdom in what you've said, Sophia. But I wonder if it might be of help to me, and to you, if you would say something about your life in very recent times.'

'Yes, perhaps I am willing to do so,' said Sophia.

Kathryn relaxed a little and, thankful that the dialogue was continuing, she pushed her advantage. 'So, Sophia, I'd find it very helpful to know where you were before you were found in the harbour yesterday? Or even which city, or suburb, were you in, say, a week ago?'

'I cannot say.' Sophia's reply was quiet.

'Why can't you say, Sophia? Is it that you don't recall or that you don't want to tell me?'

'It is a little of both but, in truth, it is more the second reason. I do not want to tell you because you may misinterpret. I am here now and that is what matters.'

'I, that is, we all here at the hospital have a responsibility to care for you in the best way we can, Sophia. And a huge part of our responsibility is returning you to safe living conditions. Do you understand?'

'I am safe, and I am living.'

Kathryn suppressed another spark of annoyance and decided to try again from a slightly different angle. 'Then, maybe you could explain how it came about that you were found in the harbour yesterday?'

'I believe we spoke of this in our first meeting. Don't you recall, Kathryn, that I told you a tale of falling out of my mother's pocket? Of course, that's a symbolic tale, a metaphor but, in general, that's what happened. I fell out of somewhere and into the harbour. Just as it happened the last time I was found there.'

Kathryn gave a start. 'The last time?' she repeated.

'Yes, in what is called 1973. You know about it, I'm sure. I was brought to this same hospital. And I was treated kindly by many. And I helped those I was called to help, and then I moved on. And now I've returned to help others in this time. I've especially come to help you, dear Kathryn.'

'I don't understand.' Kathryn's voice was weak. 'How, why, would you need to help me?'

'You *do* understand, Kathryn. You understood the instant we met; you understood earlier today when I told you about holding a child, and losing a child. You understood when you promised to listen to me.'

'Perhaps I do,' said Kathryn, conscious of the discomfit that was swirling within her. In a desperate bid to regain her equilibrium, she turned the subject back to the other surprising announcement that Sophia had just made. 'I will give proper consideration to all you have said, Sophia, but, for now, could you tell me a little more about coming to this hospital in 1973?'

'Very well, for that is of benefit to you and to others now. In 1973 I travelled the channel of my life and came to Sydney Harbour, and from there I came to this hospital where I met Dr Smith; and I helped him understand. And then I went to the hospital of St Faith where I met Sister Margery and I helped her understand. It was Margery who gave me the name "Julie". All then called me "Julie", or "Julie X", but not all understood, or chose not to understand. And that is their right. Often, it is the discerning of what we do not want, as much as the recognition of what we do want, that points us in the right direction. When I had completed my helping, I returned to my flowing life until I was again found in Sydney Harbour yesterday.'

'Sophia, that's a forty-year gap you're talking about. You are a young woman. Can you explain that?'

'No explanation would satisfy you. I have told you the truth of my life. I can say no more in that regard.'

'One last thing then, please Sophia,' begged Kathryn. Sophia made no protest so Kathryn asked, 'You've told me why you were laughing earlier. But you were also sobbing and I wondered what you were seeing that was moving you so profoundly.'

'That, dear Kathryn, was a vision of your pain.'

{ 5 }

This is what she said:

There is death, and then there are the things in life that kill us, and yet we do not die but live on in a liminal zone where pain gnaws at us, eating away at our trust, our joy, our hope, little by little, until nothing is left but our shell. And some see our shell and are attracted to it because they are also shells and so they want to be near us because we will demand no deeper substance from them, and they will demand no depth from us. The world is littered with shells, and surface-to-surface relationships. But shells are brittle and eventually shatter, disappearing into sand, long after the life in them has left.

When Tim entered the room it was dark except for the blinking pin-points of light coming from the monitoring system. He could see Kathryn on a chair at the woman's bedside. He was surprised that she was leaning forward, almost lying the upper half of her body on the hospital bed, and with her face turned toward the woman who was sitting up, legs stretched straight under the covers, the top half of the bed having been raised to support her at this almost ninety-degree angle.

'Hm, hmm.' Tim cleared his throat to signal his arrival. Neither Kathryn nor the woman seemed to hear; certainly they made no attempt to change their positions. He tried again, this time calling her name. Still Kathryn did not seem to hear, but the other woman looked in Tim's direction and smiled.

'Hello, Dr Mason,' she said. 'If you are here to inquire about my health—and I know of, and appreciate, your concern—I can tell you that my name, for now, is Sophia.'

Tim was stunned. Finally he had a name—well, at least a start on the woman's identity—but its revelation here, when he had not asked, and was not even thinking of asking such a thing, when his whole focus was on Kathryn's strange posture, unnerved him. He took some seconds to find enough composure to respond 'Thank you … Sophia. That is helpful but, um, I'm, um, needing to speak to Dr Brookley right now.'

Still Kathryn did not move and he was suddenly seized with the fear that the woman had done something terrible to her, something that had rendered her immobile. He rushed to the bedside and, touching Kathryn on the shoulder from behind, he whispered, 'Are you all right?'

Again, no response. Panicked, Tim moved his hand down Kathryn's back to check for signs of breathing when she suddenly sat upright in the chair.

Tim jumped. 'Kathryn, what is going on?' he demanded.

'Nothing, Tim. Sophia and I were just having a really good chat.'

'Would you excuse us, Sophia? I'd like to confer with Dr Brookley. Outside … ah, about another patient,' said Tim, almost lifting Kathryn off the seat, onto her feet, and propelling her toward the door with a strong hand placed firmly in the middle of her back.

In the corridor Tim could see that Kathryn was not herself. Her face was very pale, her eyes wide. He steered her to a chair in one of the vacant consultation rooms, eased her to sit down, and grabbed a cup of water from the cooler and placed it in her hands.

'I'm perfectly fine, Tim,' she volunteered before he had time to form a question. 'I'm just feeling a little … I can't put a word to it, actually. I feel surprised, and totally out of my comfort zone and, yet, at the same time, strangely elated. Does that make sense?'

'No. None at all,' replied Tim. 'What were you two talking about that's produced this reaction in you?'

Kathryn let out a heavy sigh. She shook her head. 'I don't know if I can tell you, if any explanation would make sense to you. All I can say is that she's wise, not just for someone so relatively young; she's wise in a way that most people never are. It was as if she could see into my heart. She knew things about me that no one would know. She gave me hope.'

'Now I'm totally confused and out of *my* comfort zone,' admitted Tim, scratching his head. 'Are you telling me that you think she's normal ... you know, sane?'

'Yes, I think that is what I'm saying, Tim. But I'm not so sure about my own sanity because—and, be warned, this is going to sound really crazy to you—I think it is possible that she might be the same woman who was pulled out of the harbour in 1973.'

'Whoa! What are we talking about here? Back to my extreme facelift idea?' said Tim, only half laughing.

Kathryn laughed too. 'No, Tim. There's something else going on here, something deeper, and I want to try to understand it.'

'Maybe you need a rest. That leave you're about to take, maybe the investigating is not a good idea. A proper rest is probably a better option.'

'I knew you'd think I was losing it.' Kathryn lifted her shoulders in a shrug and continued, 'You'll change your tune when I figure all of this out.'

Tim rubbed his hands together. 'Kathryn, I don't think I'm the best person for you to be talking to about this. Would you like me to call one of your senior colleagues?'

Kathryn narrowed her eyes and, through gritted teeth, hissed, 'Do not mention this to anyone, especially not to any medical colleagues of mine ... or yours. No one. Do you understand? I'm trusting you on this, Tim. Do not let me down.'

The hand of the slow-ticking wall clock pointed at him. The ceiling lights glared down at him, hot and merciless. He was welded to the spot. 'All right,' he said at last. 'You can trust me. I'll just ask one thing: please keep me in the loop about what you're doing, what you discover along the way. And, if you need any help ... you know, call, text regularly.'

'Yes, Tim. I'll tell you everything.'

But Kathryn wasn't sure that she would tell Tim everything. She wasn't sure that she would tell him about Sophia's strange story of living in the fourteenth century or of the visions that Sophia had spoken of experiencing. And she wasn't sure—not at all—that she would ever tell him about Sophia's knowledge of Matthew, the baby that she and her husband, Richard, had held in their arms for only an hour before he passed away from a congenital heart defect. She *was* sure that she could never explain the pain that the baby's death had etched in her heart, and the wide chasm of grief it had created in their marriage. And she wasn't sure that she would tell Tim that she had been emotionally dead until Sophia's strange words had begun the process of enlivening her. And she wasn't sure that she would tell anyone that she had begun to believe that it was possible that Sophia had always been alive. Always.

{ 6 }

This is what she said:

I am in a channel, a watery channel. This channel is the ebb and flow of divine life. The inhalation and the exhalation of God. I move on the breath. I am here. I am there. I am. We are. We are deeply embedded in the divine fabric, so deeply embedded that we cannot perceive our position there, cannot appreciate the certainty and beauty of the fabric itself. Like our earthly position in the great spiral-armed galaxy, the Milky Way, in which our tiny solar system swirls, we sit on the edge of a spindly limb so that when we raise our eyes to the night sky we see the Milky Way as something separate, as something beyond us. But we are IN it, we are OF it, and we are simply looking back at the centre of the Milky Way and seeing the grandeur of the whole of the galaxy, the centre of ourselves, the whole of ourselves. And the only tragedy is that we do not know it. But I know it. I have known it always.

Sleep. Deep, dark, and quiet. Dreamless at first. Then a light, bright and warm. I see the light and I am on the beam of light. And I *am* the beam of continuous light that streaks and stretches across the universe. I joyously light my own way as I dance across the galaxy. And then I flash across the planet Earth and something is pulling me toward it. Curiosity? Fascination? Gravity? As I get closer to the Earth my beam starts to attract matter; matter adheres to me, to my light. I now have a form. I am no longer pure light—I am heavy. I am earthbound. And now my light is inside me, hidden from view, and I am no longer dancing across the heavens.

When Kathryn awoke she was disorientated. It was still dark outside but the glow from the streetlight pushed into the bedroom through a slight gap in the curtains. Her eyes were wide, fixed on the light. Her body was heavy, movement not only impossible but unwanted. What was she doing here? Where had she been? Slowly, gradually, she became aware that she had been dreaming. She became aware of her own breathing—in and out, in and out. She felt her chest rising and falling with the breath. Her eyes began to flicker and she could make out other shapes in the room—the shadowy outline of the chair in the corner, the coat hanging behind the door. She heard a car engine starting up in the distance, the sudden drip-drip of a tap in the ensuite bathroom. She felt the warmth and weight of the blankets covering her motionless body. And then she felt the gentle return of energy to her fingers and her toes. She made tiny, tentative movements of her extremities, her limbs; she rolled her head softly from side to side. A long intake of cold breath and a stretch. She was back. She picked up her phone from the bedside table. It was four-fifteen am. She rose from bed; there was so much to do.

The space between Kathryn's professional and personal assessments of Sophia was immense. Both as a psychiatrist and a citizen of the twenty-first century, she knew that the acceptance of Sophia's claim that she had been alive for over six hundred years was ridiculous, irrational; but as an emotional human being Katherine found herself drawn to the fervent conviction that Sophia was presenting herself truthfully. It was not just the insights into Kathryn's own life that persuaded her of Sophia's sanity and authenticity. It was Sophia's tone, her manner, the way she had of speaking from a loving point of view. For Kathryn, there was clarity and logic in Sophia's conversation; there was no malice, and no apparent reason for misrepresenting herself.

The conclusion was distressing. For someone in Kathryn's position to admit to believing Sophia's story of having always been alive, and of turning up when people need help, was akin to admitting to a belief in some mystical version of Mary Poppins. And yet Kathryn could not shake the growing realisation that, when the time came to deliver her professional opinion on Sophia, and without evidence to the contrary, she would, in clear conscience, declare her sane and well. It was hard for Kathryn even to begin to imagine the repercussions of such a declaration. She thought of Dr Smith's admission in his letter to Dr Anderson, that he believed Julie X to be sane and she understood that he must have felt as professionally compromised as she was now feeling. She thought of the ridicule that Dr Smith must have endured from many of his colleagues, and the premature end to his career. She forced the thoughts aside, went into her home study and sat in front of her computer.

Before the morning intruded she took some time to think back to Sophia's story the previous day about her life in fourteenth-century Norwich, and was surprised by how lucidly she could recall the details. She quickly but thoroughly noted them on a piece of paper. Then, turning to the internet, she typed in the search terms 'medieval women' and 'medieval life'. Information sources flooded her screen. Too much information. Still, a scanning read of an arbitrary selection of sites gave her enough certainty that the broad details of life in medieval England, as presented to her by Sophia, were accurate.

Next, she entered the term 'anchoress' and was surprised to find that, despite her own ignorance on the subject until only the day before, there was a range of information available on that topic too. She picked a site at random from the results list and began reading bits and pieces from what seemed to be a reliable, scholarly article.

Anchoresses, and the male equivalent, anchorites, were a particular feature of medieval religious dedication and practice in England. Records relating to enclosure practices in medieval England give evidence of the existence of about one thousand hermits and anchorites between 1125–1531. (For more details see Rotha Mary Clay. The Hermits and Anchorites of England. 1914).

The term anchoress referred to an individual woman who willingly sought to be enclosed (or immured) for life in a small cell (termed 'anchorhold') attached to a church, in order to pursue a solitary contemplative life. ... The core word 'anchor' comes from the Greek anachoresis meaning 'without company'. ...

Though literature of the medieval period has provided insights into many aspects of the daily conduct of an anchoress's life, it is only recently that the harsh physical actualities of such a lifestyle have been revealed by concentrated archaeological investigation of anchorhold sites. ... Enclosure in an anchorhold was preceded by a Mass for the Dead to emphasise that the anchoress was dead to the world but alive to the spiritual life. ... Anchorholds usually featured two windows ... Though notionally solitary, the anchoress was domiciled in the physical and social centre of the medieval town—the parish church—and, thus, she remained under the scrutiny of her community. ... An interesting insight into how the occupants of anchorholds functioned within the medieval community is to be found in the person and writings of Julian of Norwich. Fourteenth-century Norwich was a thriving market town ... And the situation of Julian's anchorhold in Carrow placed her in one of Norwich's most populous areas, ensuring that she was both 'in' and 'out' of the community simultaneously ...

Abruptly, Kathryn stopped reading. The mention of Norwich, and of a well-known anchoress in Carrow specifically, jumped out at her. Was it only (another) coincidence that Sophia had told her of being enclosed in that very place? Yes, all the other details that Sophia so readily gave her about the anchoritic life were supported by this article, but what did that prove? Was the wealth of correlating detail a confirmation or refutation of Sophia's story? Sophia could have read the same or any number of similar articles. A prickle of doubt itched Kathryn and it would not easily be scratched away. Kathryn had no choice but to continue her research.

She clicked on the 'Julian of Norwich' hyperlink and was taken to pages and pages of site options. Why, there was even a Wikipedia entry but, again, she chose to click on a listing written by the same academic who wrote the anchoress information she had been reading.

Biographical information on the great medieval mystic, Julian of Norwich, is limited and comes primarily from her own writings. There she tells us, for example, that she was thirty and a half years old when, on 8 May 1373, following the sudden onset of a debilitating illness marked by paralysis of the limbs and breathlessness, she received sixteen divine revelations ...

Kathryn stopped and re-read the entry. The date: 8 May 1373. Julie and Sophia were found in the harbour on 7 May and experienced paralysis and breathlessness the following day, 8 May. Both women presented as being about thirty years old. It was all too much, and Kathryn was about to leave the study to get a cup of tea when her attention was caught by something at the bottom of the webpage under the heading 'Searches related to Julian of Norwich'. There she saw a link to 'Julian of Norwich quotes hazelnut'. She shook a little as she clicked on this choice, and her shaking increased when she read a quote that she knew she had seen before. She read it again, with mixed feelings of elation, confusion and caution:

And then he showed me a little thing, the size of a hazelnut. And I wondered at it and he told me it was all that was made. And I wondered how it did not fall away to nothingness because it was so small. And he replied that it was preserved because he made it and cared for it and loved it. (Julian of Norwich, *Showings* (*Revelations of Divine Love*). Short and Long Texts, Rev.1).

Kathryn grabbed the Julie X file and rummaged through it until she came to the quotation Dr Smith had scribbled on his prescription pad. The words were exactly the same; Dr Smith's attribution of the quote to 'JN, 14th cent' confirmed the Julian of Norwich connection.

⊙═╤═⊙

The State Library's reading room was busy at this time. Family history researchers, students, office workers on their lunch breaks looking for a quiet space to relax, study, and read. Kathryn's early morning discoveries sent her scurrying into the city to have a proper look at a good edition of Julian of Norwich's writings. The librarian recommended a two-volume edition in modern English but with an extensive introduction on what was known of Julian's life and times, and scholarly notes and commentaries on this important anchoress's revelations. Kathryn also requested a less 'technical' book that, from the catalogue description, looked like it might explain, in a simplified form, the main points and insights of Julian's sixteen revelations. And, for good measure, she also requested a modern edition of the *Malleus Maleficarum*, another reference—this time a direct one—in the notes of the Julie X file.

While waiting for her requested books to be retrieved, Kathryn sat at one of the large reading tables, opened her laptop and found her way back to the article she was reading earlier at home. In particular, she focused on the statement about Julian being a mystic. This is one more topic that Kathryn, with her strong scientific background, knew nothing about. She read:

A mystic is an individual who has experienced an unsought and unmediated apprehension of the Divine. The word (and its associates such as mysticism) comes from the Indo-European root 'mu' which is imitative—almost onomatopoeic—of inarticulate, unformed sounds. Words like mute and mystery come from the same root. The word mystery therefore, really means 'unspoken', 'silent', but, even in the sense that we use the word, there is the suggestion that there is something behind the silence, some solution to the mystery. In a way, this is what mysticism is—a finding of 'something' behind the silence, behind the mystery. The mystic is the one who looks behind the veil and who sees things differently; who sees the truth.

Into Kathryn's mind popped yesterday's experience of listening to Sophia's strange, wordless sounds and the insights that she went onto reveal about a life in the medieval world, a life that led her to see things very differently indeed. 'Is Sophia a mystic?' Kathryn asked herself, the answer already firming in her head.

Despite the lunchtime bustle, Kathryn's books were ready for collection and back with her at the reading table within fifteen minutes of her submitting the request. She picked the *Malleus Maleficarum* from the top of the pile. She read that the Latin title translated as 'The Witches' Hammer' and pertained to the book's original reason for publication as a handbook for witch hunters in the late Middle Ages. Written by two German Dominican friars, Heinrich Kramer and Jacob Sprenger, in 1486–1487, it was composed at the behest of the then pope, Innocent VIII, a name that Kathryn could not help but think was ironic. It was not an easy read, but it was a fascinating one as it systematically set out the procedure for identifying witches, and their signs and practices; how to protect oneself against witches; how to investigate witches; how to extract confessions from suspected witches; and, having successfully prosecuted witches, how to sentence and punish them. Clearly, it was a text of its time, full of superstition and vitriol and cruelty. In relation to the note in Julie X's file about a witch's inability to be drowned, Kathryn found the reference in Part 3, Question XV where it stated that, once detained by authorities, witches would seek to conceal all the devil's marks and tokens on, or in, their bodies and, by secretly retaining these marks and tokens, render themselves totally resistant to drowning. The belief that such marks and tokens could be hidden anywhere on and inside the body, gave the investigators a justification for 'searching' the accused women in the most probing and provocative of ways.

As she flipped through the pages, getting a general feel for the book's contents, Kathryn was struck by the abundance of references to copulation, the female body, and the power that females exerted over men; fears of removal and wrongful use of the male sex organ by witches; and particularly of the emphasis on an association between witchcraft and midwifery. Even as a doctor, Kathryn had limited knowledge of the history of medicine, but she did recall reading, in her student days, about those earlier times when pregnant and labouring women were attended not by a (male) obstetrician but by female family, friends, and the local midwife. In those times, all householding women needed to have a working knowledge of healing herbs and medicines available from their own kitchen gardens, and this knowledge usually encompassed a familiarity with herbs that could encourage pregnancy when desired, and induce abortion if required. The same women assisted other women during labour, easing the pain and facilitating the birth, receiving the baby into the world. The baby did not always survive the birth process, or would sometimes survive only to die soon after for any number of reasons. Women in general, then, and midwives in particular, came to be viewed by men in general, and men of the Church in particular, as possessing secret and specialised knowledge, and a certain degree of power over life and death. When medical schools began to spring up in the developing, and exclusively male, universities of the twelfth century and later, and men began to want a greater say in the childbirth sector, the midwives came under a cloud of suspicion, and the leap from midwife to witch was reduced to a small step.

Kathryn's thoughts flicked to an image of the birth scene Sophia described, and then to a clear recollection of Tim's observation that, as far as his understanding of the persecution of witches was concerned, it had very little to do with female misbehaviour and everything to do with male anxiety. She made a mental note to tell the young doctor that he was quite correct in his opinion.

Kathryn was suddenly annoyed by the *Malleus Maleficarum* and pushed it aside. Enough suspicion and persecution, she said quietly to herself. She was determined to proceed with an open mind as she took up the next book, a modern translation of Julian of Norwich's 'Revelations of Divine Love'. In the extensive introduction to the two-volume set, the editors confirm what Kathryn had already found out: that very few details of Julian's life were known. Kathryn's concern now was to understand more about Julian's revelations but, even though she was reading a modern English version, she found the language complex and the theological implications of the revelations difficult to grasp. The first revelation was not so daunting because she already had some familiarity with it from the Julie X note and her follow-up on Sophia's allusion to it, and so she read it again, this time in more detail:

[God] showed me a little thing, the size of a hazelnut, lying in the palm of my hand, as it seemed to me, and it was as round as a ball. I looked on it with the eye of my understanding, and thought: What can this be? And I was answered generally thus: It is all that is made. I marvelled that it endured, for I thought it might have suddenly fallen into nothingness because it was so little. And I was answered in my understanding: It endures and always shall, for God loves it; … the reason that it looked so little to my sight was because I saw it in the presence of Him who is the Creator. For a soul that sees the Creator of all things, all that is created seems very little.

And then Kathryn read the explanatory comment on this section:

Here Julian goes beyond the medieval understanding of Earth's place in the scheme of things because she is not just observing Earth but is experiencing a physically, mentally and spiritually heightened view of all the cosmos, of all creation; she is seeing 'all that is made'. Her description suggests that she has travelled—at least metaphorically—in space to a place outside creation and the vantage point to which she is raised is the equivalent of the Empyrean, the place of God. Her account implies that, for a privileged moment, she is sharing God's view of creation. She is really seeing things differently.

Kathryn wondered if this 'sharing God's view of creation' might be what Sophia was talking about. But Sophia was not Julian, was she? Was she? And the 'hazelnut' was just one tiny part of the first revelation, and there were sixteen in all. Kathryn began to feel overwhelmed. She put the book down and clasped her hands together on the table, closed her eyes and tried to clear her mind. This quietened her and she started to think that, perhaps, it was not appropriate or necessary for her to understand the theology of Julian of Norwich in order for her to understand Sophia. Just the knowledge that such insights existed, and that women like Julian experienced these heightened perceptions as long ago as the fourteenth century was, perhaps, enough for Kathryn. Nevertheless, she decided to look over the editor's summary of the sixteen 'showings' and make a few notes for later reference if needed. All of them piqued her interest, but a phrase in the summary of the four-teenth revelation jumped out at her. It said, 'God is our mother', and Kathryn was about to turn to the full revelation to read more when her mobile, in silent mode and resting on the table near her laptop, started to vibrate, indicating an incoming call from Tim Mason. She picked up the phone and said quietly, 'Hi Tim. I can't really talk. I'm in the library. But I'll call you soon because I've got some really interesting information to share with you.'

'Great, I'll look forward to it. But even if you can't talk, I think you'll want to listen to what I have to say right now.'

'Okay,' she agreed.

'The police called me with some information on our mystery woman. They've found evidence that someone matching Sophia's description was in Melbourne last week, hanging around the university—in lec-tures, the library, and even turning up at an academic conference.'

Kathryn forgot for a moment that she was in a library and pressed Tim for more information. 'How sure are the police that this woman in Melbourne is the same woman we now have here?'

'Not that sure at all,' Tim replied. 'The detective told me that, con-sidering the number of days this woman seems to have been hang-ing around on the campus, as captured on the security cameras, it's surprising how fleeting her appearances on the footage are. And even then, the images aren't that clear. But they do show someone who is definitely around Sophia's age, height, weight, and with the same cropped hairstyle.'

'That's hardly conclusive.' Kathryn could hear relief in her own voice as she continued: 'What about the Melbourne woman's speech? Sophia's way of talking is very distinctive, you know.'

'Interesting you should ask that. Apparently the woman never spoke, not even in the small conference break-out groups that other delegates report she attended. That's why they noticed and recalled her. The conference was on a small, specialised area of study and people in it generally know each other. But nobody knew her; she didn't wear a name badge because she wasn't registered to attend. And, on the cou-ple of occasions she was approached by an attendee, she just smiled and hurried off, although apparently, she would reappear just as a new session or talk began, but she'd sit at the back and then leave the instant the session finished.'

'Interesting. What kind of conference?'

'Well, this is weird but, I guess Sophia is weird too, so it matches, doesn't it?' Tim laughed, and Kathryn caught her breath as he went on to say, 'Anyway, the conference was about medieval mystics and their revelations and visions.'

Kathryn hit 'End' on her phone and, pushing the two volumes on Julian of Norwich to the side, she hastily gathered up her belongings and ran from the library.

<hr/>

The dinner trays were being distributed to the patients when Kathryn burst in, breathless and agitated, to Sophia's room. She rushed at the bed but Sophia, apparently unperturbed by Kathryn's unexpected arrival, continued to lift the warming covers from the array of food on her tray, taking a keen interest in the contents of each plate as she went.

Kathryn dropped her handbag to the floor and stood at the bedside, hands on her hips. Slowly, almost absently, Sophia turned to look at Kathryn. 'I'm happy to see you here again, dear Kathryn,' she purred.

'Don't "dear Kathryn" me,' she boomed. 'I trusted you. You owe me an explanation.'

'In truth, all that I owe you, all that any of us owes anyone else, is loving respect.'

'Put the bullshit aside and speak sensibly to me. Now,' Kathryn shouted.

Unflappable, no reaction. Sophia turned back to her tray, picked up a spoon, dipped it into the soup, raised it to her mouth and slurped. 'Delicious. Potato and leek. Full of nourishment.'

Kathryn stamped her foot. 'You were not drifting benevolently around the universe last week. You were in Melbourne. I demand that you tell me what's going on.'

Sophia took another mouthful of soup. And another. And another. Kathryn felt the sour taste of fury collecting in her throat. She shot her hand out, grabbed the bowl of soup from the tray and flung it across the room. It hit the opposite wall and dropped to the floor, leaving a trail of thick, creamy liquid in its wake. When a nurse appeared at the door in response to the noise, Kathryn waved her away with a 'Don't worry, all under control,' spoken through gritted teeth.

'So sorry. I didn't realise you were in here, Dr Brookley,' said the nurse, retreating quickly.

'Kathryn, please sit down. I am willing to talk to you when you are calm,' said Sophia, her tone quiet and even.

Despite her anger, Kathryn found herself complying with the direction. She sat, took a deep breath, and then squared her gaze onto Sophia.

'I am quite calm, calm enough to explain why I am very upset with you, Sophia,' she began. 'I have received news that someone closely fitting your description was reported to have been in Melbourne, and at Melbourne University specifically, last week. At the university, this person fitting your description attended a conference on medieval mystics and their visions and revelations. Now, I'm no specialist in that area, but I now know from my own research that Julian of Norwich was a medieval mystic who wrote about her revelations; she was also an anchoress, enclosed in an anchorhold in Norwich in the fourteenth century. And I find it more than a coincidence that you also happened to tell me, only yesterday, in one of your "tales", that you were an anchoress in Norwich at that same time.' Kathryn paused and tilted her head in question toward Sophia, but the young woman simply stared back at her, her face set in a blank expression.

'What have you got to say for yourself?' Kathryn demanded.

'I don't know what you're asking me, Kathryn. What do you want me to say?'

'You've been lying to me. I want the truth.' Kathryn was almost screaming.

'Kathryn, I have not lied to you. Everything I have told you is the truth. If you are asking whether I am the same woman as the one seen in Melbourne last week, I say "perhaps". As I've explained, I do not exist in time as you count it and, as cities and places emerge and change and then disappear in time, I cannot say for certain that I was in a particular place at a particular time. Perhaps it was me, perhaps it was someone else. But, if it was me, of what consequence is that to you?'

'It is of consequence to me because it is my professional duty to oversee your health, your mental health, your welfare, while in this hospital. It is of consequence to me because I trusted you, but now I suspect that you've been gathering information about other eras and people of those eras so that you can pass yourself off as those people,' Kathryn spat out the accusation. 'I have spent the morning in the library, and I have been reading about Julian of Norwich. The last part of the story you told me yesterday was almost identical to the little that is known of Julian of Norwich. Have you modelled yourself on her? Are you pretending to be her?

'For what advantage?' queried Sophia.

'If I knew the answer to that question,' snapped Kathryn, 'we wouldn't need to have this conversation, would we?'

'Kathryn,' sighed Sophia, 'we all need conversation, and so much conversation is question and answer. Ideally, that's because we're interested in others although, often, people speak to others only in the hope of finding themselves reflected in the other person, of building up their own egos and assuaging their own insecurities by imposing themselves on others. My life has taught me humility so I never desire to impose on others; that is the main reason that I choose to speak with very few people. I do not want to deceive or hurt anyone. Just as you want to help others in your work, I want to help others too. So, if I was in Melbourne—and by saying this, I am not confirming that I *was* there—it would have been because, in your comprehension of life, I had to be somewhere before I was here and because I had work to do there, and because I find the things of the medieval world to be of interest. You recall I told you the fourteenth century was the advent of my understanding?'

Kathryn was not ready to let down her guard or give up her indignation. 'What do you know about the medieval mystic Julian of Norwich?' she demanded.

'Less than some but more than most,' replied Sophia. 'In the fourteenth century, there were others beside me who reached understanding too. It was a time of great hardship, of plague, of upheaval, of death all around. Whenever there is great sadness, great trials, thinking and feeling people gain understanding. Tragedy breaks our heart, breaks it in two, breaks it open, and it can only be made whole again with love, with faith, and with honesty and trust. Thus, you could say that Julian and I are identical in our brokenness, and identical in our healing, and identical in our understanding, our understanding of love. I know Julian of Norwich because I understand.'

Reluctantly, Kathryn had to admire the persuasive clarity, the cunning logic with which Sophia spoke. She lifted her hands in a gesture of surrender and said, 'Oh, Sophia. I don't know what to think about you, about anything, anymore. I don't know whether to believe you or not. I concede that, actually, very little is known about Julian, apart from the few biographical details she gives in her own writings about her revelations. I'm just disturbed that those scant personal details—birth year, entering an anchorhold, receiving revelations—seem almost identical to the details you've framed your story with. On the other hand, I know that the moving account you gave me of your life, your family, your heartbreaking losses, has no equivalent in Julian's writings. And I acknowledge that, even if you were in Melbourne, and even if you attended that conference, your reasons for doing so are consistent with all that you've been telling me over the past few days. Consistency, however, is not necessarily the same as truth. I'm just very confused. I want to believe you, and in my heart I can almost believe you. But, in my head, none of it makes sense. Help me with it, Sophia, can you?'

'Kathryn, if you think back to your reading of this morning, perhaps you came across a reference to a study on the hermits and anchorites of England by Rotha Mary Clay.' Sophia paused, as if waiting for a sign of recognition, but Kathryn just stared intently, saying nothing, and Sophia continued. 'That study gives evidence of upward of thirty anchorites and anchoresses in the Norwich area around the same time as Julian's enclosure. And probably there were more, some of the records having been lost or destroyed over time.'

This was not the response Kathryn had expected. Her thoughts whirled. More than one anchoress in Norwich at the time? She hadn't even considered such a thing. Strange but true, the vocation of anchorite had been a feature of medieval life in England. Rotha Mary Clay? Hermits and anchorites? Had she seen that reference? She knew she had. Why hadn't she followed it up? Why had Sophia read such a reference? But more, more, more … disturbingly … how did Sophia know that she had read of it this morning?

'Are you telling me you know what I read this morning, Sophia?' It was a challenge.

'I never said that, Kathryn. I merely suggested that you might have come across Clay's study.' Sophia's voice was calm, direct. 'However, as we're being honest with each other, I am aware that you have been reading about witches today. Is there something you want to ask me in that regard?'

'Oh my God. You do know what I've been reading. How can you?'

'I am not a witch, if that's what you're thinking; though I'm sure you know that women through the ages have been accused of such things only because of men's fears and ignorance. Some have looked for deceit when there is nothing more to find than the marvellous operation of the natural and supernatural world. The world is alive, woven through, with the miraculous. Deception exists only in humans' lack of openness, in their fear. Fear and deception versus Love and Truth. And I think, perhaps, you also read of mystics and mysticism this morning, and if I must explain and label myself for you, I would accept the epithet of "mystic" with equanimity. Because mysticism is about looking behind the veil of the deception and illusion of the day-to-day world, and accessing the true reality that is alive with creativity and beauty and love. And I shall say one more thing on the subject of your investigations this morning. You may have read of the great motherhood of God. God is our father, our brother, our spouse, but God is especially our mother. And motherhood is expressed in great caring and love, so that whenever any of us care and love a thing or a person, we are a reflection of the divine motherhood that is part of our divine reality. The mother I told you of in my story of fourteenth century life cared for and loved me as I cared for and loved her, and as I loved my brother and my husband and my son. A midwife assists a mother to bring a child into the world—that is a wonderful work. It is miraculous, and in our lives we are all mothers and we are all midwives when we stand and ease another's pain and another's passage into life, or life beyond life. Do you understand me, Kathryn?'

Kathryn couldn't answer because, in truth, she did not understand and, yet, at the same time, she was moved beyond words. She kept her head down but lifted her eyes to Sophia, the faith and doubt inscribed in one look.

'I understand your conflict, Kathryn.' Sophia reached across to the side of the bed and took both of Kathryn's hands in hers. Kathryn was aware of a tremendous warmth and an absolute feeling of peace washing over her. Her churning and anxiety evaporated at the young woman's touch and she felt herself to be more alert, her mind clearer than it had ever been, as if it were being gently opened, expanded. In little more than a whisper, Sophia spoke: 'Faith is always tested, otherwise it is not faith. Sometimes, however, in the face of evidence to the contrary, we must choose to trust our hearts. Heart over head. Why do we usually regard the latter as superior to the former? It is the heart that sustains us, even when our heads are asleep. If your head tells you one thing and your heart another, why accept the one and reject the other?'

And Kathryn found herself believing what Sophia was saying. It was not rational necessarily but, in the context of all that Sophia had revealed of herself, believable nonetheless. And rather than this acknowledgment irritating her, Kathryn felt comforted, grateful, alive.

The two women remained in silence for some time. Yesterday, Kathryn had been convinced of Sophia's authenticity when the young woman had shared her insights into Kathryn's pain. This morning Kathryn had doubted not only Sophia's honesty but also her own experience and professional insights. Now, Kathryn's opinion had swung back to a full-hearted acceptance of Sophia and her claims, and she wanted to act only in the young woman's best interests. She knew, though, the tenuous path she would be walking if, and when, she made her opinion public. And Kathryn was not just worried for herself. She spoke sincerely when she asked, 'Is there anything else you want to tell me? Anything else that would help me do the best for you?'

'Yes, Kathryn, there is. I want to remind you of life's most important lesson. All you have to do is proceed with love.'

Kathryn cried quietly. She had no idea how long she had been listening to Sophia, but now the young woman was handing her a tissue.

The room around her was coming back into focus. There was the flat-screen television suspended above the bed; next to her was the bedside table with its water jug and glass, and the box of tissues. The lights over the bed were dimmed but, to her far right, Kathryn was aware of the harsher lights of the ward's wide corridor streaming in through the half-closed door. Suddenly, she could hear the bustle and clatter of medication trolleys and tea trolleys being wheeled along that corridor, and then there was the chatter of ward visitors—arriving or leaving—as they passed the door. There was a strange shadow in the doorway, and then it spoke, loudly.

'Evening, Sophia. Evening, Dr Brookley. Mind if I come in? Would you like a cup of tea? Or a hot chocolate?' And, from the bed next to which she was sitting, she heard a voice answer, 'Yes. Thank you. I think we'd both like a cup of tea.' And then Kathryn was accepting a mug into her hands, feeling the warmth of its contents on her palms. She had not realised how cold her hands had become. She raised the mug to her lips and felt the milky tea warm her mouth and her throat and then continue down into her chest where it radiated outward, all the way to her arms which were resting at the sides of her body and which, until the moment of that warmth, she had forgotten she had. Arms, then legs, her buttocks on the seat of the chair, her feet in leather boots together on the floor, all slowly came back into her awareness. And then she remembered where she was, and who she was, and who this woman sitting in the hospital bed was. One was the doctor, one was the patient; she just didn't remember which of the two she was.

'What am I to do with you?' whispered Kathryn, sensing the return of her voice.

'I shall accept whatever decision you come to about me,' said Sophia. 'Whatever happens, all shall be well. But, if I may suggest a way forward that might help you in your indecision ...'

'All suggestions gratefully accepted,' Kathryn smiled.

'Very well. First, as you're taking some time off, recommend a short-term placement for me so that I am not of concern to you. Secondly, speak to your husband. Tell him what we have spoken of. He may not accept it immediately but it needs to be said, just the same. Lastly, enjoy your time away—you will learn much. When you return we will complete the lessons.' She lifted her hands and clasped them in a sort of prayer position over her own heart.

Kathryn stood and left the room. She walked toward the nurses' station, pulled up a chair, logged in to Sophia's ward notes and inserted her recommendation that Sophia be transferred the next day to a private room at one of the hospital's rehabilitation units for the purpose of rest and observation for two weeks. She copied the relevant people in on her recommendation so that it would be actioned promptly, appending a further note that she would be on leave but could be contacted on her mobile. And then she left the ward. She knew that she had not told Sophia that she was taking two weeks leave as of tomorrow. She knew that she had not told Sophia anything about the rift in her marriage that had resulted in her husband moving out of their home. But most of all, she knew that her life would never be the same again.

{ 7 }

This is what she said:

There are tightly locked doors behind which we put our pain so that the main rooms of our life remain uncluttered to those who observe us. But sometimes we forget to bar the doors sufficiently and, if the pressure of the pain behind the doors becomes too great, the detritus of our lives spills out into plain view, taking the doors down with it. And those who knew us in our tightly closed state are shocked and say that we are 'unhinged'. But the unhinging of the door is a gift because, once the door is down, all is revealed to the bright light of day; and then, like a plant, we can absorb the light, and grow.

The next evening, with her work in order and two weeks leave stretching ahead of her, Kathryn sat in the armchair opposite her husband. She noticed the intensity of his gaze, and his nervous habit of rubbing his thumbs against his fingertips. He smiled awkwardly at her.

'I want to thank you for coming over to see me,' Kathryn began.

'Why wouldn't I see you? We're still married … we're still able to be civil to each other. And this is still my house too.'

Kathryn chose to ignore the last part of Richard's retort and continued, 'I wanted to talk to you about a patient of mine.'

She noticed Richard's smile drop away. 'I had hoped it might have been to talk about us. About me moving back in. I miss you Kathryn.'

'Perhaps that will happen. I'm starting to see things differently. That's what I wanted to explain.'

Richard sat forward in the chair. 'Kathryn, this is … this means so much.'

'I'd like you to listen to what I have to say first, about this patient of mine, before any decision about us.'

'Okay. I'm listening. Full attention.'

'You may have seen the news reports a few days ago about a young woman who was found, alive and well, in the harbour,' Kathryn began, handing a typed page over to him. 'Here's what we know so far. She calls herself Sophia and, as you'll see there, it seems that she, or someone very like her—given the name "Julie X"—was admitted to hospital under very similar circumstances forty years ago.'

Kathryn watched Richard reading the summary. He seemed to be taking a long time over it and she was moved to prompt him. 'Well, what do you make of it all? You must have heard about her?'

Richard's voice was quiet, faltering, as he replied. 'Funnily enough, I was the one who spotted her in the water. From the ferry … that morning. I raised the alarm, stayed with her till we reached the quay.'

Now it was Kathryn's turn to be quiet. She felt like her mouth was filled with cottonwool when she finally managed to say, 'Oh my God. Why didn't you tell me? What does all this mean?'

'What do you mean "what does all this mean"? No need to be upset, Kathryn. It's just a coincidence. And not so unusual, really. I was on the ferry—the one I often take to work—and you're a psychiatrist at a big public hospital near the harbour where this woman would, naturally, be taken to be assessed. As for not telling you—well, why would I? Remember, we don't see each other every day anymore.'

'No, Richard. You don't understand. There are so many apparent coincidences with this patient that … that I don't think anything is a coincidence with her. You felt it, too. I know you did. I saw you hesitate before you told me you'd discovered her.'

'Okay, I'll admit it is a bit coincidental.'

'A bit? Richard, come on, be honest. What did you think when you found her? What did you make of her?'

'Look, it was a strange day all round. Dark, overcast skies, rough seas. The whole ferry ride, the whole atmosphere was … unnatural. So, yes, I was surprised, even a bit rattled, to discover a body floating in the middle of the main ferry route, and very surprised that the body, the woman, was alive. But so what? Who wouldn't feel like that? You're not making sense, Kathryn.'

Kathryn shifted uncomfortably in the chair. 'Richard, I think she meant you to find her. And I think she meant to find me. I think that, somehow, she's been sent to help me.'

Richard straightened up on the sofa, inhaled with force, and then spat out a derisive breath. 'Sent to help you? Sent from where? To help you with what? Kathryn, you can't be serious.'

'But I am serious. What Sophia says, what she's told me, has touched me, struck a chord of truth. Deep truth. She knows things about me, about us. Things that have been revealed to her. Yes, revelations. I find myself thinking about her all the time,' Kathryn confessed.

'You're a doctor, her psychiatrist. You cannot be actually telling me that you've been taken in by a crazy woman's pronouncements. This is ridiculous. Complete nonsense.'

'But that's the thing, Richard. I don't think it is nonsense. I did at first. But the more I've talked with her, the more she's helped me begin to … to …'

'Oh, spare me.' Richard thumped the chair arms with his fists as he sprang to standing. 'And I don't know why I'm telling you—the psychiatrist—that these so-called *revelations* are hallucinations and they'll disappear very quickly once the medication takes effect.'

Kathryn was stony-faced when she responded. 'I'm not prescribing any medication for her, Richard. I'm letting her be. In fact, I'm on leave as of now and I'm going to spend that leave finding out more about her, and about the earlier Julie X. There's a connection between them and I'm going to find it. And it's going to help me, to help us.'

'I can't believe what I'm hearing.' Richard paused, rubbed his hand across his forehead. His next words were gentle. 'Look, I'm not speaking only as your husband here. It's your professional duty to do the best for your patient. She's plainly very ill.'

'No, Richard. She is plainly very well. Very insightful, very remarkable. And it's my professional duty to declare that someone is well if they are well. And Sophia, I believe, does not need a psychiatrist.' Kathryn stood up, her confidence growing now that she had stated her professional and personal view of the situation. Richard stared at her, distress clearly visible on his face. She crossed the room to him, took his hands in hers and looked up at him, holding his gaze. 'Please, Richard. I need to tell you something else, but I'm a little afraid of how you'll react, given your views so far on Sophia.'

Kathryn's touch seemed to take the edges off Richard's anger. 'Okay. Let's sit down. Tell me what you need to tell me. I'll play the good doctor and husband and listen without judgment for a while.'

Kathryn knew it was a kind concession on his part, but she was still nervous. As they sat side by side on the sofa, she kneaded her left hand with her right. She gulped and then whispered to him, 'She helps me … with Matthew.'

Silence. Long silence. A choking intake of breath. Richard slumped back into the sofa. More silence. Unspeakable silence.

From a place that Kathryn imagined to be somewhere behind his heart, Richard produced a small voice that said, 'Kathryn. Please. The loss of our baby breaks my heart every day, but Matthew is dead. Ten years dead. Don't do this to me, to yourself. To us. Our grief tore us apart. Don't add to it.'

'I think she could help you too,' Kathryn dared.

Richard shook his head. With effort he found his feet and let them walk him slowly out of the room. He slammed the door behind him.

{ 8 }

This is what she said:

Sometimes we long for the light of day because we think that our way will be then clear to us. Of the dark night we are fearful. There we cannot see our way forward and we are beset by doubt and imaginings. And yet, the unexpected can occur on the brightest of days and throw all that we have trusted to that point into chaos. Thus, daylight is no assurance of certainty. It is in the darkness that we endure, through our uncertainties, till morning light. And thus, we are stronger, more courageous, when we see no hope and no way and yet continue than when we set off in sunshine without care. We are blind when we think we can most clearly see. We are clear-sighted when we proceed despite the darkness.

14 May 2013

A mild day, bright and clear, unfurled ahead of Kathryn as she set off. It was just past nine am when she crossed the Harbour Bridge. To her left, the white sails of the Opera House, billowing in the light breeze of the autumn morning; to her right, the sandstone perfection of the historic Observatory; below her, the deep water of the harbour, sparkling and pulsing beneath its load of ferries, water taxis, passenger liners, yachts, and service craft. She drove on past the airport and the wide stretch of Botany Bay, its blinding clarity reflecting incoming and outgoing flights, and then on through the southern suburbs of Sydney, flashing and glistening in the Saturday morning sun. On she drove as, on her left, the glorious Royal National Park filled the expanse between the Princes Highway and the Pacific Ocean. And then she was at the pinnacle of Bulli Tops, the great city of Wollongong spreading confidently far below her and the South Coast ahead.

It had been easier than Kathryn had thought it would be to track down Sister Margery and the broad story of the demise of the order of nuns to which she had belonged. Tim's remark about the association between the public hospital and the smaller Catholic private hospital's uptake of suitable convalescing patients gave her the starting clue. Such an association was, of course, a matter of public record and she had been able to find the basic information on Google under the search term 'history of Harbourside Public Hospital'.

In the late 1960s the Catholic private hospital, St Faith's, was one of a number of private hospitals with which the public hospital established an association, to ease the pressure on increasing demands for its beds by patients who were in need of good quality nursing care during their convalescence following medical and surgical treatment.

From there, the simple entry of the search term 'St Faith's Hospital, Sydney' produced more information.

Located in the suburb of Willoughby, St Faith's Hospital was administered and largely staffed by nursing nuns of the order of St Faith of Peace and Devotion and, at its peak occupancy in the mid-1970s, could accommodate forty-seven patients in single or twin bed rooms. The original buildings on the site of the hospital had served as a private boarding school in the late nineteenth century and up until the outbreak of the First World War. From that time, and until shortly after the Second World War, the buildings were used by the Army as a storage facility. The site and its structures were completely abandoned in 1952 and fell into disrepair until 1960 when the Catholic Church purchased the property and converted it into a modern convalescent and rehabilitation centre with facilities that included an indoor therapy pool, an activities room, and a prize-winning rose garden. Changes to government funding for reciprocal arrangements between public and private hospitals, and problems within the St Faith of Peace and Devotion order, saw the hospital's closure in 1976. The complex was released for sale in 1980 and, subsequently, the hospital was razed to make way for town houses.

The next step on the search trail was 'St Faith of Peace and Devotion nuns in Australia' and, again, the information was readily available.

The Order of the Holy Sisters of St Faith of Peace and Devotion was founded in East Anglia in 1847 by Georgette Crofter with the express purpose of ministering to the sick and dying who had no family to care for them in their final stages of life. Miss Crofter, who was the daughter of Jeremiah Crofter, a successful ship builder, turned her back on her wealthy family when they tried to force her to marry, instead following her vocation of a life devoted to God and the service of others. The Order was approved by Pope Pius IX in 1848 and, by 1850, had attracted twenty-five dedicated women to work among the poor. Numbers joining the order grew steadily and, in 1877, a small group of fifteen sisters set out to establish a branch of the order in Australia where, despite never drawing huge numbers to its fold, the sisters were able to establish a solid identity as caring and prayerful nurses. With the securing of an agreement with Royal Harbourside Public Hospital in 1967, the order administered and staffed St Faith's Private Hospital in suburban Sydney. Under the direction of the order's then leader, Mother Augusta, the hospital and the nuns themselves gained a reputation for excellence which, unfortunately, took a spectacular downturn in 1973 following the attempted suicide of one of the order's nuns after this same nun had attempted to persuade a number of her fellow sisters to join a breakaway order based on the revelations and teachings of the mysterious Julie X. This scandal and changes in government funding saw the closure of St Faith's Hospital in 1976 and the general disbanding of the order.

The electronic trail ended there. Googling 'the mysterious Julie X' and 'revelations of Julie X' turned up no results, as did Kathryn's further searches on what had happened to the nuns after the disbanding. But a solution of sorts had presented itself quite quickly and unexpectedly in the form of one of the hospital's staff. Kathryn, her laptop open in front of her, had been sitting at a table in the hospital café all morning of the day after her library discoveries, finalising patient notes prior to her leave. After the upheaval of the previous few days, she found her office to be too sterile, too lonely; she needed to be around people. She was debating with herself whether to walk to the counter to order another coffee when Freda, the café supervisor, came over to wipe some nearby tables.

'You've been working away here all morning, Dr Brookley,' said Freda. 'Can I bring you over another coffee? On the house.'

'Thanks, Freda. Just what I was thinking about. You don't usually do table service here,' replied Kathryn.

'No, you're right, love. But we're quiet at the moment so I'm happy to do something for good customers like you.'

Kathryn watched Freda shuffle over to the coffee machine and in no time she was back with a cappuccino.

'That was quick. Great service.'

'It should be great,' said Freda, laughing. 'I've been working at it a long time.'

'Really?' said Kathryn, looking more closely at the woman and realising that she would have to be well past retirement age. 'How long, exactly?'

'Well, nearly forty years. Since late 1976. I've been here through three expansions and renovations of this café. And, before that, I worked in the kitchen at St Faith's from the day it opened till the day it closed. So, this hospital's been very important to me over many years.'

Kathryn couldn't believe what she was hearing. 'Freda, could you sit and talk to me for a few minutes? I think you might be able to help me.'

'Of course, love. What's bothering you?' Freda pulled out the chair next to Kathryn and sat down, her face full of concern and interest.

'I need some insights into St Faith's Hospital—its nuns and the closure, in particular.'

'Don't you worry, I know the whole story,' Freda confided. 'Of course, certain people might rather it was all covered up. But I was there, on the spot. Where would you like me to start?'

Kathryn felt as if she had been handed a box of beautifully wrapped Christmas presents. She wasn't sure which one to open first so decided on a lucky dip. 'Well, can you tell me anything about a Sister Margery?'

'Of course. She was made out to be the baddie but, in my opinion, she was the best of the lot. They drove her to it, you know.' Freda looked off into the distance and Kathryn reached to gently pat her forearm by way of encouragement for her to continue.

'Oh yes. Where was I?' Freda laughed, shaking her head. 'Sister Margery was lovely. Not very old at the time, maybe forty-five. And so dedicated to the patients. Nothing was a trouble to her. And that suited the others—they were happy to let Margery do the majority of the work. Until Julie X arrived, that is. Margery took a real interest in that young woman. Well, really, neither of them seemed to have anyone else. Margery never mentioned her parents except to say they'd given her into the care of the nuns when she was a teenager. As for Julie, she was at St Faith's for nearly six months, I think, because they just didn't know what to do with her. She'd been in a psych hospital initially but that didn't last long. I don't think it was the right place for her. You see, she was healthy enough, she just made some people feel uncomfortable.'

'So, you knew the young mystery woman?'

'Knew her? Why, I served her breakfast, lunch and dinner, and morning and afternoon tea every weekday—and some weekends—the whole time she was at St Faith's,' Freda announced proudly.

'What did you make of her?'

'Well, she was nice. At first I felt sorry for her, having no one. But I don't think she cared that she was alone. She had this way about her. Confident, kind, otherworldly. To be honest, I envied her; I looked up to her. You know, we were pretty close in age. I think she was around thirty and I was only a bit older, thirty-five or thirty-six. But there she was, interesting, doing her own thing. And there I was, bringing up two kids after my husband had shot through, and working long hours in a hospital kitchen. I was in the background of life. Julie was out in front. People took notice of her. And that was the problem.' Freda smiled ruefully at the memory.

'How was that a problem, Freda?'

'Well, it's difficult to explain when you haven't met her. When she talked, she spoke of seeing things differently, living differently. And, on the one-to-one level, when she spoke to you it was as if she knew everything about you—like she could see inside your heart. Not in a mean way; in a loving, positive way. She could tell you about your deepest hurts, and then she could help you get over them. So, some of the nuns didn't think that was right. You know, God's the one who's meant to help you; the one you're supposed to pray to for help. Not that he ever answered any of my prayers. Anyway, I think you can understand the problem. Patients, and even some of the staff, stopped going to pray in the chapel about their sorrows; they went to talk to Julie instead. And when Sister Margery and a couple of the other nuns started to confide in Julie, and take notice of her advice, there was hell to pay—if you'll excuse the expression.'

'What was she advising them, do you know?'

'Not exactly,' confessed Freda. 'I can guess, though. I know what she told me about my heartaches. She said that pain and love were part of the same package. The package of life. You know, if you don't love something or someone then it's no big loss if that something or someone is taken away. As dreadful as losing the thing you love is, your only alternative is to love nothing at all, and that's not living. That's pretending to live when, really, you're a frightened, empty shell. Love or fear, they're our choices, she said. Press on with love despite the heartaches, or shut down with fear. Of course, there was always lots of gossip about what she'd told the nuns, but I suspect her advice was the same; it was just that the nuns might have had different troubles to people like me. So, overall, I don't think the nuns heard much more than I did. Then again, whatever she said to Margery made quite an impact. But I never blamed Julie for Margery's suicide attempt. I reckon it was the hounding Margery got from those superior nuns, and those pesky priests, and those nosey do-gooders. Mother Augusta did her best to protect Margery but, really, too many people felt threatened. They didn't like their comfortable little world being shaken up, their precious beliefs being challenged.'

Kathryn had suspected that Margery was the nun referred to in the internet article, the one who had attempted suicide and brought shame on the order.

'What happened to Margery? And to Julie? And what about the other nuns? What happened to all of them?' Kathryn had so many questions.

The café was starting to fill with the first wave of the lunchtime crowd and Freda shifted uneasily. 'Sorry, Doc, I'll have to be brief because it looks like Dawn and Joe will need my help with this lot,' she apologised. 'But, I'll do my best for you. So, last question first. The nuns. Hmm. It was a long time ago. Well, obviously, the ones who were following Margery's lead and taking notice of Julie weren't welcome in the convent anymore. So I guess they left and got on with their lives. As for the others—the 'anti-Julie brigade'—I remember hearing that some of them joined other orders of nuns. And I know for a fact that Mother Augusta and a couple of the older remaining nuns took up a more contemplative life in some backwater, you know, in one of those isolated Church-owned mansions.'

Freda paused for a moment to signal to Dawn at the service counter that she'd be there very soon, then she continued, in a rush. 'Now, Julie. She disappeared, probably drowned. After all the commotion at the hospital, it was decided that Julie couldn't stay there any longer. And she wasn't ill, anyway. So one of the doctors offered his own family holiday house to Julie. Somewhere on Pittwater or the northern beaches. I can't remember exactly. It was a sad end to an extraordinary young woman. As for Margery, she was carted off to an old people's home. That seemed very wrong to me. Margery wasn't old, and she wasn't crazy. They just wanted her out of the way.'

'Freda, I don't want to hold you up, just one more thing if possible,' begged Kathryn. Freda nodded. 'You were saying that Margery was about forty-five when all this took place. So, she would be eighty-five now, if she's still alive.'

'Oh, she's alive,' said Freda. 'We exchange Christmas cards every year. So, unless she's died in the last five months, she's still at the old folks' home, bright and breezy as ever.'

'Where's the home? Have you got an address?' Kathryn could not contain her excitement.

'Yes, yes. Calm down. I've got all the details in my head. St Monica's Home for the Aged. If you're going to see her, give her my best. I visited her a couple of times when she first went there but it's out of the way. Beautiful spot, on one of those South Coast beaches, beyond Kiama, but a long way for someone like me who never owned a car. It would take me from early morning to very late at night to get there and back by train and bus. And then the bus stopped running on weekends, and I was too busy looking after my kids when I wasn't working here. And then I was too old to even think about making the trek, so Christmas cards are our only contact now.' Freda sighed, took a little notepad and pen out of her apron pocket and jotted down the address.

'Freda, you're an angel,' said Kathryn.

Some kilometres south of Kiama, Kathryn turned left off the highway and onto a smooth-surfaced road that wound between rolling green pastureland dotted with small groups of fat, glossy dairy cattle. The pastureland ended abruptly in a towering rock incline that forced the road to curve suddenly down toward the ocean and then follow the shoreline before it rose up again to hug the edges of a spectacularly steep headland. Up and over, around and down the other side of the headland, another beach stretched out under the sun. And there Kathryn came to St Monica's. She'd seen the building long before she saw its name sign, an imposing edifice facing the sea, owning the view, dwarfing the few small holiday cottages dotted at other points along the sea road. On a morning like this, Kathryn thought that St Monica's was beautiful, a place where anyone, of any age, would be happy to be.

She had called ahead the previous afternoon and spoken to the Director of Nursing, Geoff Briar. He had been more than accommodating in saying that he would be there to welcome her, show her around, and introduce her to Margery. He had even invited her to stay a few days at St Monica's so that she and Margery would have time for thorough conversations and, as she parked her car in the visitors' area, she suddenly felt very glad that she had accepted the invitation. Kathryn took her bag from the back of the car and, looking up, saw a young man approaching and smiling broadly.

'Hi, you must be Dr Brookley. I'm Geoff Briar. I've been looking out for you. My office overlooks the main driveway entrance,' he said, indicating generally with a wave of the hand.

'Yes, that's me. Kathryn, please,' she said, reaching to shake the hand he was extending to her.

'Any problems finding us?' he asked as he guided her in the direction of the home's main door.

'No, easy, thanks to your directions. And a gorgeous drive, especially on such a lovely day.'

'Yeah, if you have to be in an old folks' home, at least you're doing it in style here. And I don't just mean the view.' He laughed.

And he was right. As they cleared the main doors, Kathryn was stunned by the opulence of the reception area in which she found herself. It looked more like an upmarket hotel lobby than a nursing home's entrance. To her left was a long reception counter of polished timber, its grain clearly indicative of its solid and authentic origins. No veneers here. Behind the counter were what looked like office doors of the same timber with the occupants' names etched on brass plates. To her far right was a glass-fronted elevator. Directly in front of her, opposite the entrance, was a magnificent marble staircase, wide and edged with full-marble balustrades. After the first eight or so steps of the staircase, a wide landing—at the rear of which sat an antique velvet sofa—branched into two equally generous staircases, one leading to the right, the other to the left. Kathryn's eyes followed the branches and saw that they led onto broad marble-floored walkways, bordered by marble banisters on the open side overlooking the reception area. Along the lengths of the walkways, doors (to what she presumed were the residents' rooms) of the signature polished wood stood closed but full of the promise of further luxury inside. At various points around the foyer, huge brass vases were filled with exquisite arrangements of fresh flowers and, behind the opulent staircase, and through two huge doors that had been thrown open, Kathryn glimpsed a dining room in which uniformed staff were laying tables with linen cloths and silverware.

'Wow,' she heard herself say. 'I see what you mean about style. I'm guessing that residents here have to make quite a sizeable weekly payment beyond the government contribution.'

'You could say that the residents are a very select group,' Geoff agreed.

'Um, what about Margery then?' Kathryn ventured. 'Nuns, poverty, all that.'

'There's a story there,' said Geoff. 'Let's go into my office. I'll have some coffee brought for us and we can talk a bit about Margery before you meet her.'

He led the way behind the timber counter and down a panelled corridor before opening the door with his brass nameplate on it to reveal a ridiculously spacious office with a huge desk positioned to take in a full view of the ocean through floor to ceiling glass doors and windows.

'Oh, and excuse me. I should have shown you the guest ladies' room. Just out of my office and down the second corridor to the left. You can't miss it. And while you're there, I'll have someone take your bag up to your guest room.'

Kathryn nodded and left the office, more to get a grip on the surprising surroundings than the need for a toilet visit. Nevertheless, as she could have predicted, the ladies' room was just as luxurious as the other areas of this aged-care facility.

When Kathryn returned to Geoff's office, a rich coffee aroma greeted her. She took a moment to locate its source. Then she noticed one of the glass doors near Geoff's desk was open and she crossed the room to it. The beach, sparkling in the sunshine between its two spectacular headlands, filled her field of vision as she stepped over the threshold onto a colonnaded terrace.

'Pretty impressive, isn't it?' Geoff said, wrestling her attention away from the view. 'It's such a beautiful morning I thought you'd enjoy having our coffee and chat here,' he continued, motioning for her to sit down opposite him in one of four matching high-backed cane chairs arranged around a small but exquisitely crafted cane table. Kathryn took her seat and allowed her eyes to flick from the view to the table where a large tray with a silver coffee pot, milk jug and sugar bowl, Wedgewood cups and saucers and cake plates, and a delicate cake stand displaying a selection of tortes and pastries, rested.

'Kathryn, please help yourself. I can guarantee it's all delicious,' he said, turning the coffee pot so that she could easily take its handle.

'I want to work here,' joked Kathryn as she took up the pot and poured the rich, dark coffee into her cup. 'How did you get so lucky, Geoff?'

'This is a surprising place, Kathryn. And it's all courtesy of Margery.'

Kathryn frowned. 'I don't understand.'

'I'll try to explain. This is why I wanted to speak to you before you meet Margery. She's, well, extraordinary, but she won't necessarily talk about the things you want her to talk about.' Geoff put down his cup and spread his palms on the table, as if he were stalling, or looking for the right words. 'Look, it's hard to know where best to begin with this,' he confided, 'so I'll give you the short version and you can ask questions if you need to fill in any gaps.'

'Fine,' agreed Kathryn, all ears now.

'When Margery came here forty years ago, it was a very different place. Of course I wasn't here then—I was employed after the conversion of the home into the luxury retreat you now see; that was seventeen years ago. At the time of Margery's arrival back in the 1970s, St Monica's was run by the Church as a regular aged-care facility, with a Matron in charge and sisters, nurses, nurses' aides and so on working under her. The patients then were your usual assortment of older people requiring high-level nursing care as a result of various severe physical problems—hemiplegia following strokes, advanced Parkinson's disease and MS, myasthenia gravis, last stage cancers, etc—and, of course, a lot of patients with dementia. Margery was the youngest admission by far but, apparently, she saw it as God's will, as a way that she could offer her services up for others. Now, remember, she wasn't sent here to work, even though she was a fully qualified nurse. She was here because of her behaviour at her former place of work, St Faith's.

There, as I'm sure you already know, she befriended the woman pulled from the harbour, Julie X, and Margery became what you might call a 'disciple' of Julie's. Margery might tell you more about her involvement with Julie but, here, suffice to say, the Church wanted Margery out of the way and St Monica's fitted the bill.' Geoff paused to refill his coffee cup. 'More coffee for you, Kathryn?'

'Yes, thank you,' she replied, holding up her cup. 'But, please, go on with your story.'

'Right. Now where was I? Oh, yes, as I said, Margery wasn't sent to St Monica's to work, but she was still only in her forties when she arrived, and very good-hearted and so, naturally, she helped the patients, made time for them when the nurses were too busy to attend to their needs. One of the patients, Miss Taylor, suffered from an extremely rare and debilitating skin condition. Today there would be treatment to help her, but she'd been born in a time that saw her as a problem not a person, and she'd been shunned at birth by her family. Anyway, Miss Taylor's skin was so thickened and constantly shedding that her room had to be vacuumed hourly to clear the large flakes of skin that she produced. And, poor woman, so many years of this disease with its thick, constantly cracking skin had affected her mobility and rendered her totally hairless; it was reported in her medical file that, ultimately, she resembled a snake. She was a difficult nursing case, and not just because she was physically confronting to look at. Years of this pain, this ugliness, had made her a bitter, nasty woman. Who could blame her? The nurses and other staff avoided her, doing only the bare necessities for her. Now Margery, fired with kindness and zeal, loved and socialised with all the patients, but she especially loved Miss Taylor.

'When Miss Taylor died about twenty years ago, she left a fortune to Margery. Fortuitously, too, the Church was looking to sell off a number of its holdings to private enterprise around that time and, Margery, through a solicitor, used part of her inheritance to buy St Monica's. She then set about organising its transformation into the magnificent facility that you see now. The families of some residents chose to move them on to other facilities, but those who wished to stay were housed in temporary accommodation until the renovations were complete. After the transformation, St Monica's had twenty-four remaining residents, including Margery herself, but there was available accommodation for another ninety-two people. Margery, as owner, refused to consider any applicants who were not below the poverty line. In fact, she gave preference to the sick and elderly who were living on the streets. Even the staff are drawn largely from the homeless population. Margery's team found me in a boarding house in Kings Cross. I was a trained nurse but I'd let it all slide because of a heroin addiction. My family had given up on me. It was Margery who paid for my rehabilitation, sent me back to university for a refresher course, helped me with new accreditation, paid my removal costs to St Monica's, and, as they say, the rest is history. No resident here pays anything. Margery's trust account is well managed and has sufficient funds to continue in its present mode of operation for at least forty years.'

The coffee was cold and the cakes untouched when Geoff finished his story. Kathryn was stunned.

'Why haven't I heard about this?' she asked.

'Margery has fought hard to keep it quiet, set up contingencies to ensure her own anonymity as far as the ownership goes. And, as you've experienced, we're out of the way here; there's a bit of truth to the "out of sight, out of mind" saying. Most of the people here do not have family and they're so grateful that they won't do anything to jeopardise their good fortune. The staff are in the same situation. We operate out of love and respect for each other. And of course the Church is not going to draw attention to it.'

'Wow. Rags to riches indeed.' Kathryn smiled. 'I'm a bit overwhelmed.'

'Yes, I know what you mean. Life is full of surprises. And there's another one waiting for you, Kathryn. Are you ready to meet Sister Margery?' asked Geoff, standing up from the table and extending his hand in a flourish of invitation toward the door.

Kathryn nodded and followed him back through his office, into the foyer, up the central staircase and then its right branch, and along a wide corridor to a pair of solid timber doors with ornate golden handles. Geoff put a hand on each of the handles, pushed down on them simultaneously, and flung back both doors to reveal a sitting room so vast and magnificent that Kathryn's mouth fell open in awe. The floor, visible around the perimeter of a huge Persian rug of rich reds, blues and cream silk, was of mirror-polished, darkly honeyed timber. On three sides of the room, smooth walls the colour of a shallow sea on a clear blue day stretched up to wide white cornices, patterned in bas-relief with seabirds of the region, and bordering a ceiling in the same soft blue colour as the walls. The central third of the left-hand wall was taken up by a huge fireplace that looked to be built of spectacular, hand-hewn blocks of Sydney sandstone and in which, today, a fire glowed in its hearth, the yellow and red flames bouncing off the ceiling's crystal chandelier. Above the fireplace, a gilt-edged mirror took in the whole room and reflected it back unstintingly. The right-hand wall was covered in diverse artworks and, even at a glance, Kathryn recognised several original works of great Australian artists—the distinctive landscape of an Albert Namatjira, the vivid still life of a Margaret Olley, and the voluptuous details of a Norman Lindsay. It was too much to take in, but all the opulence of the room paled into insignificance when compared to the 'wall' opposite the entrance doors: floor-to-ceiling glass presenting an uninterrupted vista of the ocean.

Plump, gold brocade sofas and matching high-backed armchairs were tastefully dotted around the room, some near the wall of books that bordered the room's entrance doors, others in groupings around polished coffee tables with turned legs; still another cosy grouping nearer the fireplace; and one especially inviting set of chairs, sofa and coffee table were positioned to directly face the ocean view.

'She's over there,' said Geoff in a whisper. 'On that sofa, looking out to sea. Come on, I'll introduce you.'

Kathryn hadn't realised anyone else was in the room and, suddenly, she was overcome with nerves at the thought of meeting Sister Margery. Gingerly, she stepped onto the magic Persian carpet, following Geoff as he walked toward the sea.

And then they were standing with their backs to the view and Kathryn saw that there had, indeed, been someone sitting on the sofa the whole time she had been surveying the room. A small woman, with grey cropped hair and clear blue eyes, dressed in a plain woollen smock, thick black stocking and solid black shoes, stood up to face her visitors and extended a delicate hand in welcome.

'Dr Brookley, I presume,' said the woman, laughing.

'Yes, Sister Margery, this is Dr Kathryn Brookley. Kathryn, I'd like to present our dear Sister Margery,' said Geoff, looking from one woman to the other and back again.

'I'm .. I'm … delighted to meet you,' began Kathryn.

'And, I you,' responded Margery, motioning for her visitors to take a seat.

'If you'll excuse me, I've got some things to attend to,' said Geoff, taking a step back. 'I don't think you two will need me to help the discussion along. So why don't we meet up at lunch? That gives you nearly an hour for your first conversation.'

'I'm sure you're right, Geoff. And speaking of lunch, would you mind asking Maurice to pop down to the cellar to get that special wine I wanted in honour of Kathryn's visit? Make sure he opens it to let it breathe a little. It's always much better that way, don't you agree?'

Geoff gave a friendly nod and headed for the door, leaving Kathryn to marvel and puzzle at the woman.

'You're wondering about my diamond earrings, aren't you, dear Kathryn.' It was a statement not a question, and Margery didn't wait for a response. 'I know they are rather decadent. Over a carat each. They were a gift; a gift to myself. And look at the rest of me. Positively drab. Of course, that's as it should be for a woman in my state but, well, as I'm sure you understand, a little of what you fancy is good for the soul. Can I offer you a whiskey?' Margery reached toward a cut-glass decanter set on a silver tray on the low table in front of her. She picked up the vessel and, removing its heavy stopper, poured a large shot of the golden liquid into two matching glasses. She handed one to Kathryn, saying, 'Marvellous for piquing the appetite and warming the soul.' Then she moved her glass toward Kathyrn's and, with a smile, effected a clink punctuated with, 'Cheers, dears, and down the hatch.' She had drained her glass and was refilling it before Kathryn had even registered what was happening. 'Don't worry, Dr Brookley,' Margery went on, 'I promise this second drink is much smaller and I will sip it delicately and soberly. Now, let's talk.'

Kathryn felt as if she'd lost her way and had somehow wandered onto the stage of a sitcom. She took a good gulp of the whiskey, aware of its rich malt taste in her mouth, its full body over her tongue, and its warmth as it coursed down her throat and spread across her upper chest. She relaxed back into the opulent comfort of the chair and let the beauty of the room wash over her.

'It's lovely here,' she heard herself say. 'It's a blessing to be here. A blessing to have found you.'

'You are correct, Kathryn. Life is full of blessings, from the bright yellow rising of the sun in the morning to its pink descent each evening. I hadn't noticed the exquisite beauty and the abundant blessings until I met Julie. I know you want to talk about her, and I'm delighted to do so. She taught me how to truly live, you know.'

And so the subject had been not only broached but split wide open.

'I've read your report, your nursing report, on how you met Julie.' Kathryn's nerves had dissipated and she felt certain she could speak with confidence to Margery, though she didn't know why.

'That first meeting. Wow,' enthused Margery, clapping her hands together. 'That shook me up. But it was nothing compared to what followed.'

'Margery … may I call you Margery, or should it be "Sister"?' asked Kathryn.

'Now, Kathryn, do I look like someone who stands on ceremony? You can call me whatever you want to. My mother used to call me "Topsy", my brother used to call me "Pain in the guts", and I won't even mention what I know the bishop and some of his clergy called me when I started to stir up trouble. So, "Margery", please.'

'Margery, then. Margery, in the report—' and as she spoke Kathryn fumbled in her briefcase to locate a copy of the report, which she handed to Margery before continuing, '—in the report you tell of remembering every detail of that first meeting.'

'Yes, dear. To this very day.'

'I especially loved the detail you gave about those early conversations with Julie. Her talk of home being exactly where she happens to be; and the wonderful little tale she told. But then you say that you stopped asking her more questions after the tale. Why was that? What impact did it have on you?'

'My life changed that night.' Margery put her untouched second whiskey back on the table and rested her hands neatly in her lap. 'It was as if Julie could see straight through me. Or, perhaps, it's more accurate to say that she was like a mirror, reflecting back to me all my pride and all my mistaken ideas and rigid, unloving beliefs. It was not the tale on its own that had this effect; perhaps it was not the tale at all. It was just Julie. She called me to account for my life, without me having to give any actual account of it. Do I make any sense?'

'Yes, Margery, you make perfect sense to me because—and I wasn't going to tell you this, or certainly not tell you so early in our acquaintance—I've had the same experience with a young woman, Sophia, who came under my professional care only a few days ago after being pulled from Sydney Harbour, alive and well.'

Margery turned her gaze toward the waves curling endlessly onto the shore beyond the window. After a long silence she murmured, 'So, she's back.'

❧ 9 ❧

This is what she said:

A golden beam of slim, flexible—but infinitely strong—light stretches into the distance. At numerous intervals along the shining beam, little leaves, dry and curled up, adhere to it. Suddenly, something makes one leaf quiver and then unfurl. And in the leaf's opening can be glimpsed a moment of our life. And then it curls up again, drier than before, and soon drops off the beam, falling down to the ground of Earth's being where it becomes dust and is absorbed without trace. Another leaf on the beam, another unfurling and re-furling and falling and going to dust in the great ground. And then another, and another. The leaves are like our life experiences, momentarily exquisite but barely visible to our memory as we streak onward, shining.

9 August 1973

It was on a cold day of snapping wind that Sister Margery farewelled the convent that had been her home for over twenty-five years. She had packed her battered suitcase the night before her departure, the whole exercise taking less than ten minutes. Her sombre room was furnished with only a single bed, a cracked wash basin, a small table that did double duty as a desk and nightstand, an unpadded upright chair, and an old chest of drawers. From the bottom drawer, Margery took two jumpers her mother had knitted for her long ago, a red woollen scarf, and a cheap navy blue acrylic cardigan. From the middle drawer, she took two long-sleeved cotton nighties, four pairs of socks, two pairs of black, ribbed tights, and three sets of cotton underwear. From the top drawer she took her toiletries bag with its cake of soap, toothbrush and toothpaste, talcum powder, and some lavender hand lotion that a patient had given her for Christmas two years earlier. With the exception of the scarf, she placed all of the items into the square brown suitcase that lay open on her bed. Then she walked the three steps toward the room's closed door where on the wall to the left of it, high up, her only other clothes were on wooden coat hangers on a metal towel rail. Two winter skirts, two summer skirts, two long-sleeved blouses, two short-sleeved blouses, one lightweight jacket, and one heavier winter coat occupied the short length of the rail. Standing on tiptoes, she took down the clothing, one item at a time, draping them over her arm to form a modest bundle, and then walked the three steps back to her bed and put all but the winter coat into the case. Bending down, she reached under the bed for a tattered pair of pale blue slippers and her flat-heeled brown walking shoes. She wrapped each shoe and slipper individually in newspaper and crammed the resulting packages into the sides of the suitcase, then she closed the lid, clipped the locks, and carried the case to the door in readiness for her departure the next day.

Then she reverently undressed from the habit that she had taken to wearing since her epiphany and in which she would leave the following morning. She had devised this uniform herself. She had retrieved the basis of the outfit—an ankle-length white shift—from the convent's laundry cupboard where it had been placed, along with other similar outfits, after the nuns had abandoned them for more 'normal', less obviously 'religious' garb after the changes to religious life that were introduced following the second Vatican Council. To the shift, Margery added a blue kirtle and matching waist-length veil, fashioning both from a discarded piece of fabric she had found in the sewing room. Her footwear consisted of simple black lace-up shoes over black socks. Mother Superior and the other sisters had been shocked when Margery first paraded the outfit at the monthly formal dinner to which the bishop and leading clergy of the diocese were invited. The fashion statement—following so swiftly on Margery's return to physical health after her scandalous suicide attempt—had certainly steeled the bishop's resolve to have Margery moved on. No one, least of all Mother Superior, was surprised when, on the morning following the dinner, a letter from the bishop arrived advising that, 'Due to our sincere concern for the psychological health of Sister Margery Plimsoll, it has been decided that she be re-accommodated at St Monica's Home for the Aged until such time as she is able to resume her conventual duties faithfully and obediently.'

In an earlier incarnation, St Monica's Aged Care Home had been a solid, no-nonsense structure of little charm and fewer windows, hidden behind high walls and substantial trees. Then, it had served as a correctional facility for wayward girls. Any young woman who found herself confined to this building was usually from a rural or regional area of the state where, on a balmy night in a boring town, she had succumbed briefly and naïvely to a moment's fumbling, adolescent pleasure with a local pimply (though surprisingly persuasive) youth with the result that she was, shortly after, moved hastily to this out of the way facility by an outraged father and mortified mother into the care of the good sisters until the baby was born and adopted by a decent family. When the advent and proliferation of the Pill started to impact on the number of girls that the sisters were correcting, the decision was taken to transform the building into something more socially and economically useful. The gates and walls that had hidden the building from the view of the respectable locals came down and, under the property's substantial trees, lawns and gardens of bright blooms were planted, and benches and fountains were sprinkled around the grounds like nuts on a sundae. To the sprawling residential buildings, windows were added and the ground-floor assembly hall was partially gutted and its most obstinate brick wall knocked out to enable the hall's transformation into a glassy, light-filled sitting room. Unlike the dwindling population of fatherless newborns, the number of befuddled older folk was burgeoning and St Monica's Aged Care Home was at full capacity from its first day of opening.

No one said goodbye to Sister Margery when she left her convent home, but she was accompanied to St Monica's by Sister Anselm, one of the convent's most reliable and unemotional sisters.

'Here, Margery. Leave your bag with me and go and take a seat over there. I'll get everything sorted for you,' Sister Anselm instructed as they approached the main reception desk while, at the same time, wrestling Margery's little suitcase from her hand.

'Oh, no need, dear Anselm,' said Margery. 'I think I know my way around a hospital.'

'You're here to be admitted, not to run the place,' she barked. 'Now move aside while I get the paperwork finalised for you.'

Margery shrugged, smiled, and acquiesced. She began to walk toward the reception lounge's plush couch when her attention was caught by the brilliance of the midday sunshine on the garden just outside the bay window. A glance over her shoulder confirmed that Sister Anselm was deep in organisation with the reception clerk and so Margery seized the opportunity to exit the foyer and head off for a closer look at the roses. Outside, the wind was still biting but the rose garden was protected on one side by a high sandstone wall and, at right angles to that wall, by a high green hedge. Standing near the apex of the two protective barriers, Margery found herself bathed in a determined winter sunshine but safe from the wind's more vicious gusts. She stretched her arms overhead, closed her eyes and took a deep, deep breath, inhaling the air's sweet perfume into her expanded nostrils. She shivered with joy and, dropping to her knees, breathed a prayer of gratitude for the beauty of the garden in which she had been planted. From her kneeling position, she let her palms make contact with the grass and then with the mulch atop the nearest rose bed. And then she stretched her whole body out, prone, on the garden bed in between two rows of fuchsia pink blooms and breathed in deeply again, savouring the earthy tang of the soil, feeling the softness of fallen petals on her warm face.

'Are you mad?' roared a voice from somewhere above her head. 'Get out of the dirt immediately.'

Margery rolled over onto her back and, shielding her eyes with one mud-caked forearm, saw that Sister Anselm and another woman whom she hadn't met were staring down at her. Anselm looked like she had discovered two dogs copulating in the convent chapel and Margery was confused by the nun's violent stare.

'I was just enjoying the garden,' explained Margery.

'You are lying in it. Get up,' Sister Anselm ordered.

Margery scrambled to her feet. She began to brush soil off her white habit but, noticing that the action was adding rather than subtracting dirt, she stopped and merely folded her hands neatly in front of her waist. She looked sweetly at the other two women and, extending her hand to the one she did not know she said, 'I'm Margery. I've very pleased to meet you.'

Sister Anselm slapped Margery's hand out of the way. 'Matron Pierce does not want to shake that filthy hand. Have you lost your mind completely, Margery?' Anselm pivoted to face the Matron and, in a syrupy voice, said, 'I hope you will accept my apologies for Sister Margery. You can appreciate now, perhaps, the difficulties that my sisters and I have been facing in the last several weeks. Obviously we are most grateful to you for accepting Margery here and, after what you have just witnessed, we would understand if you thought it best to confine Sister Margery to her room for the duration.'

Matron Pierce shook her head. 'I don't think that will be necessary. I'm sure Sister Margery is just getting used to the change.' Turning her attention to Margery directly she added, 'I hope you'll be happy here, Margery. I'm sure you'll settle in. Why don't you follow me? I'll have someone show you to your room and then help you to shower. You'll be as good as new by lunchtime.'

Margery nodded and smiled and followed the two women back into the home. As they entered, Matron looked at Sister Anselm and said, 'I hope you'll join us for lunch, Sister.'

'Ah, ah, no. Unfortunately, I'm expected back at the convent this afternoon,' she stammered. And with that, she was out the door.

❦

The dining room was filled with noise by the time Margery was clean enough to enter. A young, plump blonde in a tightly fitting pink uniform came up to take Margery from Matron and escort her to a table.

She chatted brightly as she walked with the new arrival. 'Hi Margery. I'm Lucy, one of the nurses here. I'm usually on first shift so I'll be bringing you in here for lunch quite often. You'll get to know the others and, mostly, we're a pretty nice lot. Watch out for Nurse Phillips, though. When she's supervising, we all have a rotten day.'

'Oh, I will, dear,' agreed Margery.

'Now, I'll sit you with Betty and Ada and Marie,' said Lucy, leading Margery by the hand to a sunny table near the dining room's bay window.

'Betty, this is Margery. Margery meet Betty,' said the nurse as she sat Margery opposite a stocky woman with stringy grey hair and a large plastic bib around her neck, covering the front of the blue dressing gown in which she was clothed. 'And, here, next to you, is Ada.' Lucy waved her hand in the direction of a painfully thin old lady with her sparse white hair tied back in a meagre ponytail with a purple ribbon, and her body tied into a wheelchair with a beige restraint strap. 'And, next to Betty, across the table from you, is Marie.' Lucy bent to whisper in Margery's ear. 'Marie's a bit cranky so don't be offended if she's not that friendly to you. She's not that friendly to anyone.'

'I'm very pleased to meet all of you,' said Margery, extending her hand to each one. Betty looked at the new arrival, mumbled, and then dropped her head back down onto her bib. Ada and Marie ignored her completely. Unperturbed, Margery continued, 'It's a lovely day today. A bit cold, but the sun is brilliant. I love a winter day, don't you?'

'You're a nasty old bitch,' Marie said.

Betty mumbled again and then stuck a finger into one nostril and began picking, only to be distracted from the activity very quickly when the lunch of beef stew and mashed potatoes arrived. Ada picked a spoon off the table and began banging it into Margery's left shoulder.

'Now, now, Ada, that's not nice,' said Lucy. 'Here's your lunch. Use your spoon for this.' Ada could not use her spoon. She gripped it tightly when the nurse handed it to her, but she had no idea, nor desire, to use it for the transportation of food from the plate to her mouth. Instead, she began combing the spoon through her hair, causing the nurse to grab it from her in annoyance. 'Now I'll have to feed you,' she huffed.

'Oh, no need,' said Margery. 'I'll help her, if you like.'

'That would be fantastic, Margery. If you don't mind,' Lucy responded, already hurrying off in the direction of another table. Margery carefully put a small combination of mashed potato and gravy onto the spoon and held it to Ada's mouth. Ada took the food at once, rolling it over her tongue before noisily swallowing, licking her lips and then holding her mouth open for more. This time Margery made a spoonful of some soft meat, gravy and pureed carrot and put it to Ada's mouth. Again, Ada savoured it, gumming the meat until it was pulpy enough to swallow.

'Thank you, dear. Thank you, dear. Thank you, dear,' Ada sang in monotone and Margery felt her heart swell with joy.

These people are old and ill, Margery thought, but they're speaking from their hearts. I think I've been called by God to work here, to help them. I am truly privileged. Oh how right I was to trust you, dear Lord. At first glance, I was fearful, I admit, about being taken out of the convent, my home for so long. But it's just as Julie advised me—the Lord knows best. She told me that I would be guided, sometimes along a path that I really won't want to take. Sometimes, the way will be easy and pleasant but often it will be difficult. Treacherous. 'You will have to look for the beauty in the ugly, the positive in the negative, the love in the fear,' she had said. And here I will be able to let my compassion soar to new heights. Here I will put the animating power of the Divine and the fullness of life back into these blank faces. Oh, how fortunate I am.

Margery looked with love across the table at Betty, who had responded to the stew by upending it onto the table, spreading its constituent ingredients broadly, picking out the carrot pieces and flinging them on the floor, and then scooping up the meat chunks with her hands and placing them in the dessert bowl with the apple pie and custard. Margery watched as the dear old thing plunged a fork into the middle of the pie and, managing to skewer it successfully, raised it in one whole piece, directing it first back toward her right shoulder and then, with remarkable strength and accurate aim, catapulting it across the room to hit the back of the head of a patient at the next table. Nurses rushed to the old man who had been targeted, but he held up his hands to wave them away and, swivelling his body around in his chair to see who had fired at him, stared straight at Betty and, with a shout, declared, 'Bloody good shot, old girl.'

After this joyous introduction to her new home, there was no stopping Margery and her selfless acts of kindness and compassion. Patients who had not been outside in the fresh air since their arrival at St Monica's found themselves wheeled into the garden for a change of scene at any time of the day or night, wind and frost being no barrier to their enjoyment because, as far as Margery was concerned, 'all weather is lovely'. Any flowers or plants that patients admired on their outing were promptly picked, plucked, or uprooted and given into their keeping or arranged in profuse bunches in their rooms. Magazines that the cleaners had piled neatly on the tables in the recreation room at the end of each day were generously distributed by Margery, left on the floor at the doors of each patient's room before they even woke up each morning. Impromptu songs were dispensed when anyone looked unhappy. Visitors were greeted, escorted to patients' rooms, and given cups of tea and plates of cakes and biscuits.

Within a month of Margery's arrival, most of the staff—with the notable exception of the nurses' aides whose jobs Margery had largely taken over—were ready to mutiny. A representation, led by Nurse Phillips, approached Matron to request that Margery be forbidden to continue with her annoying, charitable works. Margery was duly summoned to the Matron's office.

'It's all too much,' began Matron.

'Oh no, Matron, not for me. I have energy to spare,' Margery assured her.

'Yes, I see that Margery, but most of the patients here are very old, very frail. You cannot be exposing them to the cold winds of winter, certainly not without consulting the nursing staff first. We have a duty of care to them and, remember, even though you were a registered nurse, now you are a patient and not a staff member.'

Margery was dejected. 'But I'm young, only forty-five years old. I want to help, I want to be of use,' she pleaded.

'I understand that, Margery, and to be honest, I don't know if this is the right place for you but ...'

'Oh, it is the place for me,' Margery interrupted. 'I understand ...

I have understanding of so much. I see things differently. It's a joy for me to help.'

'Margery, listen to me.' Matron's tone was stern now. 'You cannot take the patients into the garden without the express permission of the supervising nurse, do you understand that?'

'Yes, Matron.'

'And the magazines all over the floor are an occupational health hazard for my nurses and any ambulatory patients. Do you understand that?'

Margery nodded.

'The gardeners have also requested that you stop pulling up the plants. Do you understand that?'

'Yes, Matron, I do. So, then, what can I do to help these lovely people?'

'Well, you can still help feed them at allocated meal times in the dining room, as long as the supervising nurse agrees. And you can still talk and laugh and sing to them. Sit with them, tell them about things, keep them in touch. All those type of activities. Anything, as long as it's "hands-off" the patients.'

It was the 'hands-off' directive that gave Margery her greatest idea. Miss Taylor was a patient no one ever wanted to touch because of her most disfiguring and disturbing skin condition. Margery had read Miss Taylor's patient notes (along with all the other patients' notes) on the second night after her arrival. On that evening, the patients were all settled and the night nurses were gathered in the staff room to celebrate Nurse Staples' birthday. Margery took herself into the ward office and, uninterrupted for an hour, caught up on the details of her fellow residents. It was fascinating reading and necessary, Margery felt, if she was to minister effectively to these people.

Of Miss Taylor, she learnt that the rare skin condition had been present since birth and the unfortunate lady had spent her life in high-care facilities. Margery read the doctor's directive that this patient was never to leave her room because the continual and profuse shedding of her skin created piles and flurries of thick, grey flakes wherever she was, and that these could be detrimental to other patients. Margery understood that Matron certainly could not permit Miss Taylor in the dining room, for instance, because the flakes would contribute a topping—the texture of desiccated coconut—to all the patients' meals. Even the nurses wore masks when they went into Miss Taylor's room to prevent their mouths and nostrils being clogged with dead skin. No wonder Miss Taylor had yelled at Margery to 'get out' the first time she attempted to make contact. It was clear that no one had ever made the effort to do anything more than turn their back on Miss Taylor, no one had ever shown her anything but revulsion and rejection. Margery's mission was to change that, to show Miss Taylor that her skin disease was not sickening to everyone and that she was a perfectly acceptable human being in every way.

On a warm morning in early October, Margery put her plan into action. The first ray of light through the slightly parted curtains caught onto the thick layer of dead skin cells on the floor around old Miss Taylor's bed. Margery had been crouched in a corner of the room, waiting for this moment for over an hour, waiting to marvel at the way the tiny motes of dust danced in welcome of the dawn above the heavier scaly white flakes of dermal detritus. Joy filled her heart as she passed her moist tongue along the palmar surface of her right index finger and then pressed the finger into the flakes. Several stuck and, with a smile, she raised the coated finger to her mouth and ingested the skin. Another lick, another press, and another mouthful followed.

The night nurse, coming into the room for a final check before handing over to the morning staff, interrupted Margery's next mouthful. Startled to find someone on the floor of her patient's room, Nurse Molloy took a few moments to understand what she was seeing.

'Oh my God,' she screamed when the exact nature of Margery's actions registered. She held back an overpowering urge to vomit just long enough to shout, 'Get up off the floor and go back to your own room immediately.'

'But Miss Taylor deserves our compassion,' Margery protested.

Margery was put in a room at the very end of the corridor after this, and contact with the other patients was forbidden.

'It's only for a short time, Margery,' Lucy tried to comfort her. 'What you were doing with Miss Taylor's scabs was pretty disgusting, you know. Like, I have to clean up all sorts of weird stuff here and, yeah, I feel sorry for the poor old things, losing control like that, even if they don't know that they've got shit all over themselves. But, Margery, eating scabs—that makes even me feel ill. Do you know what I'm saying?'

'Dear Lucy,' Margery said, smiling, 'you are a very sweet girl. And you're young so, perhaps, you don't understand why I did such a thing. It was my way of trying to show Miss Taylor that, even though she'd been shunned all her life, there was someone—me—who accepted all of her. Do *you* understand what I'm saying?'

'Well, not exactly, Margery. Like, couldn't you have just held her hand—which is really yucky, really revolting when you get right down to it. You'd have been the only one who'd ever done that.'

'That's my point,' said Margery. 'I have, on many occasions, sat and held her hand, talked with her and listened to her. Something more was needed. Do you know what her life has been like?'

'No, I can't say that I do,' confessed Lucy.

'Well, let me tell you a little about Miss Taylor.'

'Is this going to be one of your stories, Margery? I mean, that's good if it is, because I really like your stories. I just want to know so I can close the door and get comfortable. I'm off duty in five minutes anyway, so I don't want old Fish Face Phillips getting on my case. She can just get stuffed.'

'It is a story but it's a true one, about Miss Taylor's sufferings. She told me the latter part of this story herself and, well, you know me, I've filled in the gaps up to that point,' explained Margery. 'And, I can assure you, old Fish Face won't bother us. She hasn't been near me since the little scab incident.'

'That makes it seem almost worthwhile to me,' said Lucy, settling herself into the recliner opposite the straight-backed chair that the nun favoured.

'Now, Lucy, I'm going to make us a cup of tea and we'll begin.' Margery stepped over to the little shelf under the window and flicked on the electric kettle she kept there. While the water was heating, she took two mugs and two teabags from the cupboard underneath the shelf and then, from her mini-fridge, she took a small jug of milk. When the tea was ready, she returned to her chair, passed a mug to Lucy and then put her own cup on the table in between them. She reached into the deep pocket of the gingham apron she had taken to wearing over her signature habit and brought out a hip flask.

'Splash of whiskey in your tea, dear?' she inquired as she poured a nip into her own mug. 'Something to fortify you.'

'Why not?' Lucy laughed. 'As of thirty seconds ago, I'm off duty.'

Miss Taylor was born in 1895 to a wealthy Queensland family who had a beef cattle property. Miss Taylor's mother had gone to stay with relatives in Brisbane while awaiting the birth of her first two children but, as she was young and healthy and as this, her third birth, was expected to be straightforward, she and her husband had decided that she would stay on the property and be attended in her labour by a midwife from the nearest town, only thirty-five miles away. Two months before the due date, on a scorching December day, Mrs Taylor sat in a comfortable chair in her cool and tastefully decorated living room, her legs elevated on a cushioned footstool in an attempt to decrease the puffiness around her ankles. Absently she called to the house-maid, Sarah, to fetch the children from their nursery and bring them in to sit with her.

The clock ticked loudly in the hall. Minutes passed. A pang of panic seized Sarah and she could barely put one foot in front of the other as she walked along the corridor from the nursery back toward her mistress.

'Why are you taking so long, Sarah? I know it's hot, but you're young. Hurry up.' Mrs Taylor was irate.

Sarah entered the living room, wringing her hands on her apron. 'I'm sorry, Mrs Taylor. I don't know where the children are,' she stammered.

The blood drained from Mrs Taylor's face as she struggled to her feet. 'What are you saying, Sarah?' she screeched. 'Florence is four years old. Henry is barely two. They awake from their afternoon rest at this time. And you are responsible for them.'

'I know, Mrs Taylor. I put them down for their rest after luncheon, but I can't find them anywhere now.'

'They must be somewhere in the house. Call all the staff and keep looking until you find them.'

But Florence and Henry were not in the house. Not under the beds, playing hide and seek. And not in the kitchen, which was separated from the main house by a long, airy breezeway and where the children often went to pester the cook for shelled peas or sugar lumps to munch on.

By the time Mr Taylor returned from stock business in the town, the homestead was a flurry of distress. He hopped straight back on his horse and, with his men, went off to scour the yard's extensive perimeter. Mrs Taylor, meanwhile, walked nervously toward the billabong at the bottom of the dusty hill behind the house, mouthing prayers with each step.

'Please, dear Lord,' she prayed, and in her anguish made a terrible bargain with God. 'Deliver my two darlings back to me safe and sound and you may take this third child from me.' Down the dusty hill she went, her eyes swollen with tears and sweat and dry earth that the scorching wind had whipped up. Then she saw them: her two darlings sitting side by side on a log near the muddy waterhole.

'My sweethearts,' she cried as she ran toward them, arms out-stretched. 'Why ever are you sitting here in the hot sun? Come to Mother.' But the children did not move; they sat and stared at her, their faces fixed in fright. And when Mrs Taylor was almost upon them, she understood their fear. There, at their feet, the wide, coppery-tinged head of a mulga snake—sometimes called a King Brown—extended from under the log, its robust body writhing in response to every tiny move the children attempted to make.

The baby in her womb writhed too, echoing Mrs Taylor's shocked dilemma. But the mother was fearless in the face of a threat to her offspring, and carefully taking up a large stick, she advanced stealthily but surely toward the log, instructing her children to stay perfectly still until she told them other-wise. When she was only yards from the log, the snake turned its attention to her, darting like lightning out into the open to reveal its full six-foot length, its mid-brown and copper scales glistening in the late afternoon sun. Mother and snake glowered at each other. And then, without warning, she struck. Mrs Taylor brought the forked end of the stick down over the snake, just below its head, pinning it to the ground.

'Move, run now, my dears,' she screamed. And the children obeyed. And she herself picked up her skirts and lumbered after them up the hill, safely out of range before the snake managed to shake off the stick and slither back under the log.

Florence and Henry were bathed and fed and put to bed. Mrs Taylor, tired and overwrought, bathed too and downed some brandy and prepared for rest. At three am she arose to use the chamber pot. Instead, her waters broke all over the bedroom floor and a labour, one hundred-fold more excruciating than her previous two labours, gripped her.

She was still labouring in agony when the midwife, Tess, arrived at ten the next morning. Mrs Taylor writhed in pain until ten in the evening when, finally, Tess had to manually assist the birth in order to save the mother. At midnight Mrs Taylor was delivered of a snake-child. Female, small but robust, and covered in coppery-brown scales. Mrs Taylor recoiled in horror when Tess tried to place the lidless-eyed girl in her arms.

Tess's services as a midwife were no longer sought by anyone in the area after that. And the little baby girl, unnamed by her parents, was dispatched to the nuns in Brisbane for an upbringing and education behind closed doors. The nuns had her christened 'Miss Taylor' and the baby matured in a desert of emotional neglect, shedding her scaly skin daily to make room for her growing body. Few could bear to look at her, so startling was the thickness and shedding of her scales. 'Skin disease, extreme and rare form of icthyosis' announced the specialists, whom her distant parents paid handsomely to attend their daughter. It was the price of guilt. Emollients were prepared and applied to the skin, but nothing was applied to the dry flaking cracks of the little girl's heart, and she grew clever and cunning and bitter. And who could blame her?

In due course her parents died and responsibility for Miss Taylor's upkeep fell to her sister, Florence. Her brother, Henry, had perished in the Great War. Florence was a beauty with long, thick, chestnut hair, deep blue eyes fringed with curling black lashes, and the softest, creamiest skin. She visited Miss Taylor once in 1922 and was so shocked by the experience that she had to take an extended trip to the Continent. She next had cause to visit her sister when, having reached the age of seventy years, and her little sister reaching sixty-six years, she decided that an opportunity for herself and her wealthy and distinguished husband to live in London, where the couple's two clever sons now lived with their families, was too tempting an option to pass up. The couple's Australian business dealings, however, were being managed from Sydney and so it was arranged that Miss Taylor would leave the only home she had known in all her sixty-six years and be moved into St Monica's Home for the Aged on the New South Wales south coast because it was more convenient for the couple's lawyer, should he have to make funeral arrangements for Miss Taylor.

As it happened, funeral matters took the lawyer all the way to London quite soon after Miss Taylor's relocation because his clients, Miss Taylor's creamy sister and rich brother-in-law, were sadly wiped out by a lorry on the motorway during a pea soup fog in the first winter after their arrival in the British Isles.

The snake-child, now an old and lonely woman whose life had been one long misfortune, was left a fortune.

'That is the sad, sad tale of Miss Taylor,' concluded Margery. 'More tea, Lucy?'

'Oh, Margery, that's a tragic story,' sighed Lucy. 'I'd never really thought about how unhappy and lonely Miss Taylor must have been because of her affliction. I did look up a bit about her condition when she first came here. They can do a lot more to help babies born with that problem now.'

'Yes, all true, Lucy. But that's the thing. Miss Taylor was born a long time ago. And nobody even thought to give her a chance, not at any time through her life. Her family abandoned her, she had no friends. The first time she left that Brisbane care facility was to be moved to this one. No wonder she's mean and grumpy. So, perhaps you understand why I went a little overboard in trying to show her that there is nothing repugnant about her, not even all that flaked skin.'

Lucy shuddered. 'I get what you're saying, Margery, but what you did is still pretty revolting.'

'Not everyone's cup of tea.' Margery laughed. 'And, Lucy, now that I see you understand, I'm going to let you in on a little secret.'

'Ooh, good,' said Lucy, leaning forward in her chair.

'Yes. Tomorrow it's the summer solstice. So, I've decided to give Miss Taylor and myself a little Christmas treat. In the morning, before dawn, I'm sneaking out of my room and into Miss Taylor's. Without me laying a helping hand on her—as per Matron's express orders—she will get herself into a wheelchair and I shall push it out the back door and down to the beach where we shall watch the sunrise.'

Lucy's mouth fell open. 'But, Margery, Fish Face will kill you.'

'Fish Face will not know until after it's done. I had Millie, the tea lady, sneak a peek at the nurses' roster and Fish Face is on leave as of today. That pesky night supervisor, Nurse Molloy, is off for the week too. There's new staff assigned to both Miss Taylor and me from tonight. It's perfect. By the time they figure out what's going on, Miss Taylor and I will be in the dining room and ready for breakfast as if nothing's happened.'

'Can I come with you, Margery? I'm not on till the afternoon.'

'Six am, south end of the beach. Bring a cake. I'll bring a rug for us to sit on and a thermos of fortified tea.'

❧[10]❧

This is what she said:

We think we know ourselves. But then I look in the mirror and the person looking back at me is not me but a reflection of me. And I am surprised by my appearance. Surely that's not me, I think. And then I remember that the mirror tricks me by reflecting my left side as my right side and my right side as my left side. And then I remember that the retinas of the eyes with which I look at myself in the mirror invert the things I see so that all is upside down. And then I remember that my brain makes an adjustment and reinverts received images so that things appear right-way up. And then I remember that the eye can only see if there is a light source. So then I realise that I was correct all along—what I see is NOT me. And when I look at others, I am not really seeing them either. We only truly see when we look with our hearts and not with our eyes.

The bed was soft and warm. She was asleep before she could even arrange herself into her preferred sleeping position. Dreams enfolded her, gently cradling her, hushing her, rocking her.

The sea is a millpond, its only motion a soft, lapping caress of the shore. Overhead, the full moon of a perfect spring night scatters diamonds over the water's surface and lights a straight path from the beach to

the rock platform. She follows the moon's path, her bare feet imprint-
ing neat steps in the sand, her trailing nightdress erasing them. She
leaves the sand and alights on the lunar-lit rock shelf, its surface still
warm from the day's sunshine. The moon leads her on to a shallow
salty pool worn out of flat rock and she kneels at its side, gazes into
its waters. And there she sees her face reflected. And then a wind ruf-
fles the pool's surface and when the wind has passed, she stares at the
reflection again. It is not her face she sees; it is Sophia's. And the wind
breathes on the pool again and when the breath has resolved she looks
and sees that it is not her face that is reflected; it is Margery's. And the
diamond lights on the water have convened to sparkle like the earrings on Margery's ears. And the salty pool is changed from water to
whiskey and she dips a cupped hand into the pool and takes out a
refreshing draught. And all is well, and all shall be well, and all manner
of things shall be well.

A soft tapping on the door drew Kathryn back from the moonlit
pool and into the plump warmth and comfort of the bed. Her eyes flut-
tered open and she remembered where she was—in a luxury suite of
St Monica's Home. Through the thick velvet drapes across the room's
bay window, a sliver of sunshine made a line across the soft carpet.
Another tap on the door, and a quiet voice said, 'I've brought you some
tea, Dr Brookley. May I come in?'

Kathryn slowly eased herself to sit up in the bed and, reluctantly,
moved the warm covers back from over her arms. 'Yes, please, come
in.'

In the doorway appeared an attractive young woman, dressed in
a smart light-blue suit, clear stockings and black, low-heeled pumps.
Her auburn hair was pulled back into a bun on the back of her head.

'Good morning, Dr Brookley. I'm Nicola, the Guests' Manager.
Hope I didn't wake you, but you did say to Margery last night that you
wanted to be up by seven because you have a lot to do,' said Nicola, setting a tray with small silver teapot, milk jug, strainer, and sugar bowl
and spoon on the bedside table.

'Thank you, Nicola. And I'm sure I did say that.' Kathryn stopped,
casting her mind back to the previous night, the previous afternoon.

She realised that Nicola was waiting for her to say something more. 'I'm sorry, Nicola. You know, I must have been really tired yesterday. I can't quite remember much about yesterday beyond my meeting with Sister Margery before lunch.' Kathryn laughed nervously, apologetically. 'That's sounds a bit strange, doesn't it? I guess I'm more exhausted than I thought.'

'No need to apologise or explain to me, Dr Brookley. This place is wonderful, but it's overwhelming. You'll take more of it in now you're over the initial shock. Sister Margery's told me you're staying a whole week so there's plenty of time to talk and discover.'

'Am I? Yes, that's true, I am staying longer than I'd first planned. But I do want to get down to some solid talking today, getting to know more about Margery. She's … um …'

'She's amazing,' put in Nicola. 'And she, and Geoff, and this place saved my life. I'm grateful for them all every single day.'

'How did you come to be here, Nicola, if you don't mind me asking?' Kathryn reached over to the teapot and poured hot tea into the cup.

'Mind? No, not at all. It's the happiest coincidence of my life,' said Nicola, turning back from the door. 'Short version: my stepfather abused me, my mother didn't stop him. And so I left home and ended up working on the streets, trading tricks for hits, if you know what I mean. And along comes this guy who says he wants to pay me fifty thousand dollars to get off the streets now. Well, I think you know what I would have thought of that. Two things, actually. One, he's a nutter and, two, if he's for real, what would I have to do for that kind of money? So I say both these things to him. And you know what he says? He says, I'm Geoff, I've been given the opportunity to turn my life around and I've been asked to find others who want a chance to do the same. What's the deal? I ask. Get on this bus right now, he says, pointing to this mini-bus across the road, full of bewildered street people, just like me. You'll be taken to rehab and, when you've successfully completed that, you'll be given a comfortable place to live, and a wonderful job so that you can get ahead. I didn't know if it was a joke, like a TV show, you know, or if Geoff was some kind of religious do-gooder recruiting me for his cult but, for some reason I trusted him and I got on the bus. And here I am. I've been working here for nearly two years.'

'You took a chance,' Kathryn reflected, 'trusting a stranger like that, I mean.'

'Yes, I *did* take a chance, the only chance I'd be offered in a long, long time. You know, if you never take a chance, if you never risk anything, the only thing you can be sure of is that nothing will change. You either want to stay in the same place, or you want to get somewhere. And to get somewhere, you've got to get on the bus.' Nicola smiled, gave herself a pat on the chest, and headed for the door again, calling over her shoulder, 'Breakfast in the Seaview Café in thirty minutes. See you there.'

❦

The Seaview Café was a grand conservatory of shimmering glass and bold steel supports, built onto but separate from the northern side of the building and perched on and over a lofty rock outcrop. It was accessed from the ground floor entrance foyer by a corridor of glass, over the outside and roof of which grew a magnificent tangle of climbing pink roses. Once inside the café, however, the view from its extensive easterly and northerly aspects was one of uninterrupted sand, sea, and sky. On the southern and westerly walls, reticulated water flowed over the entire glass surface, keeping the café cool in the face of the afternoon sun.

In the centre of the café, a long buffet table was decorated at either end with tall vases of white and purple irises. In between, bowls of fresh fruit, carafes of juices, a selection of cereals, pastries and muffins were set out. To the right of the table was a stainless steel cooking counter from where Johnny and Sybil, today's chefs, filled orders for hot breakfasts of eggs, bacon, fresh grilled tomatoes, mushrooms, porridge, and pancakes. Coffee and tea and toast were brought to each resident's table by the day's wait staff.

Kathryn stopped in quiet amazement when she entered the café from the rose-covered corridor, her eyes taking time to adjust to the magnificence of an entirely glass room that seemed to float above the sea. Margery's touch on her arm caught her by surprise, and Kathryn felt a moment of dizziness as she transferred her gaze from a wide sweep of the room to Margery's face at her side.

'Are you all right, Kathryn?' Margery asked, giving a slight wave to Geoff and Nicola, who were looking at them from their sunny table on the café's east side.

'Yes, I'm fine. Just a bit overwhelmed, I think, as Nicola suggested to me earlier,' Kathryn responded as she accompanied Margery across the room to their seats with Nicola and Geoff.

'How did you sleep?' Geoff inquired.

'Very well, better than I've ever slept before,' said Kathryn. 'That bed was so comfortable, and I think the sound of the waves on the shore, rhythmic and constant, lulled me into an extremely peaceful rest. So relaxing, I have to confess, that I can't remember much about yesterday beyond my meeting with Sister Margery in the upstairs sitting room.' Kathryn shrugged her shoulders in embarrassment.

'That would be Sister Margery's whiskey.' Geoff laughed.

'Oh Geoff,' Margery huffed in mock annoyance. 'I tried but I couldn't persuade Kathryn to have more than one. And, Kathryn, I'm sure you remember that you would only have a half a glass of that delicious wine I'd ordered for lunch, so take no notice of Geoff's snide comments. Although you did do a little better with the French champagne in the evening,' Margery assured her, patting her on arm.

'Well, it was the best French,' said Nicola.

Kathryn felt uneasy. If she could recall last night's dream so vividly, why couldn't she recall lunch, or dinner, or the champagne? Perhaps she had imbibed too enthusiastically. But the others didn't seem concerned as they stood up and invited her to accompany them to the buffet table to get started on breakfast.

At ten o'clock, Kathryn made her way to the upstairs sitting room, as agreed, to continue the previous day's conversation with Sister Margery. The old nun was already seated on the same long sofa opposite the ocean view when Kathryn walked in with a large handbag over her shoulder and carrying her laptop, notepad, hardcopy notes, and a head full of questions.

The room was alive with light from the cloudless late autumn day outside the expansive windows and with warmth from the glowing fire in the hearth. Kathryn was aware of Margery watching her closely as she set the laptop on the coffee table in front of her, and arranged her notes, pens, phone, and other necessities of modern communication around her on the chair, floor and table.

'We could just talk, you know,' suggested Margery.

'I know, Margery. It's just that, in this day and age, because there are so many ways of documenting and verifying things, and because I want to understand about Julie in the hope of doing the best for my patient, Sophia, I want to have a record of everything. And not only so I don't forget anything but also because it enables me to offer proof to others if necessary.'

'Proof of what?' Margery was incredulous. 'My words, and your words, are proof enough. If people do not believe that you or I speak truthfully then they will not bother to listen to us anyway. That is their choice. I would not lie to you, any more than you would lie to me. If people are not honest and open with each other, what is the point of them speaking?'

Kathryn was chastened. There was merit in what Margery had said. 'You're right,' she agreed, putting aside the mobile phone on which she had intended to record their conversation. 'But would you mind if I make a few notes on the laptop, just to help my memory?'

Margery nodded graciously and then poured herself a cup of coffee from the pot on the tray on the table. 'Coffee, Kathryn?'

'Thank you, Margery. I'll help myself in a while,' she replied.

'Are you all right, Kathryn? You look a little … confused? Uncertain?'

Kathryn waved Margery's concern away. 'I think I'm just finally relaxing into these lovely surroundings after long months of work and … other stresses. And, of course, all that's happened with Sophia has been a lot to take in. I'm trying to come to grips with the claims she has made.'

'What claims, precisely?' asked Margery, sipping from her cup but not taking her eyes off Kathryn.

'Oh, where to begin? Well, let me preface this by saying that I really like Sophia. Not only "like", I feel a tremendous rapport with her. And

I respect, if not believe, what she says. And what she says is that she has been alive, continuously, since she had some kind of mystical shift in her understanding, some alteration in her perception of life and death, over six hundred years ago, back in the fourteenth century. There, I've said it.' Kathryn breathed out heavily and looked expectantly, nervously, at Margery.

'Yes, this is no surprise to me. Perfectly believable, and exactly as Julie explained to me forty years ago,' Margery said in between sips of her coffee.

Kathryn felt relief pulse through her. She had found someone who understood. With renewed confidence she continued: 'Margery, yesterday you concluded our conversation with the words, "so, she's back". Am I correct in taking that to mean that you think Sophia is Julie, that they are actually one and the same person?'

The old nun put her cup on the table and stared unblinkingly at Kathryn. 'Not "think", my dear. I know. I know that Julie, Sophia, whatever she calls herself, or whatever others choose to call her, is the same lovely, loving, wise woman who came to understanding in the middle of the fourteenth century and who shared her visions with me in 1973 and who showed me the truth about myself, and who taught me how to truly live and truly love. And now she is back to help others in the same way. Isn't it marvellous?' Margery lifted her head, closed her eyes and clasped her hands together as if in brief but rapturous prayer.

The two women sat, unspeaking, for some minutes. The room was silent except for the crackle of the logs on the fire and the tick of the grandfather clock in the hallway outside the sitting room, its pendulum acting as the metronome to their thoughts. It was Kathryn who broke the rhythm.

'Oh, Margery. I'm not sure. It's all seems so impossible. How can you be so sure that Sophia and Julie are the same person?'

'Very good question, my dear. Well, let me just pray about this for a moment.' And Margery returned to her earlier position of closed eyes, reverently bowed head, and hands joined over her heart.

The clock's sudden striking of the hour made Kathryn jump, but Margery remained unmoved, as if she had not heard the booming toll. Kathryn counted the clock's clangs and found herself surprised that it was eleven o'clock because it meant that she and Margery had been in some sort of reverie or contemplation for almost an hour. And several more minutes passed before Margery emerged from her prayer, her eyes flickering open to look in the direction of the wide window and its ocean view before she focused on Kathryn.

'I am given to understand that Sophia told you a tale on the occasion of your first meeting and I am further given to understand that it was the same tale Julie told me about herself at our first meeting.'

'You're correct that before she even told me her name, Sophia told me a tale in relation to how and why she was in Sydney Harbour,' agreed Kathryn tentatively. 'But, to be honest, it didn't make much sense to me.'

'It was a tale about falling from her mother's pocket, wasn't it?' Margery's tone was one of assertion rather than of inquiry.

Kathryn heard herself gulp in surprise. 'Yes, it was. How did you know?'

'As I said, it is the same tale Julie told me when we first met.'

Kathryn racked her mind to see if there were some way Margery could have known about Sophia's introductory story, but she was certain she had shared it with no one but Tim; and Tim had admitted to finding it too strange to pass onto anyone else. She glanced at her laptop but, no, even if Margery had somehow hacked into it, Kathryn had not had time yet to transfer the story from her head to an actual document. She could feel Margery studying her as if she were an insect under the microscope. It was as if Margery could see her brain ticking over.

'And Kathryn, I don't want to upset you but I also know that Sophia is helping you comes to terms with the tragic loss of your child. And, so it was that Julie helped me.'

'Now I'm really confused,' confessed Kathryn. 'Yes, Sophia is helping me. Somehow she knew that my son had died very soon after his birth. And her insight and compassion about that have startled and moved me profoundly. I don't know how she knew, and I don't know how you would know this. And ... and ... I don't understand what you're saying about Julie helping you with the loss of a child.'

'Then, if you will permit me, I think it is time for another tale. And this will be the tale of "me", said Margery. 'And, for the telling of this tale, I think it is time for our pre-lunch whiskey, don't you?

'No, not for me, Margery. I want to stay alert. I want to hear your tale and understand what's going on. I feel embarrassed about the hours I lost yesterday. Truly, I cannot recall what happened after our morning's conversation. I don't want to do anything that might jeopardise today's insights so, please, you go ahead with your whiskey and your story. I am keen to just sit and listen.'

Margery rose from the sofa and walked over to the right of the fireplace where an elegant oak cabinet housed the silver tray with decanter and glasses that had been on the coffee table at the previous day's meeting. She deftly poured herself a small whiskey, neat, from the decanter and stepped happily back to her lounge chair. She crossed one little booted foot over the other and leant back in her place before throwing back the entire half-glass of spirit in one swallow. Without altering her overall position, she moved her arm to place the empty glass on the sofa next to her.

'Oh don't worry, Kathryn. There's not a drop left in it so even if the glass does roll over, this lovely sofa will be unharmed.' Margery laughed and began her story.

In the war-torn world of 1943 a fifteen-year-old girl from a town on the Murrumbidgee River was invited to her cousin's twenty-first birthday party in the big, shiny city of Sydney. As the birthday fell at the end of January before the start of the school year, the girl's parents approved of her attending the party and staying with her aunt and uncle and cousins for a whole week. It was an opportunity for the girl to see the famous Sydney Harbour, and its spectacular bridge, and to take a ferry to Manly Beach, and to visit the shops that lined George Street.

'But don't hold hands with boys and certainly don't kiss any boys,' her mother warned. 'Keep yourself nice.'

The girl agreed … she was always nice to everyone. And so she travelled from the river town to the harbour city and, as soon as she stepped from the train, she knew she was where destiny intended her to be.

Three days before the party, her aunt encouraged her to take the tram into the city for some shopping.

'Off you go, look around,' said her aunt. 'The city is full of people. You will be perfectly safe, but be home by six for your tea.'

And so she dressed up in her town outfit—a floral dress with capped sleeves, brown and white pumps, a jaunty white hat borrowed from her cousin Dulcie, and a brown handbag resting stylishly over her arm. The city was abuzz, not least of all because of all the handsome American soldiers who sauntered along Sydney's streets, smiling at every pretty young woman they passed.

'Hello, ma'am. Can I help you carry those parcels?' one of those soldiers asked her.

Oh, he was tall, and so handsome with his clear skin and straight, white teeth, and she was flattered.

'Yes, thank you,' she gushed.

'Let me buy you some lunch,' he suggested in his beautiful drawl.

'Well, I am hungry,' she replied.

Gently he put his hand in the middle of her back and steered her through the crowds to Castlereagh Street and to the polished granite and columned façade of the glamorous Hotel Australia.

'Luncheon in the Winter Garden or the Emerald Room?' asked the elegant doorman.

'The lady's choice,' said the soldier.

'But this looks so expensive,' she protested.

'Then it's the only place a gorgeous girl like you should be eating,' he said, his smooth, deep voice hypnotising her.

After lunch, he held her hand and she was very glad that he was a man and not a boy so that she could enjoy his touch without disobeying her mother's directive. They walked through the Botanic Gardens, down to the seawall, and looked across to the Harbour Bridge and out to the line-up of warships at Woolloomooloo and Garden Island. And she couldn't believe that this was real. It was a dream. Someone else's dream. And then he turned her face up toward his, and he bent down and kissed her lips, and she thought she was in heaven. But then it was time for her to take the tram back to her aunt's and uncle's house in Neutral Bay for tea at six o'clock. She did not want to leave him.

'Meet me tonight,' he pleaded in her ear.

'I will try,' she said.

It was almost nine o'clock when she was able to slip away. Her aunt and uncle had retired early and Dulcie had gone to the pictures with some friends. Dulcie had invited her to join them but she told her cousin that she did not want to go because she was tired after her long day shopping, and Dulcie decided that she was just a boring little country girl who didn't know how to have fun and was relieved to leave her behind.

Into the dazzling city she went again and met her soldier at one of the Macquarie Street entrances to the Botanic Gardens. The gates had closed at sunset but they found a way in, and they were not the only ones enjoying the quiet, private darkness of the garden after hours.

Kisses at first, soft then deeper. A man's kisses, not a boy's. Her mother had been right. She was entranced by the feeling those kisses evoked in her. And then his hands, strong and dextrous, evoked other sensations she had never known existed. And then he did something else to her that she had never known about and, at first, she was afraid but then he whispered lovingly in her ear, and he kissed her fears away and soon she was swept up in an ocean of bliss. Afterward, he helped her to her feet and straightened her clothes, and then they left the garden of her delight and he bought her strawberry ice-cream.

'Thank you for a wonderful evening,' he said. 'I am leaving tomorrow but I will never forget you.'

And she was overcome with sadness but she understood that he was a soldier and there was a war and so she thanked him for a wonderful evening too. And he accompanied her to the tram and she was tucked up in bed when Dulcie came in from the pictures.

All too soon she was back at school in the little town on the Murrumbidgee. She was sick at heart missing her one-day love, and sick of body as the scorching heat of late February and early March enveloped her and squeezed her breakfast out of her stomach each morning and left her exhausted each afternoon. The late summer's intensity leeched her of energy and even of her monthly bleeding. She welcomed the frosts of mid-May mornings with prayerful jubilation, and the coldness released such a furious appetite in her that her mother was alarmed at how plump she was becoming.

'You've never been much wider than a stick,' she said to her daughter. 'But now you're getting quite a tummy. No boy will look at you in future years if you let yourself get fat.'

The girl agreed and tried to cut back on meals but it made no difference.

By July her mother was annoyed. 'I cannot afford a new school uniform for you, especially as you will only need it till the end of this year,' she said. It had been decided that the girl would leave school and begin a shorthand and typing course in Wagga Wagga in the new year. And so her mother took her to see Mrs Clay, the seamstress, so that her uniform could be let out.

'Undress down to your petticoat,' Mrs Clay commanded, 'and I will measure you.' She obeyed, but as Mrs Clay put the tape measure around the girl's belly, she let out a cry. 'Your daughter's stomach is moving,' she told the mother. 'She has a bun in the oven.'

Mother and daughter both stared at the petticoated tummy and saw little bumps and lumps sticking out here, moving there.

'But I haven't eaten any buns,' the girl said.

'You don't get a bun like that by eating one,' scolded my mother. 'Whose is it?'

She didn't understand what they were talking about but she was marched home; the mother told the father something; and the next day she was on a train to Sydney again, but not to stay there this time. Instead, she was met by Sister Gilberta and marched onto the South Coast train and off the South Coast train and onto a bus that took her to St Monica's Home for Wayward Girls.

There she met other girls who were as fat, and fatter, than she. It was Molly who told her the facts about her tummy and the truth of the bun. And she was overcome with wonder that she should have been chosen to give birth, just like the Virgin Mary.

'No, you silly girl,' said Molly. 'That dreamboat American of yours gave you this present on the night you told me about.'

For her, that was even better than being like the Blessed Virgin. She was so grateful to her handsome American for this precious gift of a child.

'Don't be too thrilled,' said Molly. 'It might have felt good going in but it's going to hurt like hell coming out.'

And on the last day of October she learnt that Molly spoke honestly. She lay in great pain for many hours, and cried for her mother, but her mother was far away; and she cried for her one-day love, but he was even further away; and she cried for herself because she didn't know where she was but she wished she could be far away from this agony.

'Stop blubbering,' instructed Sister Gilberta, but then Sister Rosetta placed a cool washcloth on her forehead and held her sweaty hand with her own cool hand and encouraged her to breathe and picture something lovely in her head. And she pictured her handsome soldier and his tender kisses and the delights of a Sydney city garden on a summer evening.

And then her body was overcome with a powerful urge to push and when Sister Rosetta whispered, 'Good girl, you can do it. I will stay with you,' she knew she would be all right. And she pushed and pushed and there was a tiny, new life emerging from her.

'It's a girl,' announced Sister Gilberta, looking up from between the new mother's quivering legs and holding on high a round, pink, mewing life. The baby was the most beautiful thing she had ever seen. She was overjoyed and held out her arms to take her daughter, but Sister Gilberta said, 'No, she is not yours. A proper mother and father are going to have her.' The nun wrapped the baby tightly in a cream blanket and handed the bundle to Sister Rosetta before sweeping out of the room.

Sister Rosetta saw the girl's longing and passed the bundle into her still-extended arms, saying, 'Here, just for a moment. Hold your child. I will keep eyes and ears out for Gilberta's return.'

The moment of her greatest joy was too soon snatched away; the daughter of her heart's delight was too soon taken and given to proper parents. But in that moment, while she held her daughter, the newborn's face and body and little beating heart were carved into the girl's palms and arms and body and heart so deeply that, forever after the moment, the girl was left with hollow spaces, great empty chasms of scars that could never be filled.

Her tale concluded, Margery was silent. And Kathryn was silent— she could not speak. Tears that had pooled behind her eyes and filled her throat during the nun's story now overflowed onto her cheeks, her chest, and she could do nothing to stop the flood. She was drowning in sadness for the young Margery, and for herself, and the weight of the grief immobilised her. She was crushed, pinned to the seat. After a time, a long time, an indefinable time, she became aware of an arm around her shoulders, of a lavender-scented handkerchief being gently dabbed at her face, of a glass being put to her lips, of the warm fragrance of whiskey animating her mouth, radiating down her stricken throat and into her shaking chest. And when the spasms of sadness finally began to subside she heard herself say, 'I'm so sorry, Margery.'

Margery loosened her consoling arm from Kathryn's body and, instead, took the younger woman's hands into her own. 'Dear Kathryn. Thank you. I know you understand, and it means a lot to me. But, if you are strong enough, there is a little more to this story.'

Kathryn shifted back on the sofa and managed a small smile. 'Please, tell me,' she said.

'It's not a pretty story, Kathryn, but it's necessary.'

'Then I want to hear it.'

'Good girl.' Margery smiled and proceeded. 'When Julie arrived at St Faith's, pulled from the depths of the sea, I looked at her, and I knew her. I thought at first that she might be my darling daughter, so tiny and so distant, and fallen from my pocket as I travelled the inner world looking for a way to make her real and whole again, and to make myself real and whole again. And when she told me the tale of her own mother and the loss, my hopes soared. But then I understood that I was not Julie's mother and she was not my daughter and I became distraught; so distraught that one day I held a jug in my right hand, about half a metre directly above my left hand, and began to pour slowly. The water spilled over my palm then down either side of my cupped left hand and out through the spaces between my fingers. Deliberately, I closed my hand but all that remained was a cool, silky moisture, not the actuality of a body of water.

'Blood is thicker than water. I put the jug down on the table and picked up the knife. Blood is thicker. I held the knife in my right hand, about half a metre directly above my left hand and began to slowly lower it toward my upturned wrist. The blood spilled over my palm then down either side of my cupped left hand and out through the spaces between my fingers. Deliberately, I closed my hand but I could not contain the flow. All that remained was a warm, sticky moisture, not the actuality of a body's blood. Thicker but just as elusive as water.'

Margery stopped speaking. She uncrossed her neatly booted ankles and rose to standing, picking up the glass from the sofa as she did so. She walked across to the oak cabinet, lifted the decanter, and poured herself a quarter of a nip of whiskey. And then she returned to the sofa and resumed her seat, her face and its unreadable expression turned toward Kathryn, and the whiskey in its glass, awaiting consumption.

'Oh Margery. You've had so much to bear,' said Kathryn, rising from her chair and, seating herself next to the old nun, taking her turn at comforting by stretching a softly protective arm around Margery's thin back. 'Your sorrow about your baby was the reason for your suicide attempt. It was not at the instigation of Julie as everyone seemed to be speculating at the time,' she said, clarifying the situation for herself as much as for Margery.

'Yes, that's true,' agreed Margery. 'And yet, without Julie's appearance, without her courage to disrupt the *status quo* and to break open the most rusty of hearts, I might never have tried to kill myself. I would have stayed frozen till I died ... dead till I died.'

'Are you saying your attempt to kill yourself was a good thing?'

'No. I'm saying, Kathryn, that sometimes we have to realise how low we are in order to rise up to our rightful stature. And, for me, and perhaps for you, Julie showed me how mechanical, how empty, my life had become. It was Julie who saved me. It was Julie, and only Julie, who noticed my absence from the afternoon ward round the day of my attempted death, and who instantly knew that something was wrong. It was she who found me, lying unconscious on the bathroom floor, in a shallow pool of blood. It was she who shouted for help and who tore a long strip from the base of her dress to wrap around my severed wrist to staunch the flow, and who covered me with her shawl until they came to help. And it was Julie who took the time to understand my pain and the cause of my despair. And it was Julie who showed me how to be full of life despite the pain.' Margery concluded by raising her glass in a silent toast to the ocean view and taking a good swallow of the spirit.

Kathryn wanted to comfort Margery, but the words in her mind would only form themselves into more questions. Finally, two of them forced their way out. 'How did she help you? What did Julie tell you?'

'Well, Kathryn, she told me so many beautiful things. Things that changed me, changed the way I looked at everything,' Margery answered. 'She helped me look at things differently, to see the great wide and wild beauty of everything. And to see things not just for my own benefit but for the benefit of all. She helped me to become fully myself, more than myself.'

Kathryn tilted her head to one side. 'I'm trying to understand but I can't seem to grasp it.'

'Grasp? We spend our lives grasping at things that are, at best, fleeting. Grasping is pointless,' Margery advised.

'But we live *now*. We test everything. Surely that's one of the great strengths of our twenty-first century society. We are not naïve; we are not foolish. Science is a gift and a key to understanding our world.' Kathryn struggled to convey her confusion.

'I agree, Kathryn,' said Margery, smiling. 'Science is a wonderful, wonderful lens through which to view creation and our existence. And we should give to science and to reason that which rightfully belongs to science and reason. But, as Julie taught me, we should also give to heaven and the miraculous that which rightfully belongs to heaven and the miraculous. Not everything can be explained by science, but that does not mean it doesn't exist. Do you understand what I'm saying?'

'Could you give me an example?' asked Kathryn, finally managing to swivel around on the sofa so she could see the nun's face.

'I'll try,' responded Margery. 'Think of it like this: there are experiences that are beyond words and then there are experiences that are before words. When a woman first holds her newborn baby in her arms she has such an experience. There are possibilities of being that are unformed and unmediated by anything that can be known, anything that can be spoken, anything that can be thought. The artist who captures the subtle play of light with his paints on canvas does so spontaneously, out of his creative self, and though the final result may be lifelike, when you look very closely you see that it is just a dance of colour and brushstrokes. The poet who puts words together in a totally new way, outside of grammar, and yet who makes the heart contract in elation at the beauty and rhythm and power of the words. A haunting melody. The wind in your hair on an autumn day. Warm sand between your toes. A cake fresh from the oven. A joyful bride in a white, flowing dress. The groans and sighs of lovemaking express all the world's joy and despair in the very moment of union. The inarticulate mewing of a child or an animal conveys a meaning more powerful than words to those who love that child or animal; the cry of the newborn is a fierce statement of hope. The shapes we see in clouds, the taste and texture of an oyster, the joy of a good malt whiskey.'

Kathryn listened, her imagination fleshing out the images that Margery was presenting. 'I see what you're getting at, Margery. I'm struggling, but I do understand.'

'Struggle is natural to the human condition. We would never question anything, we would never have made scientific advances either, if people had not struggled and questioned. Julie taught me that those who don't question are fools, and so are those who settle for stock answers supplied by others. Sometimes science provides stock answers and refuses to discuss any possibility that falls outside its own paradigm. Religion does the same thing. And isn't that ironic? Science and religion so often in opposite camps, both stuck with a limited view; different views, but still limited, not the whole thing. Both are correct, but only partially.'

'But you were a nun. Religion must have been important to you, at least for a time. Don't you believe any of it anymore?' said Kathryn.

'Now that's a very good question.' Margery grinned. 'Let's say I don't fully disbelieve. I just choose not to reduce God to the limits of a humanly crafted box labelled "Belief". God, or whatever name you choose to give to the Divine Essence, is like the ocean. It's a real thing, the ocean, you can't deny it. But from wherever you stand, on whatever shore you find yourself, you can only see a tiny fraction of the whole of it. And while even that minute portion tells of its vastness and power, you know, intuitively almost, that the ocean doesn't end at the horizon, at the limits of your sight. It's immense, but you can't hold even a bit of it in your hand, not without some kind of container. The Church became my container but, of course, the Church only holds a little, tiny bit of the immensity of the Divine Actuality. Just like a jar can hold a miniscule bit of the sea. Now, the ocean in a jar doesn't look much like the ocean at all. In the jar, all the power and vastness and magic of it are reduced to a lifeless brine. You know it's come from the real thing, but there's not much resemblance. We're just grasping at water while the whole ocean is there, encircling us. We're trying to cling to a little piece of divinity when we are immersed in the Divine.'

The clock struck twelve. Margery rose to standing on the last chime. 'I am needed for a final check on today's luncheon,' she said. 'But, to appease your scientific sensibilities, and to make me very happy, may I make a suggestion? A request, actually.' She lowered her head slightly in a gesture of supplication.

'Of course, Margery. Anything,' agreed Kathryn.

'Could you arrange for Sophia to be brought here, and soon, so that we, together, can spend time with her?'

❦ 11 ❧

This is what she said:

> *A time for every purpose under heaven, the Bible wisely says. The challenge is to discern for ourselves at each point what the purpose is. There are times to laugh, there are times to cry, but sometimes we confuse them. Sometimes, something we fervently seek eludes us and its lack brings us to the edge of despair, but later we see that, in being forced to seek elsewhere, we find our heart's true desire. Other times, the very thing that seems to bring us joy is, in the next moment, snatched from us and we wonder at the cruelty of the joy because, in the sudden absence of the source of our joy, the grief is too much to bear. If we did not love so, we would not suffer so when the love is taken away. But love and suffering are inextricably linked and we cannot truly love without suffering for it; and we cannot truly suffer without first loving the object of our suffering.*

The most important lesson … It seemed such a long time ago that she had sat next to Sophia's bedside and listened to that lesson but, actually, it had not even been a week. And, surely, it had been something that she had always known. What makes us forget things that we are born knowing? she wondered as she sat alone in the upstairs sitting room at St Monica's. It was dusk, a short, sharp and ineffectual rally against the dying of the day at this time of year. From the window she could see the waves rolling into the shore, one after the other, and lingering as if trying to absorb the sun's last rays before it plummeted below the western hills and into a resting place far, far away from the eastern sea. In the room's hearth a bright fire crackled, but otherwise the room was beautifully quiet. By this time of day everyone else had other things to occupy them.

Kathryn had made her way back to the sitting room after Margery had trotted off for an afternoon nap following lunch, as was her usual habit. Other residents—those who skipped the snooze—spent their afternoons meeting for a cuppa and a chat in the Seaview Café or busying themselves in the light-filled activities room with an endless variety of arts and crafts. Others opted for a walk along the beach or spent time in the gym on the treadmills and weight-training machines or, perhaps, attending tai chi or yoga or pilates or ballroom dancing sessions. For the tech savvy, there was time in the state-of-the-art IT lab. They all gathered for the cocktail hour in the home's Irish pub, which took up a cosy room next to the grand dining room and, somewhat incongruously, opened on one side to a terrace that overlooked the home's outdoor swimming pool and tropical garden.

The subdued light and the peacefulness of the sitting room washed over Kathryn and she was determined to take this one hour before the social whirl that was dinner at St Monica's for some quiet reflection. She sat in a comfy recliner armchair near the fireplace, her head sinking deep into the chair's plush upholstery and her feet elevated on its pop-out footrest. 'The most important lesson, the *one* lesson,' Sophia had said, 'is this ...' Kathryn tried to remember how old she had been when she'd forgotten the lesson, when she had let it slip from her grasp and into the cracks that opened up beneath her feet; how old she had been when she'd given up all that she knew in exchange for all that the world said she *should* know.

In Kathy's head there is a house with walls made of wonderful thoughts. Kathy constructed the walls herself, in order to be protected from the multiple threats of the world and its life outside the house. Inside Kathy's house are dancing paintings of coloured points of lights, and vibrantly rhythmic music, and poems of exquisitely resonant words; and when she chooses, she can take the lights and the music and the poems outside her house and share them with others. But she doesn't choose to do this very often because these are her treasures and they are fragile, and when exposed to the air, the lights are less brilliant, the music less splendid and the poems less emotive. Or so her mother and father say. 'Why don't you stop making up those silly songs and painting those ugly pictures and do something useful with your time? Like homework, or netball,' they say. And Kathy then wonders if the lights and the music and the poems inside her head are nothing more than cobwebs hiding the grey reality to which she should be responding. So she tries to brush the spidery wisps away. But gossamer is persistent in those of a certain sensibility and so it continues to grow inside her head; it thickens, it takes over. And that which was once finely beautiful starts to become tough and twisted, and with each passing hour it becomes harder to brush away until one day there are so many tangled webs in her head that Kathy finds herself caught. 'What's wrong with you?' asks her mother. 'You used to be quite good at schoolwork. And sport. Your father and I have spent a lot of money, a lot of working hours, on your education. You owe us better than this ridiculous lethargy. Please get out of bed. You'll miss the bus.' But by now the webs have grown beyond their cranial confines. They have grown outside Kathy's skull and wrapped around and around her head so that she cannot see, or hear, or taste, or smell, or feel where she is situated in the grey reality. So she must lie very still. In order to survive, she must move out of her parents' house and into her own home, into the house in her head, with its walls of wonderful thoughts, and dancing paintings of coloured points of lights, and vibrantly rhythmic music, and poems of exquisitely resonant words … and with no doors or windows.

'Off to the psychiatrist with you, young lady,' said her mother. And though she didn't want to go, she found that her doctor listened carefully to her, and if she said the things that she knew the world wanted to hear, the doctor would tell her parents that she was cured. Kathy grew up and extended her name to match her adult height. 'Well, Kathryn,' said her father, 'we are so proud of you and your Higher School Certificate results. It's off to university for you where, because you are very clever, you will study medicine.' Kathryn's head, without doors or windows, was the perfect trap for knowledge and she stored it all away in the well-ordered compartments of her brain, opening filing drawers as needed, and regurgitating signs and symptoms and syndromes in the blink of an eye. 'Top student', they exclaimed. 'What will you specialise in?' they all asked. 'I shall specialise in the inside of heads,' Kathryn decided, because that was where she was most comfortable. As it was a psychiatrist who helped her before, she would be a psychiatrist who would help others after.

Richard was a surprise. 'I love you,' he had told her as she finished summarising the findings of her latest journal article for him. They sat close together under the jacaranda tree on the green lawn of the university's main quadrangle and, though his arm was around her waist, she had not felt its sturdiness and heat until he uttered those words. 'Do you?' she had replied. 'Yes, surely you know that,' he said, passing his other warm, sturdy arm around the front of her waist and drawing her down so that they were lying awkwardly on the grass in full public view. He moved his face toward her, covering her lips with his, and she noticed the sturdiness and heat of those lips. 'I want to marry you,' Richard breathed into her mouth. 'Do you?' she had replied. And so they were married, and again, Richard was a surprise because Kathryn discovered in him a man who was gentle and devoted to her and made her wish her head, and her heart, had some doors and windows. 'I want us to have a baby,' Richard had confessed one night as she lay in his arms in their bed. 'Do you?' she had replied, but this time she added, 'I don't think I would be a very good mother.' And Richard had laughed his deep, loving laugh and said, 'You will never know until we try.' And so they did try. And try. And try. But without success. And Richard said, 'I think we should see someone about this.'

'Do you?' she had replied, but they didn't see anyone until ten years had passed and Kathryn was nearly forty years of age and she said to Richard, 'I think I am pregnant.' 'Do you?' he had replied and, to her surprise, Kathryn was almost as happy about it as Richard.

'There seems to be a little problem with the heartbeat,' the obstetrician had told Kathryn and Richard after the ultrasound. 'Probably nothing that can't be fixed, if necessary, after birth.' But Kathryn was seized with fear for her baby. In all her life, she had never felt such fear. And in all her life, she had never felt such love. During the day, whenever she could steal away from her patients to a quiet place, she would put her hands onto her belly and wait for reassurance from the fluttering of the baby's little limbs inside her. Occasionally she would feel her belly giving regular tiny jumps and she would smile at the knowledge that the baby had hiccoughs. 'It means the baby will have a good head of hair,' Richard had told her when she told him about her jumping tummy. 'I thought heartburn, not hiccoughs, was the sign of the baby's hair,' Kathryn had said, and she and Richard would exchange old wives' tales as if they were ... well ... old and very happy wives.

Her labour began at midnight, one month exactly before the due date. 'It's too early,' she cried to Richard as they counted the time between the contractions. 'Early, yes,' agreed her husband, 'but not *too* early. It will be fine.' But progress was slow and painful and when the sun rose on that clear November morning, its sky streaked with pink and red light in ominous echo of the old wives' saying, 'Red sky in the morning—sailors' warning', Richard picked up Kathryn's packed bag and ushered her to the car for the short drive to the hospital. At midday, the labour was advancing but still ... so ... slowly. By two in the afternoon the midwife was concerned. 'The baby is in a tricky position,' she said. 'Your doctor is on his way but, in the meantime, I will try to turn the baby.' *There is a season, turn, turn, turn.* But the baby did not want to be turned; its purpose was a different one. 'Time to get this baby out; time for a caesarean,' announced the obstetrician. Kathryn was anaesthetised from the waist down, and numb with worry from the heart up. 'Here he is,' said the doctor, holding a small dark pink package up before Richard and Kathryn. 'We will check his signs and then you may hold him.' The signs were checked. They were not good, but the little boy was handed to his parents to hold and cuddle nevertheless. 'I'm so sorry,' said the doctor, 'this was unexpected.' 'I'm so sorry,' said the midwife, 'it happens, but not very often.' *A time to be born and a time to die. Why, why, did they have to be one and the same time for their tiny son Matthew?*

His life was over before it had begun, and Kathryn felt her own life was over just when it was really beginning. The ache in her empty arms and heart would not cease. 'We could try again,' suggested Richard. 'No, we cannot,' said Kathryn. And she returned to work with a vengeance. And now she was forty-five and the season of babies was past.

{ 12 }

This is what she said:

We cannot escape our dreams. They are the words and images etched on our souls and we carry them there always. In this life we catch glimpses of them when we close our eyes each night. Then, we are not really asleep; we are really awake because the deepest truths of ourselves push their way to just below the surface of our comprehension. As children we know the truth of this and, unencumbered by layers of ego, we live a dreaming life, and dream a living dream, day and night, awake and asleep. As adults, however, we are better at barriers, and the dreams of sleep and of life rarely break the surface of our egos, and so we put the dreams aside each morning when our feet touch the ground to repeat the daily run toward death. Sometimes, however, a dream is too hardy, too deeply inscribed to be shelved on waking and, instead, leads us on to difficult and beautiful places that others who have buried their dreams, find too confronting to acknowledge. 'It's all in your imagination,' they say, as if imagination is a scourge and because, sadly, they have worked to erase the sacred image in their own souls. But we who live in waking dreams know better.

She dreamed of the shallow, salty rock pool again, its surface shimmering under a mellow moon and mixing the images it reflected: Margery, Sophia, Kathryn. Faces in a pool under the moon. Again, she was awoken by a gentle knocking on her door and again, on calling out a 'Come in, I am awake,' she was greeted by Nicola and the tea tray.

'How did you sleep, Dr Brookley?' asked Nicola cheerily.

'Very well I think, thank you, Nicola. It's a remarkably comfortable bed. And I am beginning to realise how tired I am.'

'You had a busy day yesterday, I know. You and Sister Margery have so much to talk about. I wasn't surprised to see you excuse yourself from the dinner table before dessert and head upstairs to bed.'

Kathryn felt a shot of panic race through her body. She could not remember leaving the dinner table early. She could not remember anything about last night's dinner. Again.

'Are you all right, Doctor?' said Nicola. 'You look rather pale.'

Kathryn suddenly realised Nicola was next to the bed. She had already put the tea tray on the bedside table. And yet, hadn't Nicola just opened the door?

'I'm fine, Nicola. I mustn't be fully awake yet. Everything's still a bit dreamlike, if you know what I mean,' Kathryn answered, uncertain of whether she was trying to convince Nicola or herself.

'I know exactly what you mean.' Nicola laughed. 'I love this job, but sometimes, especially on a dark winter's morning, getting up at five-fifteen is a real effort. I often prepare the tea trays like I'm sleepwalking. On auto-pilot.'

Kathryn returned Nicola's smile but she was not comforted. She was conscious of her mind ticking over furiously, searching for any snippet of memory from the previous evening, and puzzling over why, in one instance she had seen Nicola standing at the door and, in the next blink, she saw her at the bedside as if she had not walked across the room at all.

'Why don't I bring your breakfast up to your room? And I'll tell Sister Margery that you'll meet her in the foyer at ten,' said Nicola, as if she sensed Kathryn's distress.

'Yes, I'd really appreciate that,' replied Kathryn, surprising herself at her quick agreement. 'I've got to catch up on some calls and emails, actually, so a bit of time alone before I meet with Sister Margery again would be a good idea. Would you apologise for my absence at breakfast?'

'No trouble at all,' Nicola assured her, smiling and moving toward the door and, this time, Kathryn was relieved that she saw Nicola's firm footsteps as she exited.

The quiet start to the morning left Kathryn feeling more in control. She managed to clear her inbox and make the call to Tim asking him to arrange, on her recommendation and authority, the transfer of Sophia from the private rehab centre she was currently in to St Monica's. Tim had been reluctant but finally acquiesced, and they set the transfer date for Friday, two days hence.

Most importantly, Kathryn used the time to call Richard. She was grateful that he picked up the call immediately, and that his tone was welcoming.

'Kathryn, so nice to hear your voice. I wanted to call and apologise about storming out on you the other night,' he said.

'Actually, I'm the one who should apologise. Richard, I don't know where to begin. I know you don't think much of Sophia, but she, and the people she has led me to, have helped me so much.'

'Kathryn, believe me, I'm pleased that she's helping you. It's just that I feel it should have been me helping you. Us, together, helping each other. Look, I want to explain, to apologise properly … for everything. This separation has been so hard …'

'I know, Richard. It's been hard for me too. But I just couldn't come to terms with losing our child. And you became so angry.'

'I *was* angry. But most of all, I was hurt. Hurt that you'd pushed me away when Matthew died; hurt that you'd pushed me away in favour of your work; hurt that you didn't want to work on our marriage. Don't you know that his death broke my heart, too? I wanted us to grieve together but, instead, we pulled apart.' A pause. A gulp. A strangled cough before Richard continued, 'Ten years since we lost him. Ten long years of pulling away from each other. And you know I wanted us to try for another child, but you wouldn't. You wouldn't even discuss it. I realise that was because of your own heartbreak, your own fear that it might happen again. I was fearful too, but don't you see that …'

Kathryn heard him sobbing. She put her free hand to her chest to soothe the deep pain in her heart. 'I see it now, Richard. I see it all,' she said. 'And I'm sorry. Sorry with all my heart. And the amazing thing is, it's taken Sophia … this whole, strange experience … to make me realise it. Do you think we could try again?'

'What? What did you say?'

'Richard, you're right. I was full of fear. I did push you away. I don't want to do that anymore. If you can forgive me, I forgive you. Can we try again?'

'Yes, Kathryn, yes. It would mean the world to me … But, there's something I need to tell you … Oh God … I hope this doesn't make you change your mind.'

'I hope it doesn't either,' she said, laughing. 'Go ahead. Tell me. Clean slate.'

'Okay. Well, I should have told you when you asked me that night. I wasn't being honest when I said my discovery of Sophia was all down to coincidence. I didn't think that at the time, and I don't think it now. She had an impact on me the instant I saw her. You know I said that the day was eerie and unnatural … well, the eeriest, the most unnatural thing of all was Sophia. In that first instant, I knew her, I knew I'd met her before.'

'But how could that be? Why didn't you tell me?'

'Because I couldn't believe it. It was crazy. Like a dream. Like a story. Kathryn, there *is* a story. Shall I tell you?'

Kathryn laughed again. 'Yes, definitely. It seems Sophia attracts stories wherever she goes.'

And so, from the other end of the phone Richard told his tale.

One day a seven-year-old boy was sent to live with his grandmother after his mother died and his father was too grief-stricken to care for him. The little boy had no siblings and was used to amusing himself and keeping his own company. But his grandmother decided that he should have a friend, and so she got him a puppy. The little boy loved the puppy and by the time the dog was fully grown and the little boy a year older, the two were inseparable. Each afternoon after school the boy and the dog would go walking together—sometimes to the park, some-times down to the creek to fish for tadpoles, but mostly to their favourite place: the old abandoned military storage huts that formed the back boundary between his grandmother's house and the rose garden of a suburban hospital. The huts were off-limits, but the boy could not resist sneaking under the barrier and into one hut in particular, which still had a container of fascinating metal objects that looked like pine cones with a pin at the top. One afternoon the dog, sensing that they were going to explore the hut this day, ran ahead of the boy who, though he ran as fast as he could, could not keep up. He called the dog's name, called for him to stop and wait, but when the air was sud-denly ripped by an explosion, the boy knew, knew why entry to the huts was forbidden and, worse, knew what had happened to his dog. People came running, holding him back from the smouldering heap that had been the hut, holding him back from his dearest friend. Then, through his tears and screams, he saw a young woman walking toward the scene from the hospital. He saw her say something to the man who was ordering people back from the area; he saw her step in front of the man; he saw her stretch her arms forward and begin to rock to and fro; and then he heard her calling his dog's name—though how she knew it he could not guess. And then he saw a section of the rubble shudder and lift, and he saw that it was his dog shaking off the timber beam as if it were a leaf; and he saw the dog running to him, wagging and yapping as if nothing had happened. And he saw the young woman walk to him and he heard her say, 'All shall be well.' And he saw her face, clear and shining, and he knew he would remember that face until the day he died.

On each end of the phone, they held a long silence together. A silent reconciliation. At last Richard said, 'I'll be home when you get back. Don't be away too long.'

Margery was waiting for Kathryn in the foyer when she went down-stairs at the agreed time. She received the news of Sophia's impending visit with great excitement.

'You can't imagine what this means to me,' she gushed, grabbing Kathryn in an embrace. 'And that being the case,' she continued, drop-ping her arms and stepping back to look squarely at Kathryn, 'we have important work to do today. Follow me.'

She led Kathryn toward the activities room. At this hour of the day, the morning sun streamed through the north-easterly facing windows and bathed the room in a golden light that was perfect for the vari-ous arts and crafts the residents were busying themselves with. At a solid wooden workbench along the entire length of one wall, several men were hammering and sanding and nailing neatly sawn pieces of pinewood into children's tables and chairs. At one of the cheery central tables, the members of the knitting group were stitching together doz-ens of colourful squares into a huge rug. At the far end of the room, on a linoleum stretch of floor, the potters' circle people were loading the first of the day's creations into the kiln for firing, while in the room's carpeted corner, the bridge club was in full and deep concentration mode.

'Ah, there's our lovely activities officer,' said Margery, waving her arm in the direction of a stout, grey-haired woman flitting between the carpentry bench and the knitting table. The woman noticed Margery's wave and had begun to make her way across to them when Margery called out, 'I'll introduce you to our guest later, Rainbow. We're just on the way to my storage unit,' stopping the woman in her tracks.

Behind the pottery area was a heavy door with spring-loaded hinges. 'Bugger,' said Margery as she leant against the door and it failed to budge.

'Here, Margery, let me help you,' said Kathryn, lending her weight to the task. 'My, this is heavy.'

'It's designed to close itself so the draught doesn't get into the activi-ties room,' explained Margery. 'You see, this is the storeroom and it's on several levels, each one accessed from a central spiral staircase. My storage unit is on the very lowest level, below the wine cellar, which is carefully temperature-controlled, so you can understand why the whole thing needs a solid door or all the busy bees upstairs would be catching their death. Of course, my level has a superb heating system so, year-round, I'm in comfort. Come on, follow me, down we go into the bowels of the earth. But don't be worried. The whole staircase and each of the levels lights up automatically like a Christmas tree all the way. Of course, I should add, there's a perfectly good elevator we could use, but the stairs are excellent exercise, don't you agree?'

There was a noticeable decrease in temperature as they spiralled downward. Kathryn didn't count how many steps they took in the descent, but she did note that they passed through four separate storage floors and then a chilly fifth level featuring walls covered in wine stacks before Margery announced, 'We're here.'

And, yes, they were somewhere, but it didn't resemble any storage unit that Kathryn had seen before. It was more like an underground living quarters with a floor-to-ceiling bookcase along one wall; a little kitchenette with a shiny sink, neat under-counter cupboards with bright yellow doors, and what appeared to be a tall pantry cupboard on another wall. A third wall had a door and, when Margery noticed Kathryn looking in that direction, she said, 'Yes, dear, that's the bathroom, if you need it.' The final wall was completely covered with massive sliding doors which, when Margery slid each one aside in turn, were shown to be shielding shelves packed with filing boxes, stationery items, and even a fold-down bed, complete with its own patchwork quilt.

'I come down here when I want to feel like I'm enclosed,' said Margery. 'You know, like an anchoress.'

Kathryn was almost too stunned to speak but she managed, 'I don't think anchoresses would have had this much space and all these amenities, nor would an anchorhold be as pleasantly warm.'

'Quite right. And look.' Margery, unperturbed by Kathryn's comment, pointed to a centrally placed work table on which sat a laptop, scanner, and printer. 'They wouldn't have had all this lovely technology either. Of course, I don't work down here all the time. I've got a perfectly sunny study aboveground but, when I need to work with my files, this little place is so handy for me. Cup of tea?' Margery had edged toward the kitchen-side of the room and was opening the pantry, taking out a large plastic basket full of tea-making necessities—electric jug, cups and saucers, milk jug, sugar bowl, spoons, plates.

They sat at the work table drinking tea and eating chocolate cake that Margery had brought out, along with the milk, from the small fridge in the corner. Kathryn was enjoying the whole experience but, after a while, felt compelled to ask, 'Is there any special reason for us to be in the storage area, Margery?'

'Oh yes, my dear. A very, very special reason. Actually, it's all part of our preparations for Julie–Sophia's arrival on Friday.'

Kathryn felt herself sitting up more alertly. She could feel her eyes widening and her ears pricking in anticipation of what would be revealed. She watched unblinkingly as Margery got up from the table and walked to the filing shelves. From a shelf at waist height she began to reach for a cardboard storage box.

Kathryn sprang to her feet. 'Here, let me help,' she called.

'No need, it's light as a feather,' said Margery, proving her claim by sweeping across the room and depositing the box on the table in front of Kathryn.

Still standing, Kathryn removed the lid and, peering into the box, immediately understood why Margery had carried it so readily. It contained only two items: a small white envelope and a slim leather-bound journal. She picked out the envelope and emptied its meagre contents of three coloured photos onto the table's surface, spreading them face-up so that all three were visible at a glance. One photo showed a group of nine women standing in a neat row, and all but one of whom was dressed in a religious habit of calf-length black dress, dark stockings, black shoes, and a short grey veil; the remaining woman wore a grey mid-length woollen dress, dark stockings and shoes, and her head was covered not with a veil but with close-cropped hair. Despite the lack of clarity of the women's faces, it was no great stretch for Kathryn to assume that these were Margery's former religious sisters with Julie X. The second photo, however, allowed no assumptions, and its inclusion in the 'Julie box' puzzled Kathryn. It was of a fish, an extraordinarily large and vividly blue fish, apparently swimming in clear, shallow water; and its image had obviously been captured by someone who was very close to, though slightly above, the fish, someone who was probably wading, ankle-deep, at the moment the fish swam by.

'This photo,' began Kathryn, pointing to the group shot, 'is of your St Faith sisters with Julie, isn't it?'

Margery nodded and, tapping her finger at a nun, second from the left, she said, 'That's me, there. Of course, I was much younger. This was taken in the early days of Julie's residence with us, before I adopted my own particular style of dress.'

'I recognise you,' said Kathryn, though, in truth, she had been more focused on the Julie figure than any of the nuns. 'But what about this fish?'

'Marvellous, isn't it? Julie took the fish photo and I kept it because it reminds me of her, in a way—it's so striking, yet gentle. It's a blue groper. It swam right up to us, Julie and I, one day when we were just wading in the shallows. Julie was entranced by it; by its beauty, its friendliness. It seemed to appear every time Julie was anywhere near the water's edge, or out further in the little run-about we'd use sometimes to go to other beaches and coves around the Pittwater area.'

'Yes, I know the area very well.' Kathryn spoke slowly, her mind flicking over furiously, trying to make sense of what she was seeing and hearing. She closed her eyes briefly and when she opened them her gaze fixed on the third, and smallest, of the photos and she realised, with a start, that it was the same as the little photo she'd found in the Julie X file from Dr Smith's office, the one that showed two women standing side by side in front of a white weatherboard house. Kathryn turned the photo over and saw that its inscription was the same as the file's photo too: 'Julie and Margery, Xmas '73'. This photo, however, perhaps because it had been stored away from any hint of sunlight, was clearer and Kathryn could easily make out a younger version of Margery posing happily next to a young woman who—all assumptions aside—looked remarkably like Sophia. She could also see the details of the weatherboard house in the background and it was with an uneasy feeling that she asked, 'Tell me about this photo, Margery. When and where it was taken? Tell me everything you remember about it.'

'Oh that's easy,' Margery replied. 'I remember as if it were yesterday. It was taken late on the hot and sunny Christmas Eve of 1973. We were on the little pier in front of the nuns' weekender at Cottage

Point. When I was first working at St Faith's Hospital, some of my sisters and I would often make the short drive from Willoughby to Terrey Hills and then on through the National Park to the weekender on a Friday afternoon. It felt like we were miles from everything there but we could be back to the hospital in thirty minutes if we were needed. Oh, but I digress. So ... where was I? Oh yes. Julie and I were both invited by Mother Superior to spend the Christmas–New Year break there. Out of pity or perhaps guilt. Both of us had arrived that morning from our separate locations. You know, I'm sure, that Julie had been sent, shortly after her discovery, to the local mental hospital. But she'd confounded them all there with her miraculous healing of a dead cat and so, with no one claiming her and no clues to her identity, she had been returned to St Faith's temporarily until someone could figure out what to do with her. That's really when I, and some of the other nuns, began to listen carefully to Julie's wise words. Of course, Mother Superior and others were not happy about the situation and well, I suppose I didn't help matters with my suicide attempt and the adoption of my special outfit. So I'd been sent off to become a permanent resident of the old St Monica's Home, and Julie had been moved out of a room in the convent and put in virtual isolation in one of three little cottages in the grounds of St Faith's. Our removals, however, didn't halt the disarray into which our little order of nuns was falling. Many blamed Julie, but others knew that she merely brought existing problems to a head, just as when rotten things are exposed to the full light of day their deterioration is accelerated. Perhaps others also realised that the impending dissolution of the order was not our faults and so, as small compensation for the ostracism we had both suffered, we were invited to be present at the weekender over the Christmas period. Anyway, whatever the motivation, on the day this photo was taken, we were happy to see each other after those months apart and looking forward to a lovely summer holiday.'

Kathryn went over to the kitchenette, filled a glass with tap water and, keeping her back to Margery, drank it all. Without turning around, she said, 'Margery, do you know who owns that weekender now?'

'No, Kathryn, I'm afraid I don't. Obviously the Church reclaimed it when the sisters of St Faith of Peace and Devotion disbanded and

I have a vague recollection of it being sold to one of the doctors who regularly saw patients at St Faith's. Why do you ask?'

'Because,' replied Kathryn, swinging back to look straight at Margery, '*I* own that Cottage Point weatherboard now. Richard and I bought it from a doctor and his wife after our baby son died so that we could get away from all the weekend functions where family and friends paraded their happy children. We bought it to get away from all the reminders of Matthew. And now you're telling me that, by some weird set of coincidences, you and I not only have the strange Julie and Sophia in common but also that we have both, at separate times, spent our weekends and holidays in the same house in Cottage Point. It's too much for me to take in.' Kathryn began to sob, collapsing at the knees and sliding her back down against the kitchen cupboards until she was crumpled on the floor.

❡{ 13 }❡

This is what she said:

I saw many things in the course of coming to understanding, but I did not see sin. An animal, beloved of its owner, and dedicated to its owner, may, in the enthusiastic pursuit of its animal instincts, become so absorbed in its own activities that it forgets, momentarily, that it has a home, that it belongs with someone who cares deeply for it, and so it becomes separated from its owner and unable to find its way home. Do we say, 'Bad dog, for running off'? No. We search for the dog, we mourn its loss and, if the dog does not, cannot, return we remember our faithful pet with great affection and thankfulness for the time it spent with us. Humbly, I began to understand that sin is just an acting out of the forgetfulness of our divine origin, an amnesia about our deep and intrinsic value. It is a lack of self-love. It is a failure to recognise love—of oneself, of others, of the Divine. But it is only forgotten, not lost. When it is found again, when it is remembered and recognised and acknowledged, then love abides. And where love abides, sin cannot.

Kathryn was dreaming again. She knew she was dreaming and yet everything was so vivid that her sleeping self seemed more real than her waking self.

She is moving backward down a dark tunnel. It is constraining, claustrophobically narrow. She wants to get out. Suddenly she is expelled from it but, immediately, she wishes to be back in the tunnel. In the world outside the tunnel she is surrounded by death. The stench is overwhelming. Cupping her hand over her mouth and nose she takes short, shallow breaths in an attempt to filter out the repugnant smell. Gagging, she raises her head from its downcast position and tries to make visual sense of the dreamscape in which she finds herself. She is leaning against a wall, a house wall. Her feet are standing on cobblestones. Everything around her is narrow. Across the narrow cobbled street she sees narrow, closely packed houses of uneven proportions, many with the upper storey protruding fifty centimetres or more over the lower storey, overhanging the street. The houses' windows are narrow, mean, without glass and covered, instead, with what looks like oiled cloth. The doors are narrow and heavy. It looks like the medieval town that Sophia had described to her. From somewhere overhead, Kathryn hears a female voice shout out something in a strange accent. 'Gardey loo, gardey loo,' calls the woman, who Kathryn can now see is hanging out of the upper storey window of the house directly opposite where she is standing. She is holding some kind of pot in her hands.

'What are you saying?' Kathryn calls back, stepping forward into the middle of the street. She is hit with a downpour of liquid and other matter; it drenches her head, sticks to her hair, and its overpowering odour tells her instantly that she is covered in urine and faeces.

'She was saying *gardez l'eau* and using the phrase to mean "watch out for the water". But I see you got more than water,' says a well-dressed gentleman as he passes by, laughing. 'These English have been bastardising the French language ever since the Norman Conquest.'

Kathryn wants to ask the gentleman more but he vanishes, clearly not belonging to this place and time. Kathryn wants to vanish from it too, but does not know how to do it. Instead, she takes a single crumpled tissue from the inside of her sleeve and tries to wipe her face with it, tries desperately to remove the smell of the chamber pot's contents from her nose.

Another woman at another second storey window a little further down the street holds a chamber pot in her hands and cries, 'Gardey loo,' and this time Kathryn does what she observes other pedestrians doing: scrambling for cover against the first storey walls of houses so that they are under cover of the overhanging second storeys. Up and down the street, the cry is repeated until the street is a shower of human waste products that splash into and up from the cobblestones, some of it clinging to the clothes and uncovered hands and faces of passers-by, the majority of it pooling in the slightly concave centre of the street and mixing with other muck that coats the cobbles to form a lumpy, brown sludge that oozes and flows along the sloping thorough-fare and into the river at the end of the road.

Kathryn hurries toward the river too, hoping that from its banks she will gain a perspective on where she is, and how she might escape. But on reaching the embankment she is assailed by an even greater stench, and it is not simply the result of the odious refuse and excre-ment that pours into the river from the streets that wind down to it. Kathryn sees that both banks are home to trades and industries that she takes some time to identify.

'Tanning and butchery,' says a scrawny woman crouched on the shore, and looking up at Kathryn as if she has read her dream-thoughts. 'Stinks, doesn't it? That's because the butchers slaughter right here, on the river's edge, and skin the animals as well. Then the skins are sold to the tanners next door and up along the river and they submerge the hides in a solution of lime and urine to dislodge the hair and fat. And then they rewash the hides by immersing them in either warm dogs' dung or birds' droppings. And then they drench in another solution of barley and urine or stale beer. They make beautiful leather here— oh, the shoes, belts, gloves, saddles and harnesses are something to behold. Still, the smell is so bad that even the rats keep away.'

Kathryn does not dare to open her mouth to thank the strange woman for the information but, instead, looks down at her to acknowl-edge that she has heard what was said and is shocked to see that the woman is washing her clothes in the river, right next to the tannery's outfall. And at various spots all along the river's edge there are women washing clothes, immersing heavy fabrics in the water, then wringing them by hand and rubbing and scrubbing them on washboards, and spreading them out on the ground to dry. She feels herself retching. She clutches her stomach and hurries toward a bridge, then crosses to the other side of the river. Running, running through more winding streets, uphill away from the river, running nowhere, anywhere, to get away. She is lost, there is no way out. And then the path widens, opens out, and she finds herself in a spacious, airy forecourt, and overhead there is blue sky. In front of her looms a magnificent building. It's an immense cathedral, a structure with four long intersecting arms that give an overall cross-shape to the edifice around the giddying height of the central tower.

Kathryn longs to enter into the cathedral, to sit quietly under its soaring vaults, but she cannot find the entrance. 'Solace for you is this way,' she hears a disembodied voice saying, and she walks toward it. On and on the voice leads her until she arrives at another church, but this one is small, humble, out of the way.

Now she is in a small, damp, dark, bitterly cold room. She does not know how she came to be inside the room but she knows that the door is barred from the outside and so she cannot escape. There are two windows in the room and she walks to one of them; she has to kneel down to peer through it and when she does so, she finds herself looking into the interior of a church. She gets up from the kneeling position and moves toward the other window. There is a small wooden chair under this opening and, when she looks through it, she can see a grassy area, a cobbled street beyond the grass, and a small row of houses lining the street. She suddenly understands that she is in an anchorhold, with its one interior window looking toward eternal life— as represented by the church—and the other exterior window looking toward the temporal life of the everyday world. In the corner away from the external window she sees a low bunk and on it a woman is lying, groaning and crying. Kathryn is surprised that she has only just noticed the woman.

'Are you all right?' Kathryn asks, going to the distraught stranger and laying a hand gently on her arm, which is extended above a coarse blanket.

'You have come,' says the woman, moving her arm to take firm hold of Kathryn's hand. 'Please sit near me. I must tell you something.'

Kathryn leaves the bedside briefly to retrieve the chair from under the window and brings it back to place near the bunk. She sits. The room grows darker. Kathryn's eyes struggle to adjust to the gloom. And then a light, bright and focused as a spotlight, illuminates the face of the anchorhold's inhabitant and she begins a soliloquy:

I am called Julian, though that is not my name. I forfeited my identity when I entered into solitude. This is the anchorhold of the church of St Julian's in Carrow, Norwich. I am regarded as a holy woman. I do not think that I am. Rather, I think all women, all people, are holy, all creation is sacred. Certainly, all people seem to be sinful but I was shown revelations of Divine Love and in those revelations, I was not shown sin. People lose their way, that is all. Fear and doubt overtake them. They forget their divine origin and divine destination. It is the unavoidable circumstance of the human condition. Suffering, however, is a different matter. I am suffering in pain now, but I have been shown an insight into the suffering. Do you know what the greatest pain is? It is to see the one person or thing you love the most suffering. I am an anchoress and the thing I have come to love the most is God, in the Christian form. You will be familiar with the Christian idea of the crucifixion of Jesus. In my revelations, Jesus appeared to me as a suffering human hanging on a cross. And I said to him in his agony, 'Even though I am ill and in pain, my worst suffering is to look upon you, dear Lord, in your suffering.' And he answered me, 'And the worst pain for me is to look upon you in your suffering.' And I know that I am one who is the representative of all. In love and suffering, we are all made divine. If you are a mother, you know that you would exchange places with your child if he or she were suffering. You or I would carry the cross of one whom we love because it is a lighter cross than watching helplessly as the loved one suffers. We all carry crosses every day and we are all on our cross every day of our life. Some people attempt to avoid their suffering, to hide from their cross. It is their prerogative. But, in doing so, they also fail to learn the lesson of life. There is only one lesson, and it is Love.

The anchorhold evaporates. Kathryn is in another room, a room she does not recognise. But it is a modern room and, thankfully, it is clean and it smells of roses. Margery appears. She gives Kathryn a cardboard box piled with yellowing, brittle papers covered in even, deliberate handwriting in fading black ink.

'Here are Julie's accounts of herself,' Margery says. 'Take your time to read over them. And note: sometimes Julie writes as if she is observing herself from outside; other times she's right in her skin; sometimes she's both. Sometimes she notices or experiences something and then she interprets it. Other times it seems that the experience and the interpretation are simultaneous. She is the "I" and the "she", the subject and the object. She is herself and she is all of us. Perhaps that is the truest way to be in this world. Inside, above, beyond, outside; being who we are where we are when we are. All human experience is the same across the ages, it is just played out against a different background. Can you or I imagine life in the fourteenth century? We can read a bit of history about it: there was a terrible plague, for example. But can we *know* what it was like to live through that plague? To see everyone we love dying a cruel and agonising death? The stench of putrefying flesh taking root in our noses? The sight of countless decomposing bodies piled up outside doorways awaiting removal by city authorities who could not do their job because they, themselves, were on a pile of the dead? And then the sight of those awaiting inevitable death, the walking dead, their bodies decorated by the black, pus-filled swellings that were the jewellery of the illness? The sound of coughing and wheezing and death throes hammering our ears? The feel of the thick, fetid air weighing on every inch of the livings' skins. The taste of fear, dread and hopelessness? Today our plagues may be different, but their results are the same.'

Kathryn chooses, at random, a yellowing page and she reads:

26 February 1974

February is the sauna of summer in Sydney, overtaking the long, hot, crackly days of January. February hangs ponderously around my little cottage in the backyard of St Faith's Hospital, dulling my senses, depleting my energy, and promising, but never delivering, an orgasmic storm to put an end to the highly charged atmosphere.

On this twenty-sixth day of the sauna, the humidity has stopped the air moving altogether so that I cannot breathe without feeling that I am drowning.

She lay on her bed, loosened her shift and decreased her inspiration to a bare necessity. Sleep came quickly and when she was awakened by the tenderest wisp of evening air entering through the window, Julie at first thought that she was receiving an early taste of autumnal relief. Instead, the wisp concentrated itself over her head on the pillow, intensified into a swirling mini-spiral of electric energy which burst into a tongue-sized ball of flame that licked at her face, assaulting her nostrils with the smell of sulphur, and searing her eyelashes until she feared to open her eyes again.

'It's the fiend,' she screamed. 'Oh my God, my God. Take this away from me.' But her prayer went unacknowledged and served only to encourage the fire to enlarge so that it threatened to cover her entire pronated form. Wildly she began hitting at it, attempting to repel, with all her human strength, something that was beyond human repelling. And then, without warning, the fire changed its tack, moving from a horizontal plane to a vertical one that stood upright at the end of the bed. Now the full height of a large man, the fire began to darken in certain parts, lighten in others, and then take form.

And then I saw that it was not the fiend but my own fear and ignorance. It was a body, covered in mud. It was my father and it was my mother, my brother, my friend, my child. All trying to rise from the mud but too sick, and tired, and filthy to get out of the mire. And I, watching, my heart torn by love for them, am unable to take away their pain, unable to cleanse them, unable to take them to my bosom and surround them with my loving arms. They are stuck, and I am stuck. But we see each other, and I cry for them because they are dying, and they cry for me because I am destined to go on living without them.

But then I was shown that between death and life there is only a moment. And that what we see as pain and suffering is changed to joy and bliss instantaneously. Between one and the other there is less than a snap of the fingers.

Still Kathryn dreams on. And now Margery is handing her what looks like the little journal that was with the photos in the Julie X storage box.

'Read it,' encourages Margery. 'Read the final pages. They tell of Julie's departure.'

In her dream-state, Kathryn flips through the diary to the last entry. But who wrote it? And then, she does not read the ending. It is not necessary to read it because it is playing out in front of her dream-eyes, and all the thoughts and feelings and visions of Julie's last moments are present to her.

Early morning. Cottage Point. A pale blue sky, full of the deeper promise of a beautiful day, drapes itself across the bay. On one side of this tranquil arm of the deep and voluptuous body of water named Pittwater, steep gumtree-covered Sydney sandstone walls stand guard all the way down to the water's edge. On the other side, holiday cottages, grand and small, cling to the narrow ledge between the base of another rock wall and the lapping, pristine water.

Most of the cottages have a small jetty with an accompanying floating pontoon to which is attached some sort of boat—a millionaire's cruiser, a run-about, a row boat. Julie is an interloper here. Long before her, long before humans, this bay existed, its tranquil beauty flourishing in the absence of eyes to admire it.

From her sitting position on the jetty she stares across the water. There is no wind but the tide is flowing in, making the surface seawater ripple and glisten and dance with shifting pinpoints of sunlight. No wind, a day of endless possibilities.

And then, a disturbance. A few jetties up to her left, she notices a man climbing into a row boat. Once seated, he adjusts his broad-brimmed hat, takes up the oars and begins rowing out. A lap, slap, lap echoes across the bay with each slice of the oars. The man doesn't paddle for long, though. He is heading for the Mary-Lou, a sleek forty-metre yacht at anchor about a hundred metres offshore. She watches as the man reaches the yacht, bringing his little boat parallel to the yacht's starboard side, then stretches his arms carefully up to gain a hold of the low deck edge. She sees him grip more firmly and then begin to manoeuvre himself, hand over hand, around to the sloping back of the yacht. Once there, very slowly, and somewhat unsteadily, he rises to his feet as the little boat rocks precariously beneath him. He leans forward then and she holds her breath, convinced that he has lost his balance and is about to crash into the water. But no, she notices the chrome cross-bars on the yacht's stern and, using these for leverage, the man climbs out of his rower and onto the Mary-Lou. Only after he secures the row boat and she sees him moving around on the yacht's deck, checking various things as he goes, can she breathe again, and look away, knowing he is safe.

Overhead a gull screeches and suddenly, without apparent motivation, arranges itself into a sleek vertical line and plunges into the water, slicing the surface with barely a sound, barely a ripple. And then, just as suddenly, the gull bursts from the water and soars back into the sky with a flapping fish in its beak.

She surveys the clear water closer in to her dangling feet. A jellyfish, plump and round with a reddish centre and pale pink edges, contracts and expands its way along to disappear under the jetty. A school of bream scurry past. And then she sees it …

The blue fish. The Blue Fish. The great blue groper that has become her talisman. Large, solid, bright blue, its tail waving casually to her. It is brighter than the day, bluer than the morning sky, longer than her arm and, at this moment in God's whole world, it is the most magnificent thing she has ever seen. It floats without fear just below the surface. It simply is. She sees its gills slowly, gently pulsating. The miraculous beauty of the fish makes her heart beat violently with joy; the miraculous beauty of the sky, and the rocks, and the trees, and the gull, and the man in the yacht all coalesce into one great and beautiful whole. The wholeness tugs at her heart, pulls her down, beckons her under. She is falling, falling in love, being immersed in love, and there is no need to grasp at anything anymore.

Kathryn awoke. She looked around the now familiar guest room that had been her accommodation for the past several days. She was securely at St Monica's. It was morning, the sun pushing a slim shaft of light through the gap in the drapes. On her bedside table, Kathryn saw Julie X's journal, the same one that revealed its mysterious final contents in her dream. She picked it up and flipped to the last pages, but she did not see the story of the blue fish there. Instead, there is a newspaper clipping glued inside the back cover.

Sydney Morning Herald, 11 May 1974.

The search for a woman who fell from a jetty at Cottage Point, in Sydney's north, four days ago, has been suspended. Several witnesses, including two fishermen and a local man on his yacht nearby, saw the young woman topple into the water at about seven o'clock on Wednesday morning. The fishermen rushed to the scene but could find no trace of the woman. Emergency services attended promptly but were also unable to locate the woman and, at this stage, she is presumed drowned. There are no suspicious circumstances. In a bizarre coincidence, while the woman's identity is not known, she is believed to be the same woman who was pulled from Sydney Harbour by a ferry operator one year ago to the day of her recent disappearance and apparent drowning.

There was a knock at the door. The handle turned and Nicola was there with the tea.

❡ 14 ❡

This is what she said:

There are always multiple possibilities in life. For every path there is another way that would lead to the same destination. I have chosen a varied path … . It might be a way that takes longer or is less pleasant or more fraught with danger or difficulty, or a path that is sunnier, or darker, but it is a way, nevertheless. And there are alternatives to the mode in which we travel the chosen way. Walking, running, sailing, flying, hurrying, lingering, even turning back. Happily, sadly, cruelly, generously, softly, loudly, intelligently, stupidly, kindly, hopefully, dejectedly. And we decide on what baggage we carry with us; we determine what is essential and what is superfluous. For every journey we select our companions and those we will leave behind. From our choices we learn our lessons and the sum total of our choices and our lessons is our life.

Tim's phone rang loudly, startling him. He had just ended a brief conversation with the head nurse at the private hospital where Sophia had been for the last few days. The nurse had called to let him know that Sophia had been collected just after breakfast and was safely on her way. Tim thought deeply about it, wondering if it had been a good idea to so readily agree to arrange transport for the young woman from the private facility to St Monica's at the request of Dr Kathryn Brookley. Sure, he trusted Kathryn's judgment, but he'd gone out on a limb in recommending an official patient transfer for Sophia when, really, she was headed for St Monica's for a few days 'recreation' with Kathryn and Sister Margery, and not for 'further treatment' as he had written on the transport request. No doubt Kathryn, as Sophia's specialist psychiatrist, would ensure the paperwork was correct when she returned but, still, Tim was uneasy enough about it to jump a little when the phone in his pocket began to ring. He was even more uneasy after he answered the call. It was a senior officer with the Australian Federal Police.

'Hello, Dr Timothy Mason?' the caller inquired.

'Yes, that's me,' Tim replied.

'This is Superintendent Rodney Mackatt. I'm with the Australian Federal Police and I'm currently working on the case of the unidentified female you have there in your hospital. The one pulled out of Sydney Harbour last week. The NSW Missing Persons Unit called us in.'

The man's voice was matter-of-fact and Tim was unsure of how he should reply to what were a series of statements. 'Ah, right. Thanks for calling, Superintendent,' Tim managed.

'I've got a few updates on the case for you,' the officer returned.

'Great,' said Tim, not very convincingly.

'The DNA sample didn't turn up anything. That's not surprising; our resources in that area are still growing. But the photos we received are a possible match with someone that Interpol's interested in.'

'Interpol?' said Tim, pulling out a chair from under the desk and lowering himself into it as his knees started to go weak.

'Yes. Nothing really sinister, but a Yellow Notice just the same, so we can't ignore it.'

'What's a Yellow Notice?' Tim asked.

'Good question. Short answer: Interpol publishes all kinds of notices and diffusions and, ah, the notices are graded, you might say. Anyway, a Yellow Notice is put out to try and locate a missing person or to identify a person who is unable to identify themselves. Now, we'd put our meagre information on your mystery woman into the international system, along with the photos the local police had sent us and we came up with a Yellow Notice on an English woman reported missing from Norwich about twenty years ago. Obviously the age isn't quite right but very similar height, build, facial features. We thought it was worth following up. Also, this English woman had a bit of form in the petty fraud area so we're interested on a number of fronts.'

As Tim listened to the superintendent his stomach became more and more knotted. He was aware of how sweaty his palms were as he nervously doodled diamonds within squares within diamonds within squares on the notepad in front of him. Behind the desk, a long window looked over the adjacent oval and he watched with envy as young men in tracksuit pants and t-shirts kicked a football back and forth in the midday sun.

'Petty fraud?' Tim was aware his voice had gone up an octave.

'Yep. Mainly posing as some sort of counsellor or do-gooder and getting board and lodgings, and sometimes a bit of money in return. Of course, that's not Interpol's interest. They're more concerned that there are reports of a woman fitting this broad description appearing and disappearing all over the United Kingdom for the past eighty years or so. Obviously, it can't be the same woman all the time—well, she's always described as looking around thirty years of age and that's impossible—but, naturally, they were interested to see us posting a similar profile and possibly similar *modus operandi* from Sydney, Australia. And, in the case of the woman who went missing from Norwich two decades ago, the fraud accusations are … well, let's say … in the eye of the beholder. I mean, she'd annoyed a few members of a church there and they'd reported her to the local police, but she'd also made quite an impact on a family there. They had nothing but good things to say about her and they're the ones who reported her missing.'

Tim's mouth had gone dry and he could hear the jagged quality of his voice as he asked, 'Have you got a name for the English woman?'

'Yes and no. It's "yes" insofar as we've got a first name but it's a "no" to any kind of surname. She called herself "Sophia" but that's not going to get us very far, is it? How about your mystery woman. Got a name for her?'

'Would it surprise you if I told you that she also gave us only a first name? Sophia,' answered Tim.

'Well, what do you know?' Superintendent Mackatt whistled into the phone. 'Okay, Doc. I've already passed on the Interpol info to your local police and they'll follow this up and liaise with me about it. In turn, I'll keep Interpol in the loop. The main thing is, then, to keep your eye on her. We don't want this one disappearing until we figure this out. Maybe there's a whole international gang of these disappearing do-gooders.' The officer laughed.

Tim, however, was not laughing. As he put the phone back in his pocket he thought of all the free meals Sophia had enjoyed in the taxpayer-funded public hospital and of Sophia reclining at this very moment in the comfortable back seat of a patient transport vehicle as it wended its way along the roads of the picturesque South Coast to the luxury aged-care facility of St Monica's-by-the-sea, where she would alight to spend several more carefree—emphasis on 'free'—days in the sun and in the lovely company of Kathryn and other unsuspecting victims of her schemes. And he was the one who had signed the authorisation.

Before he left the office, he kicked the chair across the room.

{ 15 }

This is what she said:

Our life is a story; many stories, a store of stories to which we contribute more lines. More depth, more light and shade, more meaning is added each day we live, and each time we tell our story. Our stories are lines through space, intersecting with others' stories, overlapping, interweaving, repeating, mimicking, and coalescing to create new lines and patterns until the background fabric of the universe becomes strong enough to hold us all, to support us in the Grand Narrative, unfurled through time until it is gathered to its end in eternity.

Rainbow liked to start the day, bright and early, by meditating for half an hour. Sometimes she would do this sitting on her bedroom floor in her pyjamas. But if the morning was fine, and the sun was generous, she'd dress in her comfortable working gear of vividly coloured, tie-dyed harem pants, an unstructured but equally vivid top, and sturdy shoes (because she was on her feet for most of the day and, at sixty-three years of age, those feet no longer looked attractive in strappy sandals). She would go down to the beach to meditate before grabbing some muesli and a juice at the Seaview Café, and then head to the activities room to prepare for a happy and productive day of arty and crafty creation with the lovely residents of St Monica's.

She usually set up the pottery corner first, laying thick plastic covers on the high benches, making sure that the large cubes of clay and the wire for cutting it were in place. The finer details of the firing of the pottery, and the kiln, and the wheels, she left for the experts. Then she would go to the large games cupboard and get out the most popular board games—Monopoly, draughts, Cluedo—and set them out on a number of smaller tables so that the residents could pick and choose. She entrusted all aspects of the bridge club to the members of the bridge club, its intricacies being far too challenging for her. The arrangement of easels, palettes, paints, brushes, and jars for the oil painters and watercolourists was her next task. Always last on her preparation list was the carrying out of the deep baskets of wool from the storeroom. She loved wool: its exquisite assortment of colours, its variability of textures—from the finest ply that Mrs Seymour demanded for the baby jackets she churned out like fairy floss from a machine to the thick, chunky varieties that Mr Reynolds and Mrs Birch liked to use for the shawls and hats they donated to the local hospital. Rainbow would take her time arranging the skeins in attractive piles in the middle of the large table around which the knitting group gathered. Most days there were about ten residents knitting away, and Rainbow always took the time to join them and knit a square or two for the knee rugs they whipped up for various nursing homes around the country in between their more serious knitting projects. She enjoyed the group's chatter, usually centred on tales of love and loss in their own lives or in those of their favourite soapies' characters. Sometimes she would be persuaded to tell a tale of her own, but Rainbow, like the knee rugs with their randomly coloured and unevenly knitted squares sewn together to make a whole, was also made up of randomness, and unevenness, and of many pieces that did not quite constitute a regular wholeness, and so she would begin her tales by warning her listeners that her life had been a patchwork that had not yet been crafted into an appealing pattern.

'All the better,' Mr Reynolds would say. 'We don't want the usual here. You know we've led interesting lives. I, for example, was in jail for twelve years.'

'Yes, we know.' The knitting group and Rainbow would laugh. 'You were the famous Knitting Bandit who robbed stores by holding a

Number 10 knitting needle to young shop assistants' necks.'

'Of course, I didn't mean to stab that last man I held up in the liquor store. He shouldn't have wriggled. He moved in the wrong direction, knitting while I was purling, if you understand.'

'Well, luckily they were able to stitch him up. And you certainly were stitched up, doing your time,' Mrs Murray would often say, beating him to his own punch line.

Fridays were always a popular day in the activities room. For one thing, Mr West and his rock band Old Banned Men usually set up on the room's stage area and performed a couple of sets around morning tea time. Today, though, Mr West had an appointment with his proctologist so the knitting group was enjoying each other's company and their morning tea without the background music when Rainbow sat down to knit a square or two with them. She was marvelling at the way a variegated yellow, orange and pink 8-ply was organising itself into a series of vertical stripes along the length of the square she was creating when she heard someone from behind her ask, 'Do you mind if we join the group for an hour or so?' Swinging around, she saw that it was Sister Margery accompanied by the visitor of the previous day.

'No, please, take a seat, both of you. Have you had your coffee yet? And would you like to knit a square or two while you're here?' Rainbow was flushed with the excitement of welcoming a new person to the group and, within seconds, she prevailed upon Margery to introduce the visitor to everyone before providing the newcomers with a cup of tea and a nice slice of carrot cake, and some needles and yarn with which to commence their squares. What Rainbow hadn't ascertained was the reason that Kathryn was at St Monica's.

'Are you staying long?' she ventured as a way of encouraging Kathryn to talk about herself.

'No, not long. I've been here since Monday and I think, at this stage, that I'll be leaving after the weekend, probably on Monday. So, about eight days in all.'

'Any particular reason for the visit?' Mr Reynolds was more direct.

'Well, I think that will become a little clearer as we talk,' returned Sister Margery, puzzling Rainbow even more.

'Hmmm,' huffed Mr Reynolds. 'We were just about to ask Rainbow to tell us one of her stories. But maybe you'd like to tell us *your* story, Kathryn.'

'No, as a matter of fact, I think she'd really like to hear Rainbow's story,' Margery said. 'Would you tell Kathryn your miracle story?'

'Oh yes, we love that one,' said Mrs Murray, clapping her hands.

'If you really want me to,' replied Rainbow. 'Though it's a bit tragic in parts.'

'All of our stories are tragic in parts,' said Miss Bell who, though renowned for the beauty of the baby booties she fashioned, was the quietest member of the knitting group. 'Please, I love your miracle story.'

'Very well,' agreed Rainbow, setting her knitting down on the table, draining her coffee cup and setting it down too. 'But, as most of you already know, the tale is upsetting to me in parts and so, even though it is about me, I tell it as if it is a tale about someone else. For the grammatically inclined, that means "third person".'

'Oooh, I think it makes it more exciting, too,' said Miss Bell to the others.

All eyes were glued on Rainbow as she sat, motionless, collecting her thoughts. Those at the table stopped chatting to each other and all that could be heard was the click-clack of knitting needles when Rainbow began to speak.

Once there was a young, innocent girl who lived by the sea on the far north coast of New South Wales. When she was eighteen, her parents told her that she was old enough to manage by herself and they ran away to join a hippy commune. The girl had no other family and so she took the money she had saved from her part-time job in a local haberdashery store and bought a train ticket to Sydney because she had been accepted into a course there. She rented a tiny room in a rat-infested share house in Glebe, close to her place of study. She had little money for food, so she grew vegetables and herbs in pots that she placed under her bedroom window, moving them as necessary to catch the sunlight. The vegetables did not do well with such limited natural light so she ate the stunted, flavourless produce herself; the herbs were hardier and flourished and these she sold at a

Saturday market stall. In winter, the little room was bitterly cold and she kept warm by knitting—long scarves, fat hats, coarse-textured shawls—and she sold these, too, at her market stall.

Finally, she completed her course of study, graduating as an occupational therapist and gaining a job at an important Sydney psychiatric hospital. She immediately loved working there and, only three weeks into her employment, she began to think about looking for a better place to live. Her life was improving. That was, until the day of the cat miracle.

It started as any other day but, somehow, on this particular winter's day in the great kitchen of the great hospital, a black cat was killed by one of the patients the girl was supervising. The cat lay breathless and hairless, and scalded and dead on the linoleum until another of the young woman's patients gently lifted the cat close to her mouth and breathed life back into it, breathed its fur back to wholeness and glossiness. The girl, who was called Robyn, knew that she had witnessed a miracle and that her life could never be the same again. It could not be the same because she had no one to talk about the miracle with; the doctor who attended the miracle said that it was magic and that she must forget all about it; she did not know where her parents were, nor had they provided her with any siblings to talk to. Perhaps, she thought to herself, I could tell my housemates in the rat-infested share house, and so she did. But they laughed at her and, the next morning, outside her bedroom door, she found a large cardboard box on the lid of which was written: 'See if you can bring these back to life'. And when she opened the box she discovered that it was full of dead rats. And so she screamed, packed her few belongings, and got on a train and went back up to the far north coast and to the haberdashery shop where she had worked years before. But there were new owners and the shop was now a Craft and Handmade Gift Shop and the new owners asked her if she had any special skill to offer the new enterprise. She told them her name was Rainbow No Surname because, in truth, 'Robyn' didn't fit her any longer and she had no family from which to take a family name. As her skilful offering, she said she could knit animals back to life.

'Great idea. Lifelike animals in wool,' reflected the craft shop owner, misunderstanding what Rainbow had said. But, still, his idea appealed and so Rainbow set about knitting life-size lustrous cats and faithful dogs, and their similarity to the real thing made the gift shop a 'must-see' on the tourist trail and 'Rainbow's Fabulous Felines and Captivating Canines' the most sought-after items in the whole town. The Persian cats and the golden retrievers practically walked out of the shop, such was their popularity and verisimilitude.

The money she earned from her animal creations enabled Rainbow to buy a tiny cottage, with a garden, in the hills behind the town. In the cottage she set up her spinning wheel and began to gather bits and pieces of fibre that she could spin into yarn. Lloyd, the hobby-farmer up the road, gave her some of the wool from his one and only sheep shearing effort, and this she rinsed, and beat with willow branches, and then she combed it, and started to spin, winding the yarn carefully and happily around the spindle and thinking to herself that she was a 'spinster' in every sense of the word. And then she dyed the yarn, preparing it first in a mordant to fix the dye. For this she would dissolve alum and cream of tartar in a big pot of water and, adding the pre-soaked wool and putting it all on the stove top, she would bring it to the boil, then simmer it for about an hour. When it was cooled, she would rinse the wool again, then place it in the dyes she had prepared: some made from the dried leaves of local eucalypts would yield delicious colours that ranged from beige, grey and light brown to vibrant yellow and olive green and onto chocolate brown and, sometimes, a juicy apricot; some made from the juice of boiled vegetables, such as beetroots, would produce luscious pinks and reds. Once dyed, the result-ing skeins were sorted into colours and stored in big baskets in the cosy living room, ready to be used for the replication of her extraordinary domestic animals. When knitting a Siamese she would reach for the chocolate and apricot for the cat's points; for the British shorthairs, the deep greys were needed; and the variegated reds, oranges, and browns were selected for the marble-cake pattern of the tabbies. For the dogs it was the yellows and golds for the Labradors, the pinks and whites for the poodles, the blacks for the spectacular spots on the Dalmatians. Every cat and dog was irresistibly authentic.

But her originally stated plan of knitting animals back to life was not usurped by the success of the woollen treasures. In fact, Rainbow devoted all non-knitting time to investigating remedies for the cure or succour of suffering animals. In her garden she grew flowers and herbs that she read about in books on medieval medicine, scouring the library and the bookshops for information. Oh how she would have loved the internet to have been available back in those days.

Soon she was familiar enough with the theory to start putting it into practice. Stray dogs and cats were welcomed into her cottage. Pets needing holiday accommodation were accommodated. When the local pound was full, Rainbow welcomed the overflow. And while around her feet frolicked the animals on whom she lavished her knowledge and love, Rainbow tended huge vats of potions as they bubbled on her stovetop. Her kitchen table resembled an apothecary's shop with its jars, and glass cannulas, mortars and pestles, bunches of dried herbs, and minerals and crystals of every size and hue. For the street dogs who arrived with scabies or other skin infections she prepared an ointment of sulphur, nettle seeds, mercury and butter; for those with the mange, an ointment of honey and valerian leaf. For many of her treatments Rainbow turned to the trustworthy remedies of the great twelfth century abbess and saint, Hildegard of Bingen. Her recommendation of feeding tansy cakes to the (human) sufferers of catarrh was readily translated by Rainbow into a simple treatment for canine kennel cough, while the suggestion of a salve made from apple leaves gathered in spring worked wonders for cats and dogs with eye infections. And Hildegard's recipe of ashes of the wood of grape vines mixed with wine was a favourite means of helping firm up the gums and teeth of animals with dental problems.

The animals in Rainbow's care thrived and multiplied but, despite her tireless study and loving devotion, many months had passed without her getting any nearer to discovering how to restore the life of a deceased animal. She persisted—in her apothecary kitchen and in her knitting—convinced that, somehow, between the two activities, a way forward would reveal itself. Although, it should be said that by this time, mothers were instructing their children to stay away from the witch-lady who brewed spells in her kitchen to change children into dogs and cats, which she then covered in knitted yarns and sold at the local gift shop as lifelike animals. This, the adults said, was how she managed to fulfil her promise and threat to knit animals back to life.

Things could not continue in this way. Rainbow became a little alarmed when rocks were thrown through her cottage windows at midnight. But a rock was nothing compared to what assailed her house one midday on a Tuesday in early summer, when a flighty wind shook the leaves on the peach trees in her garden. It was then that she heard an unwelcome knocking at her little red front door. When she opened it, there were two old, shabby people standing on the doorstep—a man with very few teeth, and a woman with very few manners.

'Don't you recognise us?' they said.

And Rainbow replied truthfully, 'No.'

'We are your parents, and we have nowhere to go. We are penniless so we have decided to live here.'

'But there is no room for three people and all my animals in this house,' she explained.

'Quite right,' they said. 'We have arranged to have you and your animals evicted. This house is a health hazard and you are a crazy witch-woman.'

And the council took her animals. And the parents took her house. And so Rainbow, heartbroken and broken, got on the train and went to Sydney and back to the rat-infested share house in Glebe, which was still there, though all the earlier housemates had moved to the eastern suburbs after completing their law degrees. Now, the house was condemned, awaiting demolition. It was here that Geoff found her and encouraged her to get on the bus that brought her to St Monica's.

The knitting group, who had heard this tale before, smiled and cooed and wiped away tears as Rainbow leant back in her chair to signal the tale's end. Only Kathryn remained motionless and ashen-faced. But before anyone could inquire as to Kathryn's apparent distress, from the entrance to the activities room came the sound of someone clearing their throat.

'Kathryn, look who has arrived,' announced Geoff, his booming voice turning every head in his direction. Next to him stood the small, neat figure of Sophia. She was wearing her grey woollen dress but her shoulders were wrapped in a bright red shawl.

'Actually, I've been here for about two hours,' she volunteered with surprising confidence. 'Geoff has been helping me get settled, showing me to a most amazing bedroom with a huge bed that looks straight out to the sea. Oh, it's heavenly. And then that nice young girl, Nicola, took me on a tour of this whole, wonderful establishment and we had tea in a glass palace called the Seaview Café. I am blessed beyond words. But all the more for seeing you, dear friends.' She darted across the room extended her arms. To Margery, to Rainbow, to Kathryn.

Margery was smiling, ear to ear. Kathryn was still motionless. Rainbow was shaking.

'Hello everyone. This is Pierre, your chef for today. Lunch is served,' came the announcement over the intercom.

❦ 16 ❧

This is what she said:

Many people think that they are afraid of dying but, actually, they are afraid of living. They weigh the risks, they despair of the failures, they rail against the annoyances and disappointments. On balance, they find it safer to opt for the mundane. They do not notice the blue sky in July in a clear southern hemisphere winter; they do not marvel at the way the wind changes, or how many different shapes and colours and textures there are in the leaves of a garden. They do not savour their food or their wine. They do not realise that the world is awash with fragrance. They do not indulge in laughter or crying that make their bellies and souls ache. They live within self-imposed limits so that when the thought of dying enters their head, they push it away, like all the other things in life they have relegated to oblivion, so that nothing is disrupted, nothing is examined, nothing is felt. It is life on the surface when, like an iceberg, there is so much more if they would only immerse themselves and look a little deeper.

Friday lunch at St Monica's was a grand affair. When Margery had assumed ownership of the home, she had decreed that all the residents and staff, the majority of whom had been down and out for much of their existence, should now be raised up to a life of ease and joy. This decree meant that every meal at St Monica's was celebratory but, because the residents were getting older and because it was imperative that they enjoy good health, all the meals were devised by a contingent of top class chefs in consultation with top class dieticians to ensure that 'delicious' and 'nutritious' went hand in hand. Every Friday, however, healthy options were outlawed in favour of Head Chef Pierre's Degustation Delights Day. The twelve-course extravaganza began promptly at midday and stretched until three, at which time most of the older residents would retire for an afternoon nap, allowing the weekday staff to get away early for their weekends with the family.

Today, in particular honour of the special guests, Dr Kathryn Brookley and Miss Sophia-from-the-Sea, as Margery introduced her, Pierre had created a feast of unparalleled gustatory pleasures. It began with gazpacho shots with watercress olive oil followed by dainty servings of scallop ravioli with sage butter, and grilled octopus with green apple sauce. Next came mini brioche with ricotta, avocado, and truffle oil and then a tangerine risotto with barbecued king prawns. Slightly larger plates of wagyu beef with parsley sorbet, oven-roasted peppered potatoes and baby peas were presented next but, for those who preferred it, there was also a chicken breast stuffed with apricots and sultanas and served with a sweet potato puree and tiny sautéed mushrooms, or a snapper and leek pie served with garlic mash and roasted heritage tomatoes.

Despite the unquestionable delectability of Pierre's banquet, Kathryn had little appetite. Her senses were distracted, diverted to thoughts about Rainbow. Her revelation that she had been the occupational therapist, Robyn, who had witnessed Julie X bringing a cat back to life all those years ago was disturbing enough, but Rainbow's account of her life following that incident was causing Kathryn to re-evaluate her own reactions to the mysterious Sophia. For one thing, it had not occurred to her before that the unusual actions and revelations of Julie and Sophia (and whether they were one and the same person was another question on Kathryn's mind) could have such far-reaching and negative effects on susceptible persons. And here Kathryn had surprised herself because, as a psychiatrist, she knew that, professionally, such a possibility should have been firmly on her radar. Instead, she had let herself get swept up in the wonder and mystery of it all: the good that had flowed from Julie's effect on Margery, with the establishment of St Monica's for those in need; and the uplifting of her own thoughts and mood as a result of Sophia's insights into the death of her infant son Matthew.

She needed to speak to Rainbow. Kathryn scanned the dining room until she located the staff tables in the corner area closest to the kitchen. There she could see Geoff in animated conversation with Nicola and a couple of the day-shift nurses. She could see Anne, the physiotherapist, chatting to Dave, the masseur. She recognised Ed, the onsite tai chi master, talking to Cara, the yoga teacher. A group of orderlies were enjoying a joke together. But she couldn't see Rainbow anywhere.

'Excuse me a minute, Margery, everyone,' Kathryn said, pushing her chair back from the table.

'Don't be too long,' cautioned Margery. 'The dessert courses are about to arrive and they're always spectacular. Look at the menu. You can choose from lemon and almond tart with lavender ice-cream, or churros with Belgian chocolate sauce and cinnamon cream, or honey-baked pears with crème brûlée, or fresh berries with champagne jelly.'

Kathryn smiled and then hurried toward the door. She made her way back to the activities room and there, on a low, plush chair by the window in the cosy 'conversation pit'—a specially designed sunken and carpeted lounge area that wrapped around a central, freestanding beaten-copper fireplace—sat a crumpled Rainbow, her head in her hands.

'Oh, Rainbow, I should have looked for you sooner. I should have realised that seeing Sophia might be very stressful for you,' Kathryn said, dropping onto her knees next to the woman and touching her on the forearm.

Rainbow didn't lift her head, and Kathryn gently reached for the woman's hands, moving them away from her face. 'Julie had a huge impact on your life, didn't she?' Kathryn said. 'Does Sophia remind you of her?'

Rainbow's words were slow and carefully formed when she finally spoke. 'Sophia is very like Julie. For all I know, they are the same person. What upsets me, though, is that I'm not the same, not at all.'

'I'm not sure that I understand what you mean,' Kathryn responded.

'No, I guess you don't. I'm not so sure that *I* know what I mean either. When I saw Sophia standing there earlier, it was like forty years of my life just fell away. It was like I had been transported back in time to a particular moment when I was full of hopes and dreams. And looking at that person, and that moment, should have filled me with … with … with something. Surprise, shock, sadness, happiness, recognition, anything. But there was nothing. I felt nothing. Nothing but the realisation that I have been chasing shadows for forty years. I realised I am a shadow of a person. That is why I shook. I am flimsy. I have no substance.'

'Oh Rainbow,' breathed Kathryn, not knowing what else to say.

Kathryn stayed crouched next to Rainbow for a long time, until her lower legs started to go to sleep and a small effort to move her left foot resulted in a rush of pins and needles. She struggled to standing and was beginning to shake out the numbness in her foot when Rainbow looked up at her.

'I'm scared, Kathryn. Scared that I've been alive for sixty-three years and yet I haven't live.'

'But you *have* lived,' came a voice from the other end of the room. It was Sophia, stepping slowly toward Kathryn and Rainbow. 'It may not have turned out to be the life you originally planned. And it may not have been a life full of material gain or travel or high excitement or fame. But you have lived. You have found meaning and purpose in the simple but beautiful things of everyday life. Art, craft, animals; the quiet pleasure of a little house and garden. You have looked deeply into the colour and texture of things.' By now Sophia had completed her walk across the room. She stopped briefly on the edge of the conversation pit before descending the two shallow steps into it and going to two small armchairs which she deftly moved across the carpet, placing one on either side of the seated Rainbow. She took her place on one of them and motioned to Kathryn to sit on the other. Kathryn obliged.

Kathryn spoke first. 'Did you hear all that Rainbow was saying?'

'Yes,' replied Sophia, focusing on Kathryn. 'I saw you get up to leave the dining room and I followed you. I, too, noticed Rainbow's reaction to my arrival.' Then she moved her gaze slightly so that it was fixed on Rainbow. 'Are you all right with me sitting next to you?' she asked.

'Honestly? I don't know. Here you are, so like the Julie of all those decades ago. And here I am, so ordinary. I think that I am afraid of you. I was certainly afraid of Julie, of what she could do. And now I wonder what *you* might do. I wonder why you are here.'

Sophia threw her head back and laughed gently. 'I am here to remind you that you are still alive. Too many people do not see the divine in the ordinary, but it is there nonetheless. Too many do not see the divine in themselves, but it is the true state of being. Too many have too readily traded the miraculous for the mundane, the sacred for the material. And they are impoverished because of it. Too many are becoming poorer every day, in inverse proportion to their increasing material wealth. Rainbow, do not underestimate yourself. You have seen the miraculous; you saw it when Julie brought the cat back to life. You have reflected the miraculous through your care for your animals, and the residents here, and in your creative craft. You have just not yet seen it in yourself. You are not afraid of me; you are afraid of yourself. And fear is unnecessary.'

'Such things are easy to say,' said Rainbow. 'But many people suffer terribly and I think it makes sense for those people to be afraid.'

'Well said,' agreed Sophia. 'It would certainly be foolish for such people, for any of us really, to throw caution to the wind and to charge deliberately into what we know to be dangerous. Such behaviour is not life-affirming but, rather, life-denying. What I am saying is that, more often, we are afraid in the absence of any discernible threat. We let our preconceived ideas and deeply ingrained habits determine our actions and direction when, if we took a deep breath and stepped outside our comfort zone—mentally and emotionally as well as physically—we just might discover something marvellous. Your past does not have to predict your future, you know. Not unless you let it.'

'Yes, I think I know what you're saying. Many of the dogs and cats I looked after had been mistreated by former owners. When they came to me I offered them nothing but love and kindness and yet, still, it took many of them a long time to exchange their fear for trust.'

'It is a good example, Rainbow,' said Sophia. 'Now, if you permit me, I will tell you a short tale and in the tale you may recognise something that will help you.'

Rainbow nodded and relaxed a little back into the chair as Sophia began.

Once there was a child who set out on a sea journey with her parents. When night came and they were in the middle of the ocean, a huge storm sprang up and the ship lurched and shook and rose and plummeted on the massive waves. The child lay in her bunk, crying with terror, and so the mother took her daughter's hand and, laying something on its palm, she closed the girl's shaking hand around it. 'Hold onto this through the night. It will keep you safe,' the mother assured the child. And so the little girl squeezed the charm in her hand as tightly as she could. And though the ship still rolled and dropped uncontrollably, the child felt strong and fearless, and soon she fell asleep, oblivious now to the roiling, surging sea. When she awoke in the morning, the wind had dropped, and the waves had flattened, and the sun shone. And the little girl moved her arms out from under the covers and opened her hand to look at the magic charm that had protected her through the dreadful night. But there was nothing to be seen. 'Mumma,' she cried, 'my precious charm that protected me through the night has gone.' 'No, it is still here,' said her mother. 'In your fright you did not notice that all I did was to put the scared little fist that you had made with your right hand into the careful wrapping of your left hand. All through the night you held your own hand. You were your own good luck charm and you kept yourself safe.'

Kathryn listened to Sophia's tale with great interest. Yes, she could understand the point of it but there was something more that caught her attention, something she couldn't quite put her finger on.

Kathryn heard someone calling her name. She felt someone shaking her by the shoulders. She gripped her right fist in her left hand and hung on tenaciously.

'Kathryn, Kathryn. Are you all right?'

She forced her eyes open and saw that Margery, Sophia, Rainbow, and Geoff were gathered around her, concerned looks on their faces.

Though her mouth felt as if it were stuffed with cotton wool, Kathryn heard herself say, 'Yes. Yes. I'm fine. I think all that food, and then this comfortable chair, and the warmth of the fire, and Sophia's tale had sort of mesmerised me, put me to sleep.'

'Are you sure you're okay?' asked Geoff, picking up her wrist to check her pulse.

Kathryn shook herself off and stood up, though somewhat gingerly. 'Of course I'm okay,' she replied. 'In fact, I'm so okay, I'm thinking of taking an afternoon stroll along the beach. Anyone care to join me?'

<hr />

The beach's wide sweep of sand stretched between an embankment dotted with casuarinas and the crystal blue sea. The sun was already descending behind the trees and the sand, though still warm from the cloudless day, was in partial shadow. Toward the beach's rugged southern headland, on the limen of the trees and the sand, a family of wallabies was preparing for a late afternoon forage. Toward the jagged northern headland, a lone fisherman, two long rods anchored into the wet sand, was rummaging in a yellow bucket for more bait. As Kathryn and Sophia and Rainbow watched, he took something from the bucket and carefully attached it to one of the rods. Then, taking the rod out of its fixture, he shuffled closer to the water, drew the rod back over his right shoulder and cast the line out, out, up and out into the incoming waves before sticking the rod back into its holder and turning his attention to baiting the other rod.

'Look,' Rainbow shouted, her excitement travelling up and down the beach on the increasing wind. 'Look. A whale.'

Kathryn and Sophia directed their gaze along Rainbow's extended arm and into the distance. There, far out to sea, a whale was breaching the surface.

'That one's getting a head start on its northern migration, isn't it?' Rainbow smiled, her eyes reflecting the joyous movement of the huge mammal.

'In the Anglo-Saxon language, the sea is called the "whale road",' said Sophia absently.

'Ooh. I love that,' said Rainbow, clapping her hands. 'Do you have any stories about whales, Sophia?'

'Yes. Yes, I believe I do,' said Sophia. 'Shall we sit for a few minutes?' She stepped toward an unshaded area, taking off her shawl and spreading it on the sand before sitting down and motioning to the others to join her.

Long, long ago, in the time when all things had a meaning, and all meanings found a place in things, men wrote on parchment or vellum about beasts and animals. Today, we would describe some of those animals as real and others as mythical, but then such a distinction did not exist. Myth and reality were one and the same. The men's writings were compiled into what was called a 'bestiary', and there the description of each animal was accompanied by a symbolic interpretation and a moral lesson, particular to each beast. Now, the whale was by far the largest creature in the sea and so men feared the magnificent creature, believing that its gigantic back, floating above the sea's surface, collected sand on which grass would begin to grow so that, after a while, the whale would appear to be an island on which fishermen and other mariners could go ashore to enjoy a change from the tribulations of a sea voyage. And once there, they would light a fire and begin to prepare their meal. But when the heat of the cooking fire became too much for the whale, it would dive down under the water to cool itself and, in doing so, would take all the seamen with it to their deaths. Thus the symbolic interpretation of the whale came to be that it stood for deceit, luring those who failed to be alert to deception. I prefer to think of the whale as symbolising the importance of being aware of what is truly being presented to us and ...

Sophia's story lulled Kathryn into a sort of reverie. She wrapped her shawl more tightly around her back and shoulders, blocking out the growing wind, and let her eyes close. Behind her lids she pictured the whale, floating happily, minding its own business, as a boatload of fisherman pulled up on top of its back to prepare their evening meal.

Then Sophia stood, speaking to Kathryn in a quiet but commanding voice.

'Come,' she breathed, taking Kathryn's hand and leading her to the edge, where the water and sand met. 'Lie down here, in the moist sand, and feel the last vestiges of the day's sun on our bodies.'

Kathryn obeyed and, after stripping down to her underwear, she laid in the shallows where the feathery tails of the broken waves surprised her near-naked back with their coldness. The tide was coming in, and with the next rush of water, the complete rear surface of her supine body was wet. She shivered, laughed, and felt herself sinking into the wet shore, the sure and pleasurable weight of her body holding its position against the retreating wave which arranged itself around the obstruction to return, nevertheless, to its larger self. The next wave was bigger, and broke much closer in so that she was covered in the foam, over her head and face, and her breasts, stomach, legs, feet, all submerged with surprise. There wasn't time to coordinate her breath; she went under and when the wave pulled back, she gasped at the air. She noticed her body becoming lighter, unable to withstand the wave's force, and she felt herself lifted from the sand and buoyed out to sea a little way before being deposited on the earth again.

'Don't get up,' she heard Sophia call and she became aware of Sophia also being tossed, turned, and returned into the sinking sand somewhere to her left. She was not sure how long she laid there, fearing and delighting in the incoming tide, but she knew that the waves were getting larger, the gasping for air more necessary, and the lifting, floating, and depositing more treacherous. At some point, it was not foam that engulfed her, but the sea itself. A huge, unbreaking wave appeared, towering, rushing. She felt certain that it would crush her but, instead, it surged under her, severing all her contact with the supporting sand, and then, raising her above itself, supporting her in an elongated moment of weightlessness, it carried her on its crest safely into shore, into the dry warmth of sand far from the ocean's edge.

A strange sound. A knocking. 'Good morning, Kathryn. I'm here with your tea,' said Nicola.

{ 17 }

This is what she said:

There are rights, and there is Right. There are truths and there is Truth. There are loves, and there is Love. When we concentrate only on upholding the little rights, and truths, and loves, we are in danger of missing the point of life.

Kathryn was worried. Try as she might, she could not remember leaving the beach the previous afternoon and coming back to St Monica's and getting into bed. She remembered listening to Sophia's story of a whale, and she recalled some kind of wild immersion in the incoming tide, but she couldn't tell if it had been an actual experience or part of a dream. She sipped on the tea that Nicola had left for her but it gave her no refreshment, no clarity on what had happened the night before.

A thought occurred to her and, putting the teacup back on the tray, she hopped out of bed and hurried to the bathroom to look for the clothes—underwear, in particular—that she had been wearing yesterday. She saw the jeans and jumper and shawl hanging neatly on the hook behind the door. In the cuff of the jeans she noticed some sand. Its presence confirmed that she had been at the beach. The underwear she found hanging on the towel rail above the room heater. It was slightly damp but its position suggested it had probably been hung there to dry after being handwashed the previous evening. So, she could not be sure. Why did she have to resort to checking her clothing to see what she had been doing the day before? Why could she not simply recall the details of things that had taken place less than eighteen hours earlier? Why had she been losing the latter part of every day she had been at St Monica's?

Her thoughts were interrupted by the sudden ringing of her mobile. She followed the ringing to her dressing gown, lying across the end of her bed, and retrieved the phone from its pocket.

'You took your time answering. Are you okay?' said a male voice that Kathryn did not immediately recognise.

'Who is it?' she asked.

'It's me, Tim. Did I wake you?'

'No, no. Sorry, Tim. I was just deep in thought about something,' Kathryn replied, still surprised that what should have been a familiar voice sounded so strange to her ear.

'Are you sure you're all right?' Tim persisted. 'You sound a bit … out of it.'

'Yes, I'm good. I'm great. Very relaxed. It must be the connection. You sound a bit strange too.'

'Well, I've got a reason for sounding strange,' said Tim. 'Look, I've hesitated about telling you this. I didn't want to worry you, but I think you need to know. The Federal Police called me yesterday on behalf of Interpol. Interpol are interested in Sophia. I haven't told them where she is, but what can I do? I'm a doctor, a responsible member of society. I'll have to let them know that she's down there at St Monica's with you.'

'No, Tim, you can't. She's doing so much good here. There's a woman here, Rainbow, but she used to be Robyn. You know, the one who witnessed Julie bringing the dead cat back to life.'

'Kathryn, you're rambling. I've got two days off after I finish here this afternoon. I'm coming down. That's for certain. But the only thing I'm not sure about is whether I'll ring that Interpol officer now or after I arrive.'

'Please, Tim. Don't do anything yet. And there's no need for you to drive all the way down here. I'm planning to come back to Sydney after the weekend so I'll bring Sophia with me. But what's all this about Interpol?'

'Apparently, a woman calling herself Sophia, and matching the broad description of our very own Sophia, was reported missing from Norwich about twenty years ago. In addition, there are reports of a woman, or women, of that same description, popping up and disappearing all over England for the last eighty years or so, ever since Interpol, in its earlier presence as the ICPC, has been around.'

'Well, that's not a crime, is it? To be here, then there?' Kathryn challenged.

'No, that's not a crime. But when someone is accused of fraud, specifically accepting money and accommodation from others by pretending to help them with emotional and personal issues, then it's a crime,' Tim insisted.

'I see what you're getting at, Tim. But Sophia is not manipulating me for her own profit, nor is she defrauding anyone else. It's all in the eye of the beholder.' Kathryn was definite.

'Eye of the beholder. That's what the Federal Police officer said,' reflected Tim.

'There, then, there's no issue. If the Federal Police or Interpol don't see Sophia as a risk then neither should we. If they contact you again, just direct them to me. I'll simply explain that Sophia is under my professional care until such time as a relative can be located. And, if no such person can be found, then I will explain that we will take responsibility for rehabilitating Sophia to the level of getting a job and looking after herself. See, all good,' concluded Kathryn.

'As you command, Dr Brookley. I'll stay put until you get back and I'll leave our mystery patient to you for the time being, but I hope you know what you're doing, Kathryn,' said Tim. 'Sophia may not be as she seems.'

'Then it is my job to uncover the real person, isn't it? Now, have a good day at work and then relax and enjoy your days off. I'll call you when I'm back, probably on Monday or Tuesday,' finished Kathryn, firmly pushing the phone's 'end' button.

The Seaview Café was abuzz when Kathryn arrived for breakfast. The tables were packed with residents who'd obviously lingered over their meals in the less hurried atmosphere of a sunny Saturday morning. Cheery music was piping through the café's sound system and the wait staff were bustling to replenish the buffet tables. Kathryn glanced around, looking for Geoff or Margery or Nicola or one of her other acquaintances, but to no avail. Then, through the crowd, she caught sight of Sophia's distinctive cropped head, bobbing in apparently animated conversation with someone at a table in the quieter westerly corner of the Seaview. She began to make her way across the room toward her. As she got closer, however, she saw that Sophia was sitting with Rainbow, who was dabbing her eyes with a large handkerchief.

'Why are you upsetting her?' began Kathryn, even before she was level with the table.

Sophia and Rainbow looked up in surprise.

'Upsetting me?' said Rainbow, removing the handkerchief from in front of her face and scrunching it into a ball in her palm. 'She was making me laugh with her suggestions of the kinds of animals I might knit.'

'Sit with us, Kathryn,' directed Sophia, pushing back a chair for her. 'Here, I'll pour you a coffee. We've been here so long, the waiter brought us a whole pot of it. Milk?'

'Yes, thank you,' Kathryn said tentatively. Turning her attention to Rainbow she said, 'I thought you were crying.'

'I was crying. Crying with laughter, as we discussed our idea of a new shop selling the art and craft produced at St Monica's,' explained Rainbow, her face alight with enthusiasm. 'We've already run a rough plan by Margery earlier this morning and she's agreed to fund a small retail space in the town centre. There's a vacant shop on the seaside strip and I've already phoned the agent about leasing it for a twelve-month trial. We'll be outfitting it by the end of the week. And then we'll move the stock in during the following week. I'll be, once again, creating my marvellous knitted animals. And not just dogs and cats but fish, dolphins, maybe even a whale or two. And there'll be the residents' wonderful jumpers and toys, and paintings and pottery. I'll work there a couple of days a week, and others will be there when I'm doing my activities officer job. Of course, because of Margery's need to keep St Monica's out of the public eye, we won't be advertising our creations as coming from St Monica's. We're thinking of calling it *Sea Craft*. And all the profits will go to charity.'

'That sounds really exciting,' said Kathryn, genuinely pleased to see Rainbow in such a positive mood.

'But I haven't told you the best bit yet,' Rainbow gushed, holding up her hands and waving them in little excited oscillations. 'Guess who's going to be working in the shop with me. No, don't guess. I want to tell you. Sophia. Sophia. Isn't it miraculous?'

Kathryn's mouth opened, but no words came out.

◦━━◆━━◦

The rest of the weekend passed in a blur for Kathryn. There were lunches on the grand terrace, and walks along the beach, and quiet hours for reading by the fire in the upstairs sitting room. At morning tea time on Sunday, a mariachi band appeared as if from nowhere, encouraging residents to dance and to follow them all around the home in a wild romp reminiscent of the Pied Piper leading the children away. On Sunday afternoon, an ice-cream van parked on the wide front lawn and its vendor distributed crispy cones topped with every imaginable colour and flavour. It was a riotous, joyous time and, as had been happening all during her stay, on Saturday and Sunday nights Kathryn fell into an exhausted sleep that was crammed with dreams so vivid that they seemed to take over the reality of the evenings' events.

◦━━◆━━◦

Monday morning, the day of Kathryn's planned departure from St Monica's, was cold and dismal. After drinking the hot tea Nicola had delivered, Kathryn lay in bed listening to the wind lashing heavy sheets of rain against the bedroom windows. She had little inclination to get up, let alone organise herself for the return drive to the city and her everyday life. She sank back down under the covers and let her eyes close again, savouring the softness of the mattress under her spine and the security of the blankets over her. She was aware of her chest, rising and falling gently with each inhalation and exhalation, and of the pounding rain outside stamping out a violent contra-rhythm to the peace within. This is what the time at St Monica's (and, indeed, the whole experience of meeting and interacting with Sophia) had been like: a welcome oasis within the maelstrom that whirled around Kathryn's home and work life.

She must have dozed off because when a loud knock at the bedroom door startled her to sitting, she grabbed for her phone to find that it was almost nine o'clock, a full hour since Nicola had been in with the tea and only two hours before her scheduled meeting with Geoff, Margery and Sophia.

'Just a minute,' she called in the direction of the closed door, hopping out of bed to pull on her dressing gown and slippers. 'Okay, come on in,' she continued, running fingers through her tousled hair in an effort to look presentable.

'Oh, Kathryn. I'm sorry. I had no idea that you were just awake.'

It was Sophia, standing tentatively in the doorway, a concerned expression on her face.

'No, not at all. Please come in. I confess I did fall back to sleep but I hadn't intended to. I'm very glad that you knocked on my door or I might have missed not only breakfast but also my day's numerous other commitments,' said Kathryn, beckoning the young woman into the room and toward the sofa by the window.

Sophia took a seat as directed and, swivelling her body slightly so that she could gaze out the window, she said, 'Look at this lovely rain. Water and love—both essential for life. Though, of course, you can have too much of the former but never too much of the latter.'

'Very true.' Kathryn smiled, taking a position on the other end of the sofa. 'So, Sophia, to what do I owe the honour of this visit?'

'I wanted to apologise for the manner in which you found out about the plans for the craft shop,' she began. 'I had intended to discuss the idea with you but, well, you happened in on our discussion and I think Rainbow was so excited that she forgot that I am here only under your auspices and supervision.'

'I appreciate the apology,' Kathryn responded, 'but, in fact, the incident raised a number of important issues for me so I'm glad, actually, that it happened the way it did.'

Sophia cocked her head to one side. 'Can you say a little more about those issues?'

'Well, the fact is that we are in a doctor–patient relationship but, to be honest, sometimes I'm not sure which one of us is in which role. What I mean is, you've helped me at least as much as I've helped you, Sophia. So when the idea of you staying on here and working in the craft shop was sprung on me yesterday, I didn't feel that it was really my place to tell you not to do so. Yes, from the professional standpoint, *we* don't know who you are or where you've come from but, from your own point of view, *you* have asserted that you know exactly who you are and why you're here. And, thus, if I cannot reliably say that you are in need of psychiatric care—and, I cannot—then I should declare you mentally and emotionally well and, therefore, able to make your own decisions and manage your own life. And that would entail you having the right to say that you want to stay here and work in the shop with Rainbow.'

'Are you saying, Kathryn, that I am no longer … I'm not sure what the correct term here would be … No longer under suspicion?'

'You were never under any suspicion as far as I was concerned, Sophia. It's just that I, and others at the hospital, were concerned for your health and wellbeing and so we assumed medical responsibility and oversight of your general welfare in the absence of relatives and friends. If a parent, or a sibling, or a spouse had turned up to reliably identify you, we would have discharged you into that person's care. Perhaps … probably, I would have recommended follow-up monitoring at the outpatients psych clinic for a time, maybe in the hope that your memory would return. There may have still been questions in my mind about your claims of having lived continuously too. You'll appreciate that such claims sit awkwardly with current ways of thinking and doing things, especially in the medical world.'

Sophia seemed to take no notice of Kathryn's reference to her claims of a continuous life and, instead, embraced the first part of Kathryn's statement. 'So, I'm free to stay here for a time to help Rainbow get started on her shop?'

'Not exactly,' said Kathryn, the tone of her voice tightening. 'That would have been the case until yesterday when Tim Mason phoned me to say that he had been contacted by the Australian Federal Police about you.' Kathryn paused to give Sophia a few moments to absorb this piece of information, but the young woman's expression did not change. She appeared completely unfazed by the news so Kathryn continued: 'Interpol has records of a person, or persons, matching your description in the Norwich area of England.'

'No doubt, when you say "persons" you are referring to multiple sightings of someone just like me. Sightings over time, I would think. Sightings over quite a time.'

Kathryn nodded. 'What do you know about this, Sophia?'

'I know that I have been in many places, in many times. But, as it has happened, most of the times, and most of the places, have been in England. At all times, my work has been for the good, but there are always those who condemn what they do not understand. Sometimes, it has been necessary for me to leave a place in a hurry, not just for my own good but for the good of those with whom I was working. Do you understand what I'm telling you, Kathryn?'

'I believe I do,' said Kathryn. 'But, because of the very problems that you have just described, I think it wiser that I don't set you totally free at this stage. I've been thinking that the best option is for me to continue to take professional responsibility for you, insofar as arranging for you to stay here for … say, six or eight weeks, initially … as a time of rest and recuperation. A time of therapy, let's say. That should buy us some time with Interpol. And who knows? Maybe you'll be so successful in your new retail career that when I reassess you, I'll be able to inform Interpol and hospital authorities that—firm identity or not—you are working to support yourself and can be safely discharged on your own recognisance. What do you think?'

'I agree,' said Sophia, 'though I'm sure you realise that I do not usually stay in one place for long.'

'I don't need to know that, Sophia,' Kathryn cautioned. 'If I deem you to be managing well in eight weeks' time, and if no further information—good or bad—comes to light about you from the investigative sources, then I can act in good conscience and discharge you. What you do after that is entirely your business. Now, I'm going to get ready for the day and try to fit in some coffee and toast before our meeting in Geoff's office at ten.'

'I understand. Thank you, Kathryn. See you soon,' Sophia called over her shoulder as she headed for the door.

◦══✦══◦

It was unusually quiet in the Seaview Café when Kathryn entered. The pelting rain had joined the cascading water of the clear roof's reticulation feature, making the whole room seem as if it were a giant air bubble of life underneath a surging sea.

'Hi, Kathryn. Over here,' someone called to her. It was Geoff, seated by the buffet table, which was now cleared of everything except its white cloth.

Kathryn walked across to join him. 'I'm surprised to find you in here at this hour of the day.'

'I'm surprised to see you too. You're usually up and at 'em much earlier.'

'I overslept,' Kathryn confessed. 'And then I had a visit from Sophia. So, as you see, it's extra late. Too late for breakfast it seems.' She rolled her eyes in the direction of the empty buffet table.

'Maybe. What would you like? I'm sure there's something left over. How about a croissant?' Geoff suggested.

'I really only wanted toast,' Kathryn said.

Geoff waved his arm in the air and, as if from nowhere, one of the café's wait staff appeared next to the table.

'Could you bring Dr Brookley some toast?' he asked.

'No, really, no need to go to the trouble,' said Kathryn.

'No trouble at all.' The waiter smiled. 'It's practically in the toaster now. Butter? Jam? Coffee?'

'All of the above, thank you,' she replied. The waiter hurried off toward the kitchen. 'Everyone's so nice and helpful here. Happy, too.'

'Why wouldn't they be? You've seen what this place is like. Margery lavishes love upon it and all its inhabitants—staff as well as residents. I'm not joking when I say that after I'm too old to work here I want to move in as a resident.'

'Yes, I do see how wonderful it is. I also see that Margery is wonderful but … well … a little unusual. Eccentric.' Kathryn's words were cautious. 'Hmm. I'm wondering how to open this conversation. I'll begin by saying that I'm really pleased to find you here because it gives me the chance to talk to you before our meeting with Margery and Sophia.'

Geoff's full attention was fixed on Kathryn. 'You know you can speak honestly with me. What's up?'

'Okay. Do you know that Margery has agreed to fund a craft shop in town? And that the plan is for Rainbow to work there a few days a week?'

'Yep. Margery ran it by me as soon as it came up. I think it is a great opportunity for Rainbow, and for any of St Monica's residents who want to be involved. And, as the profits are going to charity, it's a great contribution to the community too.'

'But did you know that the plan is for Sophia to stay here and to work in the shop too?'

'Yep, I know that too,' replied Geoff. 'I thought that was one of the things we'd be discussing at our meeting this morning.'

'Yes, we will. But actually, Sophia's already spoken to me and I didn't want to spring something on you.'

'Spring away, Kathryn. I trust your judgment.'

'I'll leave the details till the meeting then. But what I'd like to know, from you, Geoff, is how you feel about this idea of Sophia staying here for a while.'

'I'm fine with it,' said Geoff. 'Shouldn't I be?'

The waiter arrived with the coffee and toast then hurried off again. Kathryn began buttering a slice, keeping her eyes downcast when she next spoke. 'I'll be candid, Geoff. As you know, Sophia has told me that she has been continuously alive since the fourteenth century. In addition, my own research into the matter, and Margery's and Rainbow's views and reactions to Sophia, indicate that she is also the same woman as the Julie X who was pulled from Sydney Harbour in 1973, over forty years ago. As a psychiatrist I cannot believe it. As a woman looking at it through the eyes of my own experience, I can and do believe it. Now, I'm prepared to put myself on the line—profession-ally as well as personally—over this, but I'm worried about drawing you into something that might jeopardise your nursing career. Do you understand what I'm saying? Be honest with me. Do you believe what Sophia says? If you don't, that's fine but then the question is, are you prepared to take her in at St Monica's for eight weeks knowing that she might exert her influence over many people in your care?'

Geoff spread his palms over the table's surface, using it as a base from which to stretch his arms out and take a deep breath. Then he let his arms, his shoulders, and the features of his face relax before he smiled at Kathryn. 'When you first arrived, I told you my story. I was on the street when Margery's people found me. I regard it as a miracle that I was found, that I was chosen, that I was offered a second chance. I regard it as a miracle that I was given the job of nursing manager here at St Monica's. I regard St Monica's and all its people and all its brilliant activities as miracles. I am surrounded by miracles, even in the ordinary, everyday things such as ordering toast and having it brought to my table. My life is a blessing and a miracle. So, in answer to your question, "Do I believe what Sophia says?" I can only answer "Yes, absolutely". Whether it is actually true or not is irrelevant to me. I believe it. And I believe her because what she says affects people for the better; what she does changes people. All those years ago, Julie X changed Margery. Now Margery changes others. Whether Sophia is the same woman as Julie X matters not one bit to me. What matters is that Julie or Sophia—as the same person or two separate people—bring about transformation in others. It's what you want to do in your practice of psychiatry. It's what I want to do in my nursing practice. It's what Julie and Sophia and Margery are doing in their own unique ways. So, as to your other question of whether I'm prepared to have Sophia here for eight weeks, my answer is, without hesitation, "Yes". And if, in the process, Sophia transforms every resident and every staff member in the place—including and especially me—I will be cheering.'

Kathryn could only manage a simple 'Thank you' in response.

Geoff reached across the table and patted Kathryn's hand before he stood up. 'So, finish your toast. I'm off to do a few things in the fifteen minutes before our meeting. Don't rush. See you then.'

Geoff, Margery, and Sophia were already seated in plump armchairs around Geoff's office's coffee table and chatting noisily when Kathryn arrived for the meeting.

'Good morning all. Sorry to keep you waiting. I didn't realise I was late,' she said as she rushed in and noticed all faces turning to her.

'You're not late.' Geoff smiled. 'We're all early. This cold snap has everyone looking for comfort food. And what better than hot chocolate and these delicious scones that the kitchen has brought us for morning tea.'

'Yes, we just followed the scones into Geoff's office,' said Margery. 'When they arrived, so did we.'

'Here, Kathryn. For you,' said Sophia, handing over a mug of hot, creamy chocolate as Kathryn took her seat in the circle.

'Thank you.' Kathryn sighed, leaning back into the rich padding of the chair. 'I'm going to miss all this good food and pampering. Mind you, my bathroom scales might give me a different message.'

'Then throw them out,' Margery advised. 'A little of what you fancy is always good for the soul. That's my motto, anyway.'

'Truly, I'm going to miss you all. It's been extraordinary,' said Kathryn.

'Well, of course, you'll be back, won't you?' asked Geoff. 'So, I propose that we address this small matter of our Miss Sophia-from-the-Sea. It shouldn't take long, and once the discussion is out of the way we can give our full attention to the scones.'

There was murmured agreement all round.

'Actually, Sophia and I have had a preliminary discussion about it, haven't we?' Kathryn announced, turning to Sophia for acknowledgment. When the young woman smiled and nodded, Kathryn continued, speaking to all around the table generally but addressing her comments more directly to Geoff. 'We agreed that Sophia should stay here for a period of eight weeks, during which time she will still be officially my patient but under your professional supervision, Geoff. I will arrange an authorisation that allows her to work with Rainbow in setting up the new craft shop but, because she will remain a "rehabilitation patient" for this period, Sophia will need to report to you every day, Geoff, and you in turn will consult with me as the supervising doctor. The two of us, therefore, will be responsible for all matters of her health and wellbeing. Of course, as a patient, Sophia will receive no payment for her work in the shop, but if she does well and finds that the job suits her perhaps, after the eight weeks, and if it's agreeable to all parties, Sophia might be discharged from my care and oversight and take up employment here as a fully independent person. In such an outcome, Sophia would be responsible for funding and maintaining her own place of residence and lifestyle. And, I should add, all of this is dependent on police investigations turning up no findings on Sophia's identity and/or previous activities that would jeopardise this arrangement. That's our idea, anyway. Geoff, Margery, what do you think?'

'I love it,' said Margery, clapping her hands together. 'It will be wonderful to have Sophia around each day and, now that Rainbow is so taken with her too—and seems to have found a new confidence and purpose in life with the shop project—I see your plan as benefiting St Monica's in every way.'

'What can I say?' said Geoff, shrugging his shoulders. 'I think it's a good plan. As Margery has said, we're very happy to have Sophia here for eight weeks. And it gives you some peace of mind, too, Kathryn. I'll phone or email you each day and, in the unlikely event that there's a problem, I'll be in touch with you instantly.'

'Yes, and we'll all be looking out for her, so don't you worry about anything, Kathryn,' Margery added.

When she had finished her hot chocolate, Kathryn walked over to Geoff's desk with him and, in her official capacity as Dr Kathryn Brookley, she signed the authority that directed Sophia X into the care of Nurse Geoffrey Briar and his staff. She then signed the permission to allow Sophia X to work in the soon-to-be-opened Sea Craft shop as part of her rehabilitation. All that remained for Kathryn to do was to make her goodbyes.

Returning to the little group gathered around the coffee table, she said, 'I came here just over a week ago to see if I could resolve a few questions around our lovely Sophia. I don't know if I managed to answer those questions but I did manage to learn so much more. I've had fascinating experiences. I've had the opportunity to rest and relax in these beautiful surroundings. I've been wined and dined. But, best of all, I've met all of you. I'm so grateful.' Kathryn made her way around the circle, hugging Geoff and then Margery. As she came to Sophia she had to suppress an urge to cry.

As if reading her thoughts, Sophia said, 'You know that this is not yet goodbye. We still have work to do together.'

{ 18 }

This is what she said:

Love is never wasted, even if it is not reciprocated. For in loving—no matter what—we enlarge ourselves, becoming bigger than the small prejudices and petty jealousies and pointless vindictiveness that can engulf us if we let fear rule our lives. When we determine to love—no matter what—we lighten ourselves and become able to rise up, float above, the turmoil of doubt and indecisiveness and procrastination that can overtake us in the surging rush of time. Loving—no matter what—does not end life's pain and suffering, but it does allow us to endure in spite of it, and to embrace a larger actuality.

Exhilarating as the days at St Monica's had been, they had also been exhausting and Kathryn was very grateful, on her return to Sydney, that she still had another week's scheduled leave. She spent much of it pottering around her home or driving to the Cottage Point weekender during the day and sitting on the deck, reading, in the warm late autumn sun. For reasons that she could not quite identify—and despite the exciting events around her newest 'patient' Sophia—her past lack of motivation for her job persisted and when, the following week, she did reluctantly return to work, she found herself handing the majority of new referrals over to an eager young registrar. The settling in of winter only added to her despondency. As the days became shorter and colder, Kathryn became even less motivated to leave her warm bed and make her way into the dark morning to check on her patients. Some days she felt like she was dragging a heavy weight behind her as she left the house for her office and the hospital. Her bones had begun to ache as the chill in the air increased and, often, in the middle of a consultation, she would catch herself pushing her hands up the opposite sleeves of her cardigan or jacket in an effort to warm her freezing hands. At other times, she would suddenly become aware that she had not been listening to her patients at all but, instead, had been daydreaming about the warm upstairs sitting room at St Monica's or the soft bed there in which she had spent many nights dreaming of millponds and moonlight and balmy breezes.

Geoff's daily email or phone reports on Sophia contributed, no doubt, to St Monica's being in the forefront of her mind so, with June drawing to a close and Sophia's eight-week 'rehab' program at the home speeding on, Kathryn felt relieved to have the opportunity to rethink the situation—for all concerned. She was glad that Sophia had been managing so well at St Monica's and in the Sea Craft shop. It vindicated her professional opinion that Sophia was sane and capable of functioning in everyday life. But as July set in, bringing with it clear, cold skies, blustery southerly winds and lower than average temperatures, her previous niggling worry about nothing and everything escalated with the winds into a full-blown dread that something was about to go very wrong. It came as no surprise, therefore, when she received a call from Officer Mackatt of the Australian Federal Police.

'Good morning, Dr Brookley,' he began. 'I believe you'll have heard of me via your colleague, Dr Tim Mason. I called him several weeks ago in regard to an Interpol report on an unidentified woman. I understand she calls herself "Sophia" and that you are supervising her case at present.'

'Yes, Officer Mackatt. Dr Mason told me about your call. I am looking out for Sophia's health and general wellbeing. How can I help you?' Kathryn, in her uneasy state, wanted to get to the point.

'Nothing too much to worry about. In one way, I've got good news. As there have been no further complaints or reports about Sophia and/or the woman who matched her description, Interpol is stepping down its level of interest in her. On the other hand, as no one has come forward to identify her, and as she is still unable to firmly identify herself, the matter has been passed onto the Department of Immigration—they'll be checking on illegal entry, that sort of thing, because of the similar reports coming out of England—and also to the Attorney-General's Department under requirements laid down by the National Identity Security Strategy, or NISS as we say.'

'I see. And what does that mean for Sophia, and for me as her doctor?'

'Well, initially, it means that officials from the Department of Immigration will want to interview Sophia. If it's all right with you, the relevant paperwork will be sent to your office address on Sophia's behalf. I'm told, too, that a tentative appointment has been made for her for next Tuesday at two pm for this initial interview. It would help if you accompanied her. After that, who knows? Probably further investigation. It can be a long process so … one step at a time. No dramas. Well, not at this stage. So, would you like to tell Sophia about this or would you prefer that I contacted her directly?'

'No, thank you, Officer. I'll let Sophia know. And I'll get her to the interview next week. Anything else?'

'That's it, for the moment at least,' the officer replied. 'I'll call you if anything else comes up for us but, in the main, it's over to other government agencies now.'

'Right. Well, thanks for calling.' Kathryn noticed her hands were shaking as she ended the call. They were still shaking as she flicked through her regular contacts and selected Geoff Briar.

Geoff answered quickly, and in his usual bright manner. 'Hi Kathryn. How are you this cold, miserable day?'

'A bit miserable myself, Geoff. I've just had a call from that Federal Police officer I told you about. Anyway, he and his people aren't interested in Sophia anymore, but Immigration is. She's got an interview with them next Tuesday. She'll have to come back to Sydney earlier than planned.'

'No problem. I've got a few days off. How about I drive her back myself tomorrow?'

'That would be wonderful, Geoff. And please, bring her to our place. I'm sure Richard won't mind Sophia staying for a couple of days until I figure out what's best for her. Why don't you stay and have a few days with us too?

'Fantastic. Text me your address. We'll be there by lunchtime.'

Kathryn broached the subject of the impending arrivals at their home when she and Richard were settling down in their lounge room for a quiet after-dinner coffee that evening.

'Richard, I hope you won't mind but I've invited Sophia, and Geoff—you know the nursing manager at St Monica's—to stay here with us for a couple of days.'

Richard raised his eyebrows. 'No, I don't mind, your friends are always welcome. But why? And how long is a couple of days?'

'The fact is, Richard, the Department of Immigration is going to interview Sophia next week so she needs to come back to Sydney a bit earlier than expected. And Geoff has kindly offered to drive her so he's going to have a short break with us too.'

'Kathryn, you seem nervous about telling me this.'

'I guess I am, a little. I know how you feel about Sophia. I know you're suspicious of her claims. I feel awkward about making you feel uncomfortable in your own home … now that you're finally back,' she explained.

'Firstly, it's your home too. Secondly, I'm not going to feel uncomfortable about it because, thirdly, despite my misgivings about Sophia and all the strangeness that we've both experienced, I've softened my attitude toward her because she has, directly or indirectly, brought us back together. And who knows? Maybe she's for real after all. Open mind, I say. I can see that she and your other St Monica's friends have had a positive effect on you, so I'm going to be an exemplary host to both of your visitors.'

Kathryn smiled at Richard and had picked up her coffee cup to take a sip when the wind chime on their back veranda suddenly clattered wildly. She jumped, then started to shiver violently.

'It's only the wind,' said Richard. 'Are you okay? You're shaking.'

'Yes, I'm just feeling cold,' she replied.

'The cold never used to bother you. Now I come home each evening to find you sitting huddled in front of an electric heater, despite what I consider to be a very effective under-floor heating system in this house. Would you like me to turn it up?'

'No, just come and sit near me,' she said. She waited until Richard was at her side. 'I feel everything more intensely now. It's as if this whole thing with Sophia has made me more alert, more awake. And yes, don't laugh. I know I've been sleeping a lot more lately. But I mean that the world is more vivid, more alive to me. Colours are brighter, smells are stronger. Sounds are different. I know you weren't too sure about Sophia at first. And I realise you don't believe anything she's said about living continuously but, in a way, that doesn't matter to me. The important thing is that you recognise that she's made a difference to a lot of people. Not just me. But yes, she has made my life better.'

'Tell me more about that, Kathryn. Haven't I made you feel better too? Isn't our life good now, even if we leave Sophia out of the equation?'

'Of course it is, Richard. And yet, you know as well as I do that we were nursing a huge sadness. Losing Matthew broke our hearts, broke us in every way. But spending that time with Sophia, hearing her stories, seeing how others like Margery and Rainbow overcame their own heartbreaks, taught me something profound.'

'Which is?' asked Richard, taking her face in his hands and turning it to look directly at him.

'Well, that life is life. That there are wonderful moments, and there are times of long, drawn-out pain and suffering. No life is without some level of pain, and no life is without some level of beauty and wonder. But Sophia also showed me that life is not all that there is. Matthew is somewhere, love is somewhere and, even though they're just out of reach, I know that they're there. And that knowing, which is actually more like an "unknowing"—a letting go of what I've always thought I knew—is what Sophia gave me. Or, more truthfully, she helped me remember what I had forgotten. I'm not talking about religion here, Richard, I'm talking about something much more innate, much more important, much more powerful. I can't describe it. There are no words, because words get us through life, but they don't get us beyond it.'

'Kathryn, I don't really understand what you're saying but, yeah, I get the idea that there are things that are bigger, deeper, more important than words. Like love. That's the biggest one, isn't it? And I know that I really love you.'

'I love you too, Richard. How did we lose our way?' Kathryn asked, resting her head gently on Richard's shoulder.

'Too much pain will do that.' His voice was ragged. 'Too much.'

'But we should have known better. We're doctors. We treat people in pain, emotional pain especially, every day,' she reminded him.

'Physician heal thyself,' he said without any hint of sarcasm. 'Sometimes there's a very wide gap between theory and practice.'

He put his arms around her and drew her into a tight hug.

After a time, Kathryn gently wriggled from the embrace and moved from the sofa to sit on the floor, arranging cushions around her. Then she held her hand out to him, inviting him to sit next to her. He dipped down, stretching his long legs awkwardly in front before plumping the cushions behind his lower back. Kathryn leant into him and he responded by wrapping his arms around her. She looked up at him, grateful for the closeness, and he bent and brushed her mouth with his lips. When she didn't object, he kissed her more deeply.

Slowly, deliberately, she unbuttoned his shirt and laid her warm hand on his bare chest. More slowly, she moved her hand across the coarse chest hair and let it come to rest over his heart. She held it there for an extended time, feeling the regular beats, and the intake and release of his breath. Then she removed her hand and, lying back on a cushion, she unbuttoned her own blouse. Richard reached to hold her breast but, quietly, she redirected his hand to the space over her heart and she held it there. She sensed more than heard Richard's gasp, but she clearly heard his first sob. It shook him, and he pulled her close to him and, as if he would never let go, he cried as if his tears would fill the ocean. She cried too, as their bodies merged in all the love and sorrow of their lives.

A phone's piercing ring woke Kathryn and Richard simultaneously, propelling them both from each other's arms and up to a dazed sitting position amid a tangle of blankets.

'It's yours, Kathryn,' said Richard, indicating the shuddering mobile on her bedside table.

Kathryn was surprised to receive the call to attend a dying patient. Her surprise was not because it was three am (although, with modern medication, the late-night call-outs for specialist psychiatrists were uncommon), but because of who the patient was. She knew Dorothy, but only as a passing acquaintance—the efficient and seemingly immortal assistant to the enigmatic Dr Smith and, more recently, as the secretary to the group of doctors who had taken over Dr Smith's practice after his retirement and who had arranged her receipt of the Julie X file.

It was Tim who called Kathryn with the request. He had been rostered in Emergency when Dorothy was brought in and he had moved her quickly to Cardiac Intensive Care, but she had deteriorated rapidly. He was called back to attend her until the cardiac specialist arrived and it was there, in the little cubicle created by green curtains that Dorothy had feebly clutched his arm.

'Bring Kathryn Brookley to me, please. It's urgent.'

⟨═══◆═══⟩

'Over here,' said the nurse, ushering Kathryn swiftly into the cubicle.

'I'm here, Dorothy. It's Kathryn Brookley.'

'I need to confess,' Dorothy gasped, her breath coming at short, raspy intervals. Her body was propped up by several pillows at her back and sides but she was slumped to the left, her eyes glassy and staring, her hands distended by twisted, mauve veins. Kathryn attempted to make her more comfortable, but Dorothy gave a weak, dismissive wave.

'Shall I call a priest?' asked Kathryn.

'No. No. It's you I need to confess to,' she said, her distress hanging heavily around the bed.

'All right. Try to stay calm. I'm listening. I'm here for you,' Kathryn assured her, speaking quietly and trying to maintain professional confidence as she took the old woman's hand in hers.

Dorothy's breath was slow—five laborious in and out respirations and then nothing … nothing for long seconds. And then more laborious breaths, four, six, and then stillness. Breath, breath, breath, breath, stillness … On the breaths she tried to speak.

'I want to tell you a story,' she insisted.

Long ago, long ago, two little sisters, in the park, with their mother … A balloon seller. Please, please, Mummy, Mummy, Mummy … What colour? Red like the flowers, yellow like the sun. Red. Yellow. … Let it go, says my sister. It's yellow like the sun; let it go, to its place in the sky … No, it's mine. You let yours go. Not mine, not to the sky. No, no … She let hers go, up and up went the red balloon. She laughed. I held onto mine. It popped into shreds in my hands … I cried, at the tatters. Her balloon soared. My life, her life … Tattered. Soaring. Tattered. Soaring. Tattered …

Dorothy lapsed into sleep for fifteen minutes, but she was unsettled, groaning, clutching at Kathryn's hand. After a time she seemed to force herself awake and tried to speak, but her voice was so weak that Kathryn had to put her ears within centimetres of the old woman's mouth.

'The file … Julie X … and the other young woman, the present one I've heard about,' Dorothy began, struggling. Her lips were pale and dry, her voice as light and crackly as crumpled cellophane. 'Forty years ago … I knew Julie X. She tried … to help me … but I didn't think I needed help … Dr Smith, he believed her, believed everything she said.' Suddenly, her breathing seemed to stop, her eyes closing, and Kathryn could feel the effort that the old woman made to take another shallow inhalation, and then another, so that she could continue. 'People, colleagues … were laughing at him. Someone … had to be sensible, professional. I … just wanted … to protect him.' Dorothy smiled at this and, with palpable effort, lifted her head and eyes slightly so that she was looking into Kathryn's face. 'We were friends, you know … Dr Smith and I. … I loved him. … And I should have supported him.' Her eyes closed again and her breath became a series of fluttering sighs. 'But I worked to discredit her … I vilified her. Told everyone I could that … she was a fraud … That she was only after money. She … saw … right … through … me. She knew how empty … cold and empty … I was inside. I hated her because Dr Smith loved her. I couldn't forgive him … for loving her … and not me. … Julie said she forgave me. I didn't want her forgiveness. I wanted her … gone. I rejoiced when she disappeared.' Dorothy paused, laid her head back on the pillows and closed her eyes. She was quiet for a moment and then she took a concerted breath, which she seemed to use to push out the next part of her confession fluently, unfalteringly. 'Still, he forgave me, just like Julie. That was how they were. They had both learnt the lesson. They both reached understanding. Dr Smith understood so much that he left psychiatry. Left me. Left me far behind, in tatters. And then, before I could decide what to do, he died. He went to her, I know. And now, forty years later, she is back.' Dorothy had tears running down her cheeks from beneath her closed eyelids. Her mouth continued to move, opening and closing like a goldfish on the endless circuit of its bowl and Kathryn leant close to Dorothy in case she was trying to say more. There was no sound beyond the touching and parting of the lips and so Kathryn sat up again and asked, as gently as possible, 'Are you saying that you believe that our present young woman, Sophia, and the Julie that you knew all those years ago, are the same person?'

'I want to see her,' Dorothy replied. 'I cannot go till I see her.' Despite her failing breath Dorothy shifted restlessly on the bed, her eyes flickering open again but focusing on nothing.

Kathryn phoned Geoff. Despite it being only shortly after four am he answered promptly. 'So sorry to bother you at this crazy hour but I'm with a dying patient who is asking to see Sophia. I know you were coming up to Sydney today anyway so … um … is it possible that you could bring her here a bit earlier? Like now.'

'Kathryn. Are you wondering why I answered this call so quickly? It's because Sophia woke me about half an hour ago to tell me that we had to leave for Sydney immediately. She's already dressed, packed, and ready to go. I'm doing my best to do the same. We'll be right to leave in about ten minutes. The roads will be pretty clear at this hour so we should be there in about two and a half hours max. No problems.'

As good as his word, Geoff walked into the ward with Sophia just after six am. Sophia went confidently to Dorothy's bedside. 'I am here, Dorothy,' she whispered, gently laying her hand on the old woman's shoulder.

'Is it you? Is it too late?' Dorothy asked, reaching desperately for the young woman's hand, blindly grasping at the air around her. Sophia leant in closely to the old lady and whispered something in her ear.

'But I have wasted my chance,' declared Dorothy, beginning to sob. The sound was feeble but heart-wrenching for all present.

'Nothing is wasted, Dorothy.' Sophia's voice was strong and clear. '"Better late than never" is a very good adage,' she said, laughing. 'You do not need to fear anymore. As Julian of Norwich tells us in her fifteenth revelation, we shall all be taken from woe, and between the woe and the joy there is less than the blink of an eye.' Sophia placed her right hand on Dorothy's forehead and then moved it softly downward to close the woman's eyes. She held it there for a moment before bringing her left hand to cover the right and then she blew a light puff of breath toward her hands. Dorothy's soft sobbing evaporated and when Sophia lifted her hands and stepped back from the bedside, the others saw that Dorothy's face was exquisitely tranquil. She was dead.

The four of them—Kathryn, Tim, Geoff, and Sophia—stayed quietly by Dorothy's bedside for a time. Through the still-drawn curtains of the cubicle the dawning sun pushed its first rays through the gaps, then extended one of its beams along the length of the linoleum floor to come to rest at the foot of Dorothy's bed before it expanded to bathe the entire bed in warm light.

'That's our signal for breakfast,' declared Tim. 'Come on, it's been a long night. Let's head for the cafeteria.'

'Great idea,' said Sophia. 'But I need the ladies' room on the way.'

'Second door on the right,' said Kathryn. 'When you're through, take the lift to the ground floor and turn left. There are plenty of signs to the cafeteria. See you soon.'

'Thank you. I'll find my way,' Sophia assured them as she headed down the corridor while the rest of them got into the lift.

After ten minutes, Kathryn knew that Sophia would not join them in the cafeteria. She knew that she was gone. And she knew that she would not be found unless she wanted to be.

When Kathryn's phone signalled an incoming message, it was no surprise that it was from Sophia. It read: 'Do not worry about me. I told you that our work together is not yet finished. We will see each other again soon.'

❦ 19 ❦

This is what she said:

> *There comes a time when we must put aside arrogance and take up humility. We think we can understand all things. Those things which are not amenable to our reason, we discard as worthless. And yet, the most powerful things are beyond explanation. What is life? What is death? Why do we love? Why do we sorrow? What is beauty and why does it move us so profoundly? There is reason and there is mystery. Give to reason what is amenable to reason. But let us give to mystery all that moves us beyond words; all that causes us to hope, to wonder, to strive, and to love.*

With Sophia's disappearance, the real situation came into sharp focus. Had Richard known about the visions earlier, the outcome might have been different. As it was, he was seized by a molten anger at Kathryn for keeping the facts from him. Perhaps he could have calmed himself if she had pleaded innocence, declared an ignorance of the cause of the auditory and perceptual disturbances that had become more frequent, more intense. As minimal physical pain was associated with the visions, such ignorance would have been acceptable in an untrained person. But Kathryn was a doctor, a specialist, and yet she had persisted in ascribing the hearing of strange voices singing heavenly melodies, the alterations in the senses of smell and taste, and the extravagant visual hallucinations to a divine and not a pathological source.

Richard was shaking when he spread the test results out on the desk between them. 'Look carefully at this MRI, Kathryn. What do you note?' he demanded.

Kathryn sat quietly, hands in her lap. She leant her body forward a little so that her eyes were, more or less, looking straight down at the images. She made no attempt to pick them up and, instead, reached for the printed summary report. She moved back in the chair and, taking out glasses from her coat pocket, she began to read the neurologist's findings.

'Hmm,' she sighed. 'This changes nothing.'

When his clenched fist hit the desk the whole room reverberated. He waited for the waves to subside, taking the time to compose himself. His response was a monotone hiss. 'This changes everything. We are talking about a fast-growing astrocytoma in the temporal lobe. Why? Why has it taken so long to be diagnosed?'

'Do you know what it's like to speak with Sophia? I thought it was something else. I thought it was something wonderful. There was no pain with it. There was only beauty, and light, and sweet insights that touched my heart.' Kathryn sounded far away, as if she was speaking from underwater. 'And, in truth, Richard, even *with* the diagnosis of this tumour, I still think there's something more, something miraculous.'

Richard forced himself up from his chair, walked as if in slow motion around the desk, his feet dragging, his breath catching in his throat. Ages passed, it seemed to him, before he arrived to kneel at Kathryn's feet, to tenderly reach out his hands to feel the warmth of her forearms through her jacket sleeves, to lay his head in her lap, and to hear the sobs rip from his chest in between choking words. 'You are my life, Kathryn. You have a brain tumour. And you are going to die.'

❦ 20 ❧

This is what she said:

Look at the light. Concentrate on the light. There, in front of me in the pitch black, is a tiny glowing point. As I stare it glows more brightly, begins to grow. Bigger, bigger. It was a central footlight, illuminating an otherwise darkened stage. And on the stage, directly in front of the light stood I. Blinded, dumbfounded, I was 'on'. Time to perform. It was, I suddenly knew, the light of life. The light at the end of the tunnel, of the birth canal. And I screamed—in surprise, in terror, in indignation, at my expulsion from my life before birth, into a life in front of the footlights. Now I had to perform for others, in full view. I howled accordingly. Darkness again; my awareness of the footlights fading but their threat remaining, just out of sight. Snatches of life, snatches of forming perceptions drifted by me, overhead. A winter blue sky, bare trees with spindly branches whipped about in the cold wind; a scorching summer with ice-cream dripping from its cone down my plump little arm; a warm kitchen filled with the smell of roasting meat and onions; the green crunch of peapods being opened. Flashes, all flashes. Then, all gone. I'm hurtling toward the single footlight again. But it rises, retreats, beckons. I follow willingly, leaving behind the snatches and flashes of my life. Did any of it matter? I am consumed, subsumed, re-wombed in God, bathed in light, clothed in light, becoming light in the Being of Light. All is light.

The decision to refuse treatment had not been a difficult one for Kathryn. She was aware that, as her tumour was already Grade 4, there was minimal chance of survival beyond one year at best. In fact, surgery being considered pointless at this stage, Kathryn understood that the median survival for patients with this diagnosis was eighteen weeks and that even with radiation, it stretched to only thirty weeks.

'I do not want radiation, Richard. I love you, I do not want to leave you. And perhaps I won't. But if my time is to be limited, I want to be able to make the most of it, not to spend it in a hospital,' she explained, taking his left hand in both of hers. It was a bright, calm day in early September, and the sun was streaming onto them as they sat together on a cane lounge on the rear veranda of their home.

'Kathryn, please reconsider. Treatment would buy you more time and, during that time, who knows what progress the research might make—probably new drugs. Or even alternate approaches. Please. I understand the logic of your decision, Kathryn. I just can't think about the consequences of it yet,' said Richard quietly.

'Then don't. Let's just enjoy this beautiful spring day,' said Kathryn. 'Look, the wisteria is already in bud. Everything's about to come to life …' Realising what she had said, she let the rest of the sentence trail off, but it was too late. Richard pounced on it.

'Not everything. Not the most important thing.' The hand his wife was holding clenched into a fist. 'Please don't taunt me like that, Kathryn.'

'I'm sorry, Richard. I didn't say it to hurt you. I'm always happy to see the garden about to burst forth. You know that.'

'I know. And you shouldn't have to apologise to me. You're right. Let's just enjoy the garden, and this lovely warm day. But promise me you'll give more thought to treatment.'

Kathryn smiled at him as they settled back on the lounge and let their gaze take in the signs of new life appearing on bare twigs and stems. Richard put his arm around Kathryn's shoulders and she manoeuvred herself closer to his side.

'I'd really like to see Sophia,' Kathryn ventured.

Richard's answer surprised and comforted Kathryn. 'I know you would. And I wish I could find her for you. I've been in regular touch with Officer Mackatt, you know.'

'No, I didn't know that,' said Kathryn, pulling herself out from under Richard's arm and positioning her body so that she could look at him squarely and bless him with one of her widest smiles. 'I didn't know, but I'm so happy to hear it. Have you found out anything?'

'Sad to say, not a thing. Even the text she sent you the morning she disappeared was from a cheap pre-paid mobile. Of course, as you received the text within fifteen minutes of her disappearance, it's obvious she couldn't have been far away then. But she could be anywhere now. And Kathryn, even though she said in that text that she'll see you again, it's been nearly two months. I don't think you should get your hopes up.'

'I'm not giving up on her, Richard. She might be the very thing we need to help me get well. Miracles have happened around her before, haven't they?'

'Kathryn, you know I'm not convinced about this "miraculous" side of your mystery friend but, if you continue to refuse treatment, what hope do we have except Sophia? A miracle might be the only thing we've got at this stage. For that reason, I want to find her just as much, if not more, than you do.'

'Well, as you're in such an agreeable frame of mind, there's something I want to ask you,' said Kathryn.

'Oh, this sounds ominous.' Richard laughed. 'Go ahead.'

'I would like to go to visit Margery and everyone at St Monica's. Just for a few days.'

'The police have questioned the relevant people at St Monica's about Sophia's disappearance. They don't know anything.'

'It's not about Sophia. Well, maybe it is, to an extent. It would help me to talk to Margery about it, see what she thinks. But it's more than that. I feel I need to see them all again. Please, Richard, three or four days is all I want.'

'Kathryn, how can I deny you this request? Yes, of course you can go. But my agreement is dependent on two conditions: One, if you start to experience any distress, any escalation of your symptoms, you will come home immediately; and, two, that I can go with you. Agreed?'

Kathryn stared at him. 'You mean, you're going to come with me to St Monica's?'

'If that's where you're going, yes. I'll be in that luxury suite with you for as long as it takes. Besides, how can I pass up an opportunity to meet the fabulous Sister Margery?'

'Okay, I agree. I'd really like to go back there tomorrow. Can you be organised by then?'

'Absolutely,' Richard assured her. 'I'm off to rearrange my schedule now.'

<hr/>

But Richard could not accompany Kathryn immediately to St Monica's. Two patients presented that same afternoon with complications from surgery some weeks earlier and the severity of their conditions demanded Richard's personal and careful attention.

The next morning he stood in their driveway, hugging his wife in farewell. 'I'm so sorry, Kathryn. I can't believe it, but I know you understand. Besides, you'll be in very good hands with the good Dr Mason chauffeuring you there. And I've spoken to Geoff and he's promised to call if he has a moment's concern about you, in which case I'll drop everything and be there. You call me, too, if you need me. I'm only a two-hour drive away.'

'Don't worry, Richard,' called Tim, putting Kathryn's bags in the boot. 'Actually, I'm more than willing to spend my days off taking a scenic drive to see the famous Margery and this geriatric paradise she's created.'

As Richard opened the passenger door and helped Kathryn in, Tim reached out to shake his hand. 'I'll take good care of her on the way. And I'm staying there overnight so I'll check out what's going on.'

'Thanks, mate,' said Richard. 'I really appreciate it. I hope to have these patients sorted by tomorrow morning, then I'll be down there myself.'

Tim and Kathryn drove in silence at first, Tim concentrating on navigating smoothly through the last of the morning peak-hour traffic and Kathryn looking contentedly out the window at ordinary people going about their everyday business under a warm morning sun.

The city was well behind them before Tim summoned the courage to ask, 'Why didn't you see someone about this sooner, Kathryn? You must have known you were sick. You must have recognised the symptoms.'

Kathryn continued to look out the window at the wide vista of sea that spread out in the distance, far, far below the highway. 'But I didn't know. My symptoms, as you call them, were not symptoms to me. They were experiences of beauty, of altered consciousness, of seeing everything more clearly, just like the experiences that Sophia was having, and like the ones Julie and Margery had described themselves as having all those years ago.'

Tim chose his words carefully. 'But Kathryn, you also knew that the general medical opinion about Margery and Julie and Sophia was that they were mentally unwell.'

Kathryn turned her head and bent down to retrieve her handbag from the floor. She rummaged in it for a minute or two and then pulled out a block of dark chocolate. Neatly, she peeled back the alfoil packaging and broke off two chunks of several squares each.

'Here, Tim,' she said, handing him one of the chunks. 'This is exceptionally delicious chocolate.' She smiled as Tim took the chunk and chomped through the squares quickly and with obvious enjoyment. She, too, took a bite of her chocolate before saying quietly, 'That's the thing, isn't it, Tim? Everyone has an opinion about everyone else. Doctors are paid for their opinions. The general medical opinion was that those women were mentally ill. But I'm a psychiatrist, and Dr Smith before me was the psychiatrist for Julie X, and our personal experiences of them led us to believe that they were sane and well. So, general opinion—no matter how authoritative its proponents—and personal experience are often very different things. And who's to say that authority is more reliable, more "real" than personal experience?' Kathryn put the rest of the chocolate in her mouth.

'I agree with you to a point,' said Tim. 'But in this case, the consequences for you, personally, in choosing experience over authoritative science, have been dire. You're really, really ill, Kathryn. And maybe, probably, if you'd sought treatment sooner, there would have been a good chance of survival. And, personally, the fact that you are so ill breaks my heart.'

Kathryn could feel the emotion in Tim's words. 'I'm so sorry to see you in pain about this, Tim. It's the worst part of all this—to see those I care about suffering because of me. But, in truth, if I could go back a few months and do things differently, I don't think I would. These few months have been the best of my life. I've lived fully, all the pain, all the love, all the beauty, all the joy. I wouldn't trade it for anything, not even another twenty years of life if I had to live them as I was before Sophia appeared. Can you understand that, Tim?'

'No. I can't, not at all,' replied Tim, gripping the wheel.

'Time for more chocolate then,' said Kathryn.

They drove on to St Monica's in silence.

❦

The sun had disappeared behind increasing cloud cover by the time Tim turned the car up the main driveway of St Monica's and into a space in the visitors' carpark. Despite the sombre sky, Kathryn was excited. She got herself quickly out of the passenger seat and to a standing position from which she could take in the whole sweep of magnificent coastline to her left and the sprawling grandeur of the front façade of St Monica's Home for the Aged to her right. She grinned when she heard Tim's whistle of surprise as he took in the same vistas before grabbing their luggage from the boot.

Wordlessly, Tim accompanied Kathryn as she walked toward the main entrance, its ornate double doors wide open in welcome at this time of day. They had barely stepped over the threshold when Nicola appeared, rushing at them with arms outstretched and a beaming smile on her face.

'I've been waiting for you,' she said, wrapping Kathryn in a quick embrace and then going to Tim to shake his hand. 'Margery's beside herself with excitement and, if you're not too tired after your journey, she's asked to see you in the upstairs sitting room as soon as you've freshened up in your room, which, by the way, is the same one you had last time you stayed with us.'

'Nicola, I'm absolutely fine. Give me twenty minutes and I'll be there.'

Nicola looked at her watch. 'Perfect. That would make the meeting time right on eleven, so I'll have coffee up there ready for you. And as for you, Dr Mason, Geoff, our Director of Nursing, whom I believe you've already met briefly in Sydney, would be very pleased to have you join him for coffee in his office at the same time.'

Nicola reached for one of Kathryn's bags and, letting Tim manage his own small overnight bag and Kathryn's other piece of luggage, she gestured for them to follow her up the grand staircase. First, Tim was shown to his room which, Kathryn knew, though she did not look into it when Nicola opened the door, would have a spectacular view of the ocean as it was at the front of the building, just as her room several doors further on did. Kathryn gave Tim a cheery wave as they parted company.

Nicola said, 'You'll see each other at lunch. Remember, Kathryn, Friday is Degustation Delights Day.'

'How could I forget?' Kathryn smiled.

Shortly before eleven o'clock Kathryn made her way to the sitting room. There, on her favourite sofa with its uninterrupted view to the ocean, sat Margery, her back to the door. The old woman didn't turn to look at Kathryn as she approached and, at first, Kathryn wondered if she should cough or make some other sound to indicate that she had entered the room so as not to startle her friend. She was debating the idea when Margery herself gave a cough and said, still without turning around, 'Don't think I don't know you're here, Kathryn Brookley. I might be old but I've lost none of my senses. I'm about to pour your coffee.'

Kathryn hurried forward, launching herself onto the sofa next to Margery, who promptly surrounded the younger woman with a hug.

'It's about time you came to see me,' chided Margery, releasing her hold on Kathryn. 'What's all this illness about? Tell me everything.'

'Oh Margery, it's so good to be here, so good to see you. As for my illness, what can I say? I have a fast-growing tumour in my brain but, you know, some days I feel quite well. Like today. Today I feel like my old self. Anything is possible.'

'Anything is possible any day, my dear,' Margery assured her, taking her hand and giving it a squeeze. 'It just depends what you want to do.'

'So many possibilities, so many uncertainties. It's been a roller-coaster since I was last here. I truly didn't know I was ill—which, I acknowledge, is a bit pathetic for a doctor to have to admit. Strange things were happening to me when I was here. I was losing whole afternoons. Whole evenings were lost in dreams. But I thought the forgetfulness, the vivid imaginings, were the effect of Sophia's insights and of my own growing awareness of things beyond my narrow, scientific view,' Kathryn tried to explain.

'And no doubt they were,' Margery assured her. 'Coincidentally, you were also sick.'

'Yes, and I couldn't, and still can't separate one from the other,' Kathryn confessed.

'Pain and love are like that, Kathryn.'

'I understand that more clearly now. That was Sophia's greatest gift to me, I think.' Kathryn picked up the cup of coffee that Margery had poured for her and took a thoughtful sip. 'You know, Margery, with Sophia's grasp of such things, it really surprised me when she disappeared so suddenly, so deliberately,'

'Why should it surprise you? She helped Dorothy to die peacefully and, if she wanted to continue her work—which, of course, she does—she could not allow herself to be bogged down in wranglings with government departments. They are only concerned with her surface identity. We know her, and her truth, better than that.'

'I guess you're right,' agreed Kathryn. 'Still, I wish she had said goodbye to me, let me know where she was going. Oh, I know that she doesn't operate like that, but we were close. And I really need her now.'

'Enough sombre chat,' announced Margery, standing up abruptly. 'Put your cup down. Give me your hand and come with me. There's something I need to show you.'

Kathryn obeyed. She followed Margery out of the sitting room, along the corridor, down the main staircase to the foyer, and then on through the activities room where an animated Rainbow caught sight of them and started to move in their direction. Margery waved her away impatiently and kept walking toward the heavy door that separated the activities room from the multi-level storage facility. Once through the door, Margery eschewed the spiral staircase in favour of the elevator, which took them speedily to the lowest level where Margery's own little version of an anchorhold was situated. As they exited the lift, the automatic lights instantly blared into brightness and Kathryn's eyes took several seconds to adapt. While she stood in the semi-blindness generated by her own eyes' mechanism, she could feel that the room's temperature was perfect, indicating that the heating had been operating before their entrance. Slowly, her sight adjusted and Kathryn sensed a variation in the room's arrangement since her previous visit. At first, she couldn't quite put her finger on why the area seemed different, but then she realised that the pull-down bed was, indeed, pulled down. It was neatly made, its quilt spread smoothly and the pillows plumped, but somehow she knew someone had been sleeping in it.

'You're correct, Kathryn. "Someone's being sleeping in my bed", as they say,' came a familiar voice from somewhere behind her. Kathryn swung round to see Sophia sitting demurely at the table on a chair which, Kathryn was certain, had been vacant a few seconds earlier.

'Oh my God,' Kathryn gasped, bringing her hands to cover her gaping mouth. 'Am I dreaming this or are you really here?'

'Go and sit with her, Kathryn,' instructed Margery from the kitchen area where she was busily putting cups and plates on a tray. 'I interrupted her coffee to bring her to you, Sophia, so I'm making us all some now. And just a little slice of cake or two. Not too much though, because we have Pierre's Friday lunch in about an hour's time.'

Kathryn did as Margery directed and found herself across the table from her dear friend. Sophia looked as tranquil, as unruffled as ever. Kathryn noted that her hair was still closely cropped but the drab woollen dresses that she had sported in the months of their earlier acquaintance had been replaced by a contemporary outfit of jeans and a grey jumper. The two women sat looking at each other quietly, Kathryn feeling unsure and overwhelmed.

'I had to leave. I knew that you were about to enter your time of suffering, but I also knew that I could be of no help to you if I were to become caught up in pointless investigations into my identity. Our work is not yet, but almost, done.'

Margery set the tray on the table and sat down on a chair next to Sophia so that she, too, could look straight at Kathryn. 'I didn't lie to the police, nor did anyone here, if that's what you're wondering,' she explained. 'When the authorities came to St Monica's to question us about Sophia's disappearance, we could say, with total honesty, that we had no idea where she was, that we had not seen her since she left with Geoff on the morning of Dorothy's departure from this life. And then, last weekend, I was walking along the beach and, suddenly, a familiar figure was walking in front of me and I knew that she had returned. And so I gave her shelter in my anchorhold. It is true that nobody else as yet knows that she is here but, of course, I will tell Geoff and those who need to know so that they are not compromised. Sophia asked me to wait until you knew of her presence here. She told me that you would come to St Monica's today. And so you have and, perhaps together, we can speak to Geoff.

'Yes,' breathed Kathryn in reply. She rested her arms on the table and lowered her head to them and began to sob—in joy, in sadness, in frustration, in elation, in confusion, in understanding.

Sophia stretched her hands across the table and, laying them on the back of Kathryn's bowed head, she said, 'All shall be well. And all shall be well. All manner of things shall be well.'

This is what she said:

Soon it will be time to leave. I am not afraid. My human costume will fall away and I will reveal my true self to eternity. Already I feel I am adrift. Like a piece of wood picked up from the beach where it has fallen as a branch from a tree, I am taken from my place of firmness, my place of rootedness to the earth, and carried wherever the tides, the ebb and flow, the deep sea currents, decide. I am one of the millions of pieces of flotsam and jetsam that are pushed along in the boiling, roiling ocean until, for whatever reason—or no reason at all—I am deposited on another beach, far, far, far, from my original place of growth. But now I am transformed, beautiful in my detachment, all my roughness smoothed away by the churning saltiness of my journey. I wait, exposed on the sand, until the incoming tide gathers me again, and I am on my way.

When Richard arrived at St Monica's on the Saturday after his wife and Tim had made their way there, all seemed well. He was warmly greeted by Geoff Briar, whom he had met briefly on the day of Dorothy's death and Sophia's disappearance.

'It's good of you to give up part of your Saturday to meet me,' said Richard, shaking Geoff's hand.

'No problem,' Geoff assured him. 'Actually, I'm often at work on

Saturdays, catching up on things. And really, Kathryn's very special to all of us so it's no sacrifice to spend a bit of extra time with her, and with you.'

'Thanks, Geoff. That means a lot,' Richard confided as the two men sat down for a quiet morning coffee in Geoff's office. 'It's a real privilege for me to be here. Kathryn's told me all about how this place came into its current state of being, but I didn't imagine it would be so magnificent.'

'Impressive, isn't it? And you haven't even had the "royal tour" yet. Kathryn would have told, too, how Margery's vision and generosity are what's made it all possible,' said Geoff, 'but it's the staff's commitment, and the residents' enthusiasm and support of each other that keeps the whole thing going. Every day I thank my lucky stars that I work here.'

'I want to thank you for welcoming Kathryn here, especially now … you know, under the circumstances. It'll give her a real boost. It's just a shame that Sophia's no longer around. That woman … that strange woman … she really made an impact on my wife.'

'She made an impact on all of us when she stayed on and helped set up the craft shop. When she wasn't working there, she spent hours talking to the residents, especially the very frail and most sick. I don't know what she was saying to them but they all seemed calmer, happier, after time with Sophia. It's a real shame that she couldn't stay.'

'Why couldn't she have stayed?' asked Richard. 'I mean, I know there were issues to be sorted out with Immigration, or whatever other government department was interested in her but, maybe if she had stayed and told the truth, she could have begun to have a good life of her own.'

'Now Richard, I'm sure Kathryn's told you about Sophia's life. She *did* tell the truth about it, it just wasn't what most people wanted to hear. They couldn't accept her truth.'

'Well, I can see I've still got a way to go in the open-minded stakes,' Richard confessed good-humouredly. 'You and Kathryn are far ahead, but I'm trying. For Kathryn's sake.'

'Try it for your own sake too' advised Geoff. 'A few days at St Monica's might do the trick.'

After their conversation, Geoff showed Richard to the suite he would be sharing with Kathryn. They had both thought that Kathryn would be there, resting, after a busy earlier morning with Margery. She was not.

'That's a good thing,' said Richard. 'It means that she's feeling well enough to be up and about.'

'Yeah, good point,' agreed Geoff. 'So, I suggest that I take you on a more extensive tour of the buildings and gardens. We'll probably come across Kathryn somewhere along the way.'

They sauntered through the English garden on the south-east side of the main building first, then walked around to the back of the building where the tropical garden was situated next to the huge outdoor swimming pool. Richard was especially impressed by the grass-roofed cabana and the pool's centrally located wet bar.

'Do the residents use the pool's bar much?' inquired Richard.

'Are you kidding? That's their motivation to get into the water in the first place.'

The two men chuckled and continued back inside through the Irish pub, which was empty at this time of the morning except for three men making use of one of the billiards tables. Next, Geoff steered them into the rose-covered glass concourse that led to the Seaview Café. By now, Richard was so impressed with everything he was seeing that he had almost forgotten that the main purpose of the tour was to locate Kathryn.

'This is the place for breakfast every morning, and a snack anytime of the day or night,' explained Geoff, with a wave of his arm.

'Spectacular.' Richard whistled. 'Now why isn't Kathryn in here now? I would really enjoy sitting at that corner table by the window, just to watch the waves roll in.'

'Hmm. Why, indeed. She and Margery might be in the sitting room. Come on. If you think this view is good, wait till you see this.'

Back through the covered concourse and into the entrance foyer they went before ascending the main staircase and turning to the right along the wide sweep of the landing that introduced the grand sitting room. And while Richard was really impressed with everything about the sitting room's interior and was stunned by its outlook, he was as disappointed as Geoff to find that Kathryn was not there either.

'They might have headed to the beach for a walk,' suggested Geoff, 'though I'd be surprised if that's where they are because I know Kathryn wanted to be nearby for your arrival. She's probably lost track of time.' He thought for a moment. 'Let's try the activities room first, and if she's not there then we'll head for the beach.'

Saturday was the day for residents' independent, unsupervised arts and crafts in the activities room. Rainbow sometimes came in but such visits were unofficial as Saturday and Sunday were usually her days off. Since the opening of the Sea Craft shop, however, she usually swapped her free days around so that she could be in the shop for the increased trade that weekends brought. Today, only two keen handymen, Bob and Fred, were sanding and preparing to paint three large dollhouses for the children's hospital when Geoff and Richard came upon them in the room's woodwork area.

'You haven't seen Sister Margery in here this morning, have you?' Geoff called to them.

'Yep, sure have,' replied Bob. 'And Dr Brookley too. They went down into the storage unit about two hours ago. They're researching something, something important they said, and they didn't want to be disturbed.'

'Oh, thanks very much, Bob. By the way, Bob, Fred, this is Dr Richard Brookley, Kathryn's husband. He's going to be spending a few days with us,' Geoff explained.

'Nice to meet you,' the men said, coming forward to shake Richard's hand.

'I'm thinking we should surprise them,' said Geoff with a wink. 'And Richard, don't look so worried. Margery calls it her storage unit but it's actually a very spacious, very comfortable living and working quarters that just happens to be below ground. And fully temperature-controlled. There's an elevator we can take but, to surprise them I suggest we take the stairs, if you're up for it.'

'Lead on,' agreed Richard.

'Okay. Fred, can you do us a favour? You know where the power panel is for all the storage levels. I'm going to disable the automatic stair lights for the first four levels so that we can get down to the fifth level without Margery and Kathryn being alerted by the automatic lights coming on as we descend. Flick it on again in about five minutes, will you, so that no one else gets stuck in the dark after us?'

'Yes, no problem,' said Fred, accompanying Geoff to the power panel as he spoke.

'Thanks Fred,' said Geoff as he and Richard disappeared through the heavy door and into the darkness, his phone torch on low beam to guide their way down surreptitiously.

If an unseen third party had been witnessing what was unfolding, he or she would have been hard-pressed to guess which of the five participants in the event was the most surprised. When Geoff and Richard came to the end of the spiral staircase and stepped suddenly into the full light of Margery's storage unit, three shocked faces swung round from a pile of papers on the table to stare, wide-eyed, at the two men who stared back in open-mouthed muteness.

It was Margery who broke the silence. 'I can explain,' she began.

'That's good to hear, Margery,' said Geoff, still glued to the spot at the base of the stairs.

'Why don't you both pull up a chair and we can have a nice cup of tea and a chat about this?' Margery smiled.

Both men moved mechanically toward the table until Richard paused behind Kathryn and bent to kiss her on the head.

'Are you okay?'

She twisted around on her chair and, remaining in her seated position, stretched her arms to embrace him around his waist. 'I'm so happy to see you, Richard,' she said. 'And don't worry about this little ... issue. We've got it all sorted. You'll see.'

'Yes, we'll see,' he replied, moving a chair close to his wife, sitting down and taking her hands in his.

While everyone was rearranging themselves around the table, Margery moved toward the kitchen.

'Margery,' Geoff called to her. 'I'm thinking, if everyone agrees, we might skip the tea and have one of your whiskeys instead.'

In the hum of agreement, Margery opened a small cabinet and took out a silver tray on which stood a large cut-glass decanter and matching glasses. She counted out five tumblers and passed by the sink to fill a small jug with water before returning to the table with the loaded tray. As she set it down, she smiled warmly.

'Why don't we help ourselves? It's just what we need to lubricate this sticky conversation.'

'Sticky is one word for it,' said Geoff, pouring himself a small splash of the malt and topping it up with water. The others followed his lead. 'So, who's going to start the explanation?'

'I will,' volunteered Margery, 'as it was I who decided that the storage unit would be just the place for Sophia until she completed her work here.'

'I'm all ears,' said Geoff, putting his glass down and leaning back in his chair with his arms firmly folded across his chest.

Margery drained her drink and looked happily at her rapt audience. 'Last weekend, as I was taking an afternoon walk along the beach, who should I come across, quietly walking along the sand, but our Sophia. Both of us were aware of the awkward situation that has arisen around people's general agitation over her identity—or lack of it—and so I thought that the best thing to do was keep Sophia comfortable, but hidden, in my storage unit until such time as Kathryn could talk with her and other more suitable arrangements could be made. Obviously, dear Geoff, I was planning to tell you about this, but not until a clear plan was made so that if any of the police or government officials came back to question you, you could honestly say you still knew nothing of Sophia's whereabouts. So, that's it.'

'No, that's *not* it,' Geoff snapped. 'You're telling us that you and Sophia met coincidentally on the beach here and, without consulting me or anyone else, you both decided to use St Monica's as a hiding place.'

'Now don't upset yourself, Geoff,' Margery clucked. 'First of all, we didn't meet coincidentally because, once you've reached understanding, you know that there are no coincidences.'

'I'm a long way from reaching understanding about this,' Geoff said through gritted teeth.

'Perhaps I can explain,' offered Sophia, who, all present suddenly realised, had said nothing to this point. Her voice was quiet and steady, a balm to the Margery and Geoff exchange. 'Several weeks into the rehabilitation time I had been given so generously, I knew that my purpose at St Monica's was nearing completion and thus I was preparing to move on in order to concentrate on finalising my work with you, Kathryn. I had hoped that the work could proceed without interruption from those who were troubled with issues around my identity. The day before Dorothy's passing, however, you called Geoff, Kathryn, with news of my interview with the Department of Immigration. I could not jeopardise my work by appearing at such an interview and so, after attending at Dorothy's departure, I, too, took my leave. But with the intensification of your illness, Kathryn, I could no longer remain absent. Margery also knew this and so it was that our understanding led us to rendezvous on the beach and to decide on a short period of seclusion for me in the storage unit anchorhold until such time as you would return to St Monica's and, together, we would make a plan.'

Geoff and Richard knew enough of Sophia (and of Margery and Kathryn) to realise that pleading with her to reconsider talking to the government agencies was pointless. Sophia moved in an entirely different atmosphere, a deeply layered reality.

'So be it, Sophia,' Geoff conceded. 'I appreciate that you must follow the path that is right for you. My only concern is that the reputation of St Monica's is not affected. We all know that for this establishment to maintain its uniqueness it's necessary to keep away from the glare of publicity.'

Richard's concern was not to do with the reputation of St Monica's. It was focused only on what would be most beneficial for his wife, and so he directed his words to Sophia: 'Okay, I'll accept, too, that you're not going to do things in the conventional—lawful—way but how, exactly, are you going to assist my wife with this illness by behaving in this secretive manner?'

'Please, Richard, don't be harsh,' begged Kathryn. 'The three of us have spent the morning coming up with a plan that would enable Sophia to help me in these last weeks of my life.'

Richard's voice wavered when he spoke. 'What are you saying,

Kathryn? If Sophia is as wonderful as you've been claiming, why aren't you more positive about surviving, about overcoming this? And Sophia, with all your spiritual talk, and all your apparently miraculous powers, can't you cure her? Can't you take all this away?'

Kathryn placed her hand on her husband's shaking forearm and was about to speak on Sophia's behalf when the young woman herself stood up from her chair and walked around the table to kneel at Richard's side.

Looking up into his eyes, she said, 'I cannot cure her. That is not my place. I am not God. You are a doctor, but you cannot cure her. You are not God either. But, perhaps, I can ease her last discomfit. Perhaps, I can minimise the confusion, facilitate the sleep, and make the waking time more pleasant and productive. Perhaps, she will not suffer seizures and, perhaps, the alterations to her perceptions may be as gentle as flowing water, as soothing as sunlight on water, so that she can be present to the end. And, definitely, she will die wrapped in love.'

Once the truth was uttered, the storage unit anchorhold reverberated with the silent thoughts and longings of all its occupants. The room absorbed the unvoiced sobs and the unshed tears, and processed them all in its windowless walls, transforming the hurt into a fragile acceptance.

⊂━━◆━━⊃

Margery remained in the storage unit with Sophia after the others ascended to ground level in the elevator and went off to meet Tim in the dining room for lunch. Over the meal Kathryn and Richard and Geoff informed Tim about the latest location of the mysterious Sophia-from-the-Sea and, with his consent, they inducted him into their conspiracy of silence, its justification centred on the avowed belief that it was in Kathryn's best interests. When Kathryn left the lunch table for a visit to the ladies' room, the men decided that the thorny question of what to do about Sophia could wait.

With all in agreement, the plan was put into effect. After a few days of rest and recreation at St Monica's, Kathryn and Richard drove home to Sydney with Sophia and Margery in the back of their car. Tim followed in his own car, which was packed to capacity with everyone's luggage. Both cars detoured via Cottage Point, the first car depositing Sophia and Margery and making sure they were comfortable; the second car depositing the luggage and fresh food and other necessities of daily life that Tim had picked up at the supermarket on the way.

Richard and Kathryn's weekender at Cottage Point had been the obvious, and probably the only option for accommodating Sophia safely. The house was close enough to the city to enable Richard and Tim to easily provision Sophia and, more importantly, to allow Kathryn to visit, or even stay at the house with her friend for a day or two, now and then, if she chose and if her condition permitted it. At the same time, it was secluded enough to ensure that Sophia could stay there without being observed by any neighbours though, of course, if and when she was outside, she would be clearly visible to anyone on any number of the yachts and cruisers that plied this deep and beautiful section of Pittwater. Richard had thought about and worried about that possibility but, finally, had been persuaded by Tim that most people on those boats would be more interested in themselves and enjoying their days in the sun than in looking out for fugitive mystics.

⚬══╬══⚬

Sophia lay on her stomach on the warm sand of the little beach that revealed itself in front of the holiday house only when the tide was very low. At other times, because the main living area of the house was built out over the water as an architectural feature, the thick piers on which the house stood, and which were fastened to rock below the sandy surface, were submerged so that the house appeared to be floating. This October afternoon, the sun was unseasonably hot and had succeeded in drying out the moist top layer of the sand so that Sophia could lie prone, dry and comfortable, in her light cotton dress, and listen to the lap of the water against the jetty. A slapping sound some way out in the middle of the channel caught her ear and she propped herself up on her elbows and peered ahead. She could see where the water had been disturbed by something breaking the surface, the ripples around the disturbance sending out concentric circles.

'Sophia, I've made some tea,' Margery called out to her from the house.

'Why don't you bring it down here and sit with me on the sand? The sun is marvellous,' she called back.

Within a minute she heard the soft pat of sandaled feet approaching and, staying on her stomach but swivelling her head to the left, she saw a brightly painted wooden tray with a floral teapot, two floral mugs and a little glass jug of milk atop it being deposited on the sand next to her.

'I'll be back. Just going to grab a folding chair. My knees won't let me get down that far.'

'Wait, I'll help you,' said Sophia, scrambling up from her flat position. 'I'm getting a bit uncomfortable here myself.'

Together, each with a chair under an arm, the two women returned to the sunny spot and unfolded their chairs. Sophia didn't sit down immediately but, instead, descended to the sand on her knees and poured tea into each mug, handing one to her companion before manoeuvring herself and her own mug of tea up into her chair.

The two settled side by side, their chairs positioned so they both looked out on the expanse of sparkling water with its weekday assortment of pleasure craft, and the eucalypt-covered sandstone rock faces beyond. As they watched, the water's mirror cover was broken again by something—lightning quick—leaping up and slapping back under the surface, but this time, much closer in to the little beach. And again, closer in still. And then again, almost in front of them, very near the shore. When Sophia saw what was causing the disturbance, she sprang to her feet, wadding into the shallows. Margery saw it too and excitedly, though somewhat awkwardly, followed Sophia until both women were standing knee-deep and gazing into clear water.

'The blue fish,' breathed Sophia, slowly, reverently, as the giant electric-blue groper wove between their feet and brushed familiarly against their lower legs.

'The time is coming,' murmured Margery.

Sophia, in a prolonged nod, lifted her face to the sun, closed her eyes, and then lowered her head toward her hands which were clasped in prayer at her chest.

On the day of the reappearance of the blue fish, more than a month had passed since Sophia and Margery had arrived at the weekender. More than one month of perfect weather had passed without Sophia's whereabouts being uncovered by the authorities. And more than a month of Kathryn's dwindling life had passed. Despite her increasing weakness, however, Kathryn had insisted on spending most days with Sophia in long, deep conversation. When she wanted to stay overnight at Cottage Point, Richard would drive her there early in the morning and make his way there after work to stay with her. And although Kathryn's days were shortening in inverse proportion to the lengthening spring days, the weekender cocooned its visitors in a languid, idyllic existence that seemed to occupy a space outside of time.

❦[22]❦

This is what she said:

All things begin and all things end, or so it had once seemed to me. But now I know that one thing always was, is, and shall be. As it was in the beginning, is now, and ever shall be. There is only one necessary thing, only one lesson: Love

November had always been Kathryn's favourite month. Spring, building in beauty and intensity, reaches its spectacular climax in November. On Sydney's North Shore, the jacaranda trees cannot contain their heavy load of purple flowers and so they shed them on the ground, creating a wall-to-wall mauve carpet across the suburbs.

The heat builds, too, and the year speeds up as it approaches its frantic, carnivalesque end: the long degustation of December, with its parties, and beaches, and outdoor Christmas season's eatings; the brilliant explosion of New Year when the Harbour Bridge is surrounded by over a million revellers on the water and the spacious foreshores. And after the explosion, the quiet exhaustion of the lazy, hazy, mindless days of January.

How she had loved all the months, all the seasons, all the places of her city, of her life. And how she had loved all the people in her life, even those who had made it difficult. Because now she understood. She had come to understanding in the sharp light of Sydney in the twenty-first century. And the lesson was the same as it had been for Julian of Norwich in the fourteenth century, and for Margery and Rainbow in the 1970s, and for Julie/Sophia in unfettered time, and for all the others across the years, across the world.

On the last day of her Sydney life, Kathryn lay on a bed that Richard had made up in their living room so that she could look out over the garden. Her body was swollen with fluid and she dozed fitfully, in and out of consciousness. Sometimes when she opened her eyes she could see the tall Christmas bush to the right of the veranda, its tiny buds growing a deeper yellow-orange by the hour, ready to transform into their formal red shade for the adorning of the Christmas table. Sometimes, her newly opened eyes would alight on a pair of vividly green, red, and yellow lorikeets, munching grevillea flowers. Sometimes, her eyes would only flick open for a moment here and there, and here and there she would notice the dart of the sun's rays across the path as they headed toward the bubbling fountain to make gems of the tumbling streams of water. Sometimes her eyes would open wide, and she would encounter only purple-black darkness, still and velvety. On the last occasion she opened her eyes, she saw her husband sitting on a chair pulled close to the bed. She saw his face, the skin coloured by over fifty summers under an Australian sun; and his eyes framed by short, dark, tender lashes that flickered in the light as he blinked; and his forehead, wide and wise and marked in neat parallel lines above thick eyebrows; and his nose, straight and to the point, pointed in her direction; and his mouth, framed around a small smile of even teeth, the smile elicited, she knew, by her open eyes and her own small smile at the sight of him.

Richard reached for her hand. 'Can I get you anything?' he asked quietly.

'Yes,' she whispered. 'A walk in the garden.'

'No problem. You know I've been working on my imaginative skills with Sophia,' said her husband, lying down next to her on the daybed and enfolding her in his arms. 'Relax, close your eyes and I'll guide you through every flower and shrub, along every path, from the comfort of this very bed. Colours, textures, fragrances … all for you.'

'Oh, everything is so beautiful. Thank you, Richard,' she murmured as her eyes closed for the final time. On her last, long exhalation, she breathed out, 'You are my love … Love. All love.'

She was buried on the third day of December beneath the green lawn of a quiet cemetery. Later in the afternoon, after the mourners had gathered to lament and to share happy stories of Kathryn and after they had finished their drinks and their cakes and gone back to their own lives, Richard, Tim, Geoff, Margery, Rainbow, and Sophia drove to Kirribilli and walked on the soft grass of the park to the seawall under the vast northern pylon of the Sydney Harbour Bridge.

There, in the balmy warmth of the late afternoon, they looked across to the white sails of the Opera House, the historic sandstone edifices of the Rocks, and the multi-storey office buildings of the central business district beyond. Below them, they watched the play of light and shade in the deep harbour currents. To their right, the huge open-mouthed face of Luna Park laughed and leered. In front of them, they watched rivercats ferrying people home up river, and the green and gold Manly ferries plying in and out of Circular Quay.

There was no need for words. They stood in a quiet row, staring at the harbour's beauty through the filter of their own thoughts until a massive cruise liner—only minutes from leaving its berth on the harbour's western side—glided majestically past them, under the soaring bridge and down toward the heads and the open sea.

'That's it then,' announced Richard, informally drawing the silent liturgy to an end. 'I'm taking you all for drinks and dinner at the restaurant up the road. I've booked a table on the terrace so we can continue our harbour viewing from there.'

'Can you stay here for just a little longer with me, Richard? There's something I want to tell you,' said Sophia.

'Of course,' said Richard.

'Right, the rest of us will go on and meet you there when you're ready,' said Geoff, taking the hint and beginning to shepherd the others back onto the path that led up a serious hill and away from the harbour foreshore.

'See you soon,' Richard called after them as Sophia walked toward a bench near the sandstone seawall and sat down. Richard followed and took his place next to her. From the colourful woven bag that she had been wearing over her shoulder throughout the funeral, Sophia took out a small, leather-covered notebook. 'I know you wondered what Kathryn and I talked about during those last few weeks at the holiday house. Well, this is it. She wrote it all down for you.'

Richard accepted the notebook from Sophia and opened it to a random page. He looked at the handwriting and recognised Kathryn's neat hand, but his face registered confusion.

'During those final weeks, Richard, and actually, before that, Kathryn had been coming to understanding. Do you realise what I'm telling you? This is a book of her insights. This is what she said.'

⟞⟝

Margery, Rainbow, Geoff and Tim had almost finished their first drink when Richard joined them at a table on the balcony.

'Where's Sophia?' Rainbow asked.

'She said she'd join us a little later,' he replied.

After that, they sat in silence for some time, sipping on another drink and watching the evening descend, the sky fading from blue to pink to purple to black. Across the harbour, the city came alive with points of light.

'Sophia's taking her time,' observed Tim after a while.

'Give her a few more minutes. You know she doesn't believe in time,' said Margery. They all laughed.

Sydney Morning Herald, Saturday, 7 December 2013.

A young woman is missing, believed drowned, after falling into Sydney Harbour earlier this week. A group of men fishing near Pier One on the south side of the Harbour Bridge reported seeing a woman tumble into the water from the seawall under the bridge's northern pylon at around 6.30 pm on Tuesday evening. The men alerted

authorities immediately and the Marine Area Control were quick to respond, but despite an extensive search of the area over several days, no trace of
the woman has been found and the search has now
been scaled back. In a bizarre twist, the unidentified woman is believed to be the same one who was
found floating, alive and well, in Sydney Harbour in
May of this year.

ACKNOWLEDGMENTS

Heartfelt thanks to my 'Divines' who shared their creative wisdom and generous friendship with me throughout the whole process: to Dianne Masri and Amanda Hickey, first readers of the first draft, whose insightful advice and unbridled enthusiasm gave me the push I needed to continue with the project; to Michele Seminara and Adriana Cortazzo, later readers of later drafts, whose generous encouragement helped me complete it.

Sincerest thanks to Michelle Lovi at Odyssey Books for accepting the manuscript and for overseeing its journey to publication with such diligence and generosity of spirit.

Deepest thanks to my family for their constant love and support of me: to my husband, Adrian, whose encouragement and belief in my writing are unwavering; to my daughter, Laura, first one in the family to read a draft, whose sharp eye for detail helped hone the manuscript and whose open-hearted love for the book meant so much to me; to my daughter, Erin, whose willingness to discuss spiritual ideas, and to share marketing skills and her lovely company with me were a treasure; to my daughter, Bridget, whose precision as a writer and editor, and whose happy conversation and sharing of her love of books and ideas with me were invaluable throughout the process.

Finally, thanks to the mystics: to those brave medieval souls whose way of seeing things more deeply and truly, and whose profound writings about their experiences inspired me to write this book in the first place.

ABOUT THE AUTHOR

Carmel Bendon is a writer and presenter on 'all things medieval' to academic and general audiences. She has a PhD in Medieval Literature and a 1st Class Honours in Early English, both degrees from Macquarie University where she was a lecturer in English Literature and Medieval Studies. Her specialist research field is Medieval Mystics and this was the basis of her successful non-fiction book *Mysticism and Space*. Her other academic publications include chapters and articles on St Augustine, Julian of Norwich, and Hildegard of Bingen, and on anchorites and the practice of immurement. More generally, she has published on Geoffrey Chaucer, Jorge Luis Borges, and Oscar Wilde, and has been a contributor to the *International Dictionary of Literary Biography*. She is now concentrating on writing fiction. *Grasping at Water* is her first novel. She lives in Sydney with her husband, a faithful dog, and a wild garden, and she is the proud mother of three adult daughters.

Printed in Australia
AUOW01n1414150818
301508AU00002B/2